TRACES

Franklin J. Knight

Traces
© 2024 Franklin J. Knight

Published by
Ruhe Media LLC, 1401 21st Street, Suite R, Sacramento, CA 95811

Cover design by author Franklin J. Knight
Paperback ISBN: 979-8-9922181-0-7
eBook ISBN: 979-8-9922181-1-4

First Edition: December 2024

It is the glory of God to conceal things, but the glory of kings is to search things out.
Proverbs 25:2 (ESV)

PROLOGUE

Harriet jolted awake, a shockwave sweeping through her. *What happened?*

It was not uncommon for Harriet to retrace her steps. Her mental capacities were degrading with age, particularly in the last few years. She knew that, at least. But where was she now? She could not remember.

Her vision was blurry, blinded by light. Sounds were muddled, as if she were under water. The light around her radiated a tapestry of shades of white and gold.

She squinted. Was she outside? She felt no warmth. Just brightness. She was laying down, her head propped up slightly. She was lying in bed.

The plugs in her ears popped as clarity returned. Her senses began to orient. Harriet heard crying. She turned. The blinding light dissipated. She could see. Rebecca, her dear niece, sat in a chair with her face in her hands.

"Rebecca, what's going on, Dear? Where are we?" she asked, trembling.

Rebecca did not respond.

"Rebecca, did you hear me? I don't know what is happening."

Rebecca was silent, her sobs soft but steady. Harriet raised her voice.

"Rebecca! Why are you crying? I don't like this."

Rebecca still did not respond.

"She can't hear you," boomed a voice from the foot of the bed, causing Harriet to sit straight up at attention.

Harriet's eyes darted in the direction of the voice. Was it a voice or a gust of wind? The sound emanated from what appeared to be the center of the light in the room, glowing at the foot of what she could see was a bed.

"Hello? Is someone there? I can't see you."

The lights moved. Harriet felt her heart rate increase, nerves beginning to crawl up the back of her neck.

"Help! Someone help me! Rebecca!" she cried frantically.

1

Harriet whipped her head around to look for something. Anything. She was not sure what. Rebecca to the right. She looked down. A bed. To her left, IVs and monitors. Above, sterile, flat ceilings. A white room. A white room with a window. A hospital. She was in a hospital. That's right. The surgery. She was out of surgery. The tension in her back began to release.

"Fear not, Harriet, but it is time for us to go," whispered the voice. Harriet's panic ceased.

"Are you the doctor?" she asked.

Harriet fumbled around with her left hand trying to find her glasses as she held her right hand up towards the blinding light for a moment's relief. The milky glow of light glistened with hints of rainbow specks around its exterior. She wanted a look at this doctor with the obnoxious headlamp.

"Doctor, what's going on? I just don't—"

She threw her left hand up in exasperation to try and get a look at this doctor.

"Can you please turn out that light? I can't see a thing, and I really don't feel up for an exam."

"I am not a doctor, Harriet," said the stern voice.

Harriet looked back at her niece in confusion, hoping for some clarification. Rebecca had been by her side for the last decade or so. Between the doctor's visits, the pharmacy pickups, grocery store runs, and the mature exercise classes (Harriet refused to acknowledge them as "geriatric classes."), Rebecca sacrificed her own physical well-being for her aunt. As Harriet's mind followed her body's degradation, Rebecca became her thinking power too.

"Rebecca. Sweetie. Look at me. I don't understand a thing this man is saying. What is—"

"I am not a man, Harriet," said the voice. Harriet returned her gaze to the bright light. "My name is Aleifr. I have been with you from the beginning, and I am here with you at the end." The breathy voice punctuated the sentence with a resonant stop.

Harriet froze for a moment, once again assessing her surroundings and trying to determine what cruel games her dementia was playing on her today. She was dying. She knew that. But what—

"You are not dying, Harriet," said the voice, interrupting her thought. "You've already graduated. Now we must go."

Harriet's indignant self-defense mechanisms kicked in. "Young man, this is preposterous. Unless you are the Lord Jesus Christ himself coming to take me home, then I'm not going anywhere with you."

"He will come, but I am here now," said the voice.

"Son, who do you think you are?" she questioned, continuing to raise the tone of voice.

"Your kind would call me a guardian angel, although that is a gross oversimplification."

"You must be crazier than me to think I'd believe that."

She turned. "Rebecca? What on Earth is going on here?"

"How do you feel, Harriet?" asked the voice, softer now.

Her head turned back to the light, still unable to make out the appearance of this voice.

"What do you mean?" asked Harriet.

"Where does it hurt?"

Harriet felt the breath of his word strike her bones. This was preposterous, but Harriet paused to take stock of her body. She learned to ignore the aches and pains over the years. And even if she were in pain, the physical pain was minor by comparison to the mental anguish that she regularly found herself trapped in.

Harriet spent most of her time in a state of confused panic, constantly trying to piece together parts of life that she could not recall. The pain, however, was a friend she knew far too well.

She paused, waiting for the predictable wave of pain to wash up her back and down her arms. And yet, Harriet did not feel the familiar shutter. She looked down at her hands as she flexed and closed them, turning them over for an inspection. No twinge or trigger finger. No sharp sting or tingles. Not even the dull ache from carpal tunnel. *Strange.*

In fact, she could not even remember the last time her hands felt this good. Rheumatoid arthritis riddled those hands for the last 27 years. Probably even longer, but that's when the diagnosis came. She lived with locked fingers and deformed joints, slowly twisting over the years like a mangled tree.

Harriet ran one hand over the other. Soft and smooth. Perfectly formed. Surely, these were not her hands. She grimaced with confusion.

"This doesn't make any sense," she said, shaking her head.

3

Harriet wiggled her hips, still wringing her hands. No stiffness. She twisted her torso, surprised at the ease. These movements were once impossible. Her lower spine and hips fused years ago after a nasty fall left her immobile for too long. Her body naturally fused the joints in an attempt to protect itself from further damage, leaving her to move like an old, wrinkled robot.

Harriet set her hands on either side of herself and twisted her body to see just how far she could turn. She twisted just a bit, then a bit more. No resistance. She could keep going. Her head turned past Rebecca, then to the monitors, then to the back of the bed and the mirror.

But, there was no mirror behind the bed. Harriet's mouth dropped open as she shrieked. She stared at her own body. Confusion was an old friend of hers, but this?

"What's going on? I don't understand," said Harriet, shuttering as she tried to vocalize words. Only breathy squeaks came out. She turned back around and laid down, expecting what she just saw to disappear. This was a new level of crazy, even for her.

The voice softened further. "Harriet, your physical body was unable to withstand the stresses of the surgery. The doctors did what they could, but your heart simply could not go on any further. The stitches between your body and spirit are now broken. You are free, Harriet."

Harriet opened her eyes, twisting once again to look at the old woman behind her. She had never seen a dead body, but this body was definitely dead.

"That *is* me," she said.

She looked down at her hands, still clutching them and kneading the supple skin. She now saw herself sitting on top of the old woman in the bed. Harriet was raised in a local church, so the idea of death and afterlife was not new.

"If I'm dead, where's my Jesus?" she asked anxiously. Did this mean she was not going to Heaven? Had she served her church and her family only not to make it? Was this...you know...the bad place?

"Harriet, please, remain calm." The voice's words wrapped around her body with an embrace.

There was no reason for Harriet to do anything other than scream, yet the voice's words brought her peace.

"The realm you now exist in is far more complex than the world you are departing. The 'afterlife,' as your kind call it, is no such thing. It is the only true life. It always existed and will always exist. Your time on Earth was merely a shadow of the true reality."

Harriet closed her eyes and took a deep breath trying to calm herself. Her mind scanned scenes from her life. Perfect clarity. No fragments or partial words. She felt sharp. Razor sharp. The voice's words made no sense, but they anchored her. Harriet felt the words connect to her as she opened her eyes. She looked towards the voice, then over at Rebecca.

"She can't hear me, can she?" asked Harriet.

"No, I'm afraid not. The auditory plane of her reality does not presently intersect with ours."

Harriet didn't know what that meant.

She rose from the bed, slowly turning, hoping the dead old woman would disappear. It did not work. Her eyes locked on the body that lay before her. She saw the white curly hair that contrasted starkly against dark skin. She saw the deep wrinkles that greeted her with every glimpse in a mirror. That mole. This was her. Or at least, part of her. The hospital IV was still taped into position.

"I know this is difficult to process," said the voice. "It will take some time. All will eventually be made clear."

His words hung in the air, comforting despite the gravity as her understanding took hold.

"Take my hand, Harriet," said the voice. "We have an appointment, and we won't be late."

Despite the command, Harriet's gaze shifted to Rebecca, who was still softly crying and holding the hand of Harriet's former body.

"Will I ever see her again?" asked Harriet. She put her hand on Rebecca's shoulder, leaning down to give a kiss on the forehead as she had always done. Her fingertips touched Rebecca's shoulder, but Harriet only felt a warming pressure at the point of touch, the tips of her fingers disappearing beneath the surface of Rebecca's skin. Rebecca's face did not register any change.

"I love you, Dear. You took such good care of me."

"Come, Harriet."

She turned towards the voice. Where she previously only saw blinding light, she could now see the being clearly, and she was startled at the intimidating, masculine appearance. She instinctively took a step back. He was massive. Human-like but much larger, perhaps three meters tall. He wore a radiant brick red tunic. The fabric cascaded like water, swirling and tumbling down in tiny, shifting waves.

"Incredible," said Harriet.

The longer she stared, the more detail she saw in his clothing. Intricate and multi-layered stitching. It was as if she could see the individual threads.

"We must go, Harriet," said Aleifr.

His words brought her back to the moment. She stretched out her hand towards him, as her gaze locked with the being's for the first time, his eyes burning white hot. Aleifr had the structural features of a human but looked unlike any person she had ever seen. His skin absorbed light, a matte black color. His features appeared chiseled into granite. Aleifr's hair was chest length, metallic soft locks shining brighter than gold.

"My God..." she whispered in awe of what she saw.

"No, not yet," responded Aleifr. Rich violet glints reflected off the surface of his skin.

Harriet flashed back to her days in Sunday school, drawing simple little triangle-shaped angels with halos. Always sweet and friendly looking. Aleifr was not that. His fiery eyes pierced her.

Aleifr stretched out his hand.

Harriet extended hers with trepidation. At the moment of his touch, Harriet suddenly felt herself yanked to the side and immediately blinded by light once again. So much light. She felt herself accelerating at untold speeds. Lights whizzed past her. They were wrapped in a blue orb of what most resembled water around them that twinkled with flecks of a rainbow. Aleifr stood motionless, still holding her hand and staring in the direction of movement. Harriet looked down and saw glimmers below her feet. Flashes streamed beneath her. Harriet's eyes traced their path upwards to in front of the orb. A track of light extended into the darkness. Or was it water? Whatever it was, the gleaming streamer was alive with vibration, pulsing to an unheard beat.

"What is this?" she asked.

Before a response, just as soon as the movement started, the orb stopped and dissolved with a shimmer.

The area was dark. She clasped Aleifr's hand tighter. Harriet looked down. She couldn't see the ground, but it felt like cool grass between her toes. Her lower body disappeared about waist height into darkness. A few meters in front of them stood a single wooden door with a faint porch light hanging over top from a gooseneck fixture. It was well maintained but visibly aged.

Harriet did not let go of Aleifr, nor he of her. She still had no idea who this creature really was, but he was the only connection she had between her old life and wherever she was now. This is not what she imagined Heaven would be like.

"That is because this is not Heaven," he said.

PART ONE

1

Damiel heard the heavy clunk of the lock release from the massive door that stood before him. The thick solid wooden planks were bound together with seamless gold strapping, adorned with swirling golden filigree. The delicate patterns twisted and turned along the door's edges, momentarily leaping off the frame, sparkling. The door had no handle. It was a door that could only be opened by One.

As the final lock clicked, the door slowly began to open, and Damiel was immediately met with a gentle, warm breeze that carried with it soft whispers. The air was filled with the scent of wildflowers as he stood on the threshold, staring at the sight before him. Damiel saw the gentle undulation of the emerald hillsides, sweeping as far back as he could see. The crests of the flowers and grasses swayed with gentle movement.

"After you, Damiel," He said.

Damiel stepped from the crystal golden tile of the Throne Room over the threshold and onto vibrant green pasture. Taking a few steps further, the bustle behind him vanished as the door closed. The harmonious shouts faded, replaced by the comforting rustle of the gentle breeze swimming through the leaves of the trees and the stems of the flowers.

Billowing trees of every color speckled the land. While each tree contained a unique palette of sounds and hues, Damiel admired how the notes harmoniously blended together with one another, as if a swath of rainbow waves of paint moved through the landscape.

His eyes were drawn to one of the trees that sat perched atop one of the highest hillsides in the distance. Its glow reverberated differently, catching his attention. As his eyes adjusted, the creases and veins of the leaves became visible, and he looked beyond the cell walls to the dancing photons, swirling in an electrified ballet of color. Tiny bursts of light popped as he observed, releasing a kaleidoscope of gems. He closed his eyes, yet the brilliant display remained etched in his mind.

"Seems like just yesterday, doesn't it, Damiel," said Creator.

"I wasn't sure I would ever get to see this place again," said Damiel, taking a deep breath. "It's as beautiful as the last time."

As Damiel continued to drink in the landscape, his eyes were drawn to the river cutting through the land. His gaze traced its path—the River of Life, a river known to all in the Kingdom, though few had ever been this close to the headwaters. The River of Life was shallow and scintillating, knitting together the two pieces of land on either side and extended out to the horizon in both directions beyond his line of sight. The slowly flowing water was alive, a dynamic rainbow of textures, sounds, and emotions. But this river was no ordinary river. It was truly special.

Damiel scanned the horizon, matching the landmarks to his memories.

"We were just over there," he said, pointing a short distance to the riverbank.

"Indeed we were." Creator stood by Damiel's side, gazing into the distance just as Damiel was.

Damiel felt honored to be invited to today's assignment—his first apprenticeship. This was unusual as Hosts typically did not take on apprentices so soon after their advancement to an Order. Normally, newly graduated Hosts continued to work together in cohorts, but Creator seemed to have different plans. Damiel wondered what the creation of another Host looked like. Creator only told him that it was a "special assignment."

The rolling landscape brought back a sense of familiarity, although countless ages had passed since Damiel last laid eyes on these pastures. In fact, the only time he was here was on his own day of creation. He could remember how overwhelming that moment was, bursting forth into existence.

"I really do just love this," said Creator, smiling. "Let's go get a bit closer, shall we?"

Creator began to walk down the shallow hill they were on, and Damiel followed.

This was a true honor, but beneath the thrill was a lingering uncertainty, a feeling that had been nagging at him since Creator's selection. The birth moment of an infinite being destined for a unique service to the Kingdom. He saw many Hosts accompany Creator through the very same gold-strapped door, but those moments were always kept private. Birthed in light and Spirit, a Host's creation is a revered moment, each being a new thread woven into the complex tapestry of Creator's plan, an epic unknown to all except Creator.

Damiel belonged to the Heilen tribe, the healers of the Kingdom. He apprenticed with the well-known Asa, a fiery Host whose reputation preceded her in any mission. Upon the recent completion of his own apprenticeship, Damiel was robed with the mantle of the Order of Guardians. It was uncommon for a Heilen to be robed as such, and Creator still had yet to reveal the reason. Heilen specialized in reconciling Creator's vision, but Damiel was honored nonetheless to be chosen to embark on this new project.

"Creator, can I talk to you about the Guardians?" he asked.

"You must be wondering why you received entrance into the Order," said Creator, hopping onto a stone in the path before leaping off it with youthful enthusiasm.

That was precisely the question. But the real mystery ran deeper.

"The other Guardians aren't like me," said Damiel. "And now this new apprentice? I feel woefully unequipped to train anyone outside my cohort."

"I think you'll do a lovely job, Damiel," said Creator. "I sense your uneasiness, but your qualifications are exactly what I am looking for this new Host."

"What is different about this one?" asked Damiel. "I was unfamiliar with the notations of his Traces from his scroll."

"Over here, Damiel!" shouted Creator, picking up His pace as they neared the bottom of the hill. "It's nearly time, and I certainly will not be late. I have been waiting a long time for this moment."

Creator looked back at Damiel, a wide grin spreading across Creator's face. His radiance grew even more intense, as He quickened His pace toward the riverbank. Damiel was unsure if Creator was simply ignoring his questions or was just excited.

"Both!" shouted Creator without turning. "Do you remember how you felt just after?"

"You mean when I was ripped out of nothingness or when the knowledge of eternity was unlocked in my mind?"

"Don't be dramatic, Damiel," said Creator, unfazed.

"I could not contain myself," said Damiel, his tone lowering. He let the memories surface for a moment, unable to find words to describe the overwhelming experience. "The emotions, the sensory overload, the realities of reality."

"Yes, you will want to stay a few paces back so as not to frighten the little one," said Creator.

Damiel slowed his pace as Creator marched to the side of the river and down the final shallow embankment. Damiel came to a stop at the edge of the bank a few measures back.

Creator did not break pace at the water's edge, striding directly into the flow with determination, as water splashed and shimmered against His legs, sending out rhythmic jingles with each step. The water that passed near His legs glowed a vibrant metallic teal, a color that only shone for Creator.

"Do you need me to do anything?" asked Damiel. Creator did not answer him, instead eying the water as if looking for a fish.

Now hunched over, both hands on His knees, Creator raised one arm over His head, pausing for a moment to slowly tickle the air, and then plunged it into the river with full force. The moment of contact sent a thunderous shockwave of teal light and a tremor across the landscape. The trees and wind responded with a gleeful shriek in harmony. Damiel flinched with surprise, craning his neck to try and get a better look of what was happening in the river.

Yanking His arm out, Creator grasped the linen garment of a figure who was now screaming. The trees joined, resonating in lower octaves. The screaming figure sitting in the river was that of a new Host, his apprentice. A Host that Damiel knew nothing about.

The screams began to subside. The figure turned its head slightly, still in panic. Damiel caught his first glimpse. The Host appeared as a boy, perhaps only five Earth orbits old.

Damiel did not yet have many clues as to the type of Host this new creation would be. The only details Damiel knew were the Traces songs in the new Host's Scroll of Life, but the symbology was not one that he recognized.

Since Damiel had never witnessed a Host creation before, he only met the Hosts after they were wrapped with their Traces, which did not change their general form but did paint the colors, symbols, and vibrations around them, stamping their purpose and identifying them for all to see.

From his own experience, Damiel knew he would accompany the boy to the Ministry of Purpose and Destiny to receive the Traces ceremony. Damiel remained silent as the child's screams began to soften and turn merely into panicked deep breathing.

Damiel remembered how disorientating the moment of Creation was. There is nothing quite like going from non-existence to existence, unmatched with exception of the very next moment when the memory arrived. The new Host did not have that yet. The boy still looked around frantically. Damiel took a few paces forward to get closer to the activity.

"Hello," said Creator with a wide smile on His face, staring intently at the boy. "Welcome. I've been waiting for you."

The boy's diamond eyes locked on those of Creator, his breath slowing and drawing more shallow. The rainbow flecks of water caught the light, creating a dazzling display around the boy's form. Damiel took a few more steps forward.

"Adlai, do you know who I Am?" asked Creator.

Damiel's first clue. It did not help. There were no other Hosts with that name.

Adlai wiped the water from his face as his breath now quickened, droplets catching the wind of his breath and spraying out in front of him. Creator relaxed His grip, clutching His hands together and balancing on one knee as the River swirled around them.

"Adlai, do you know who I Am?" asked Creator once more.

A pillar of water appeared in the sky, directing itself into Adlai's head. Damiel could see the boy's demeanor change as the deluge of knowledge of eternity began to pour down.

Adlai bent under the force and appeared to struggle maintaining eye contact, unable to contain the breadth of emotions that Damiel knew all too well he was feeling. Tears of intense love turned to sobs of sorrow and betrayal only to be drowned out by laughter and joy.

Damiel could almost see himself sitting there in the river with the same feelings. He took the moment to examine the boy, who seemed oblivious to Damiel's presence. Perhaps there was a clue somewhere.

Adlai's features were soft and his skin unblemished, yet untouched by the battles that lay ahead of him. All Hosts had scars of some kind, even those that were not destined for battle within any of the Orders that comprised the military.

Adlai had no defining characteristics, except his eyes. His diamond eyes shone like a beacon. Damiel had seen this type of mighty light before, but he could not imagine how it would end up in a new Host.

Adlai began to gain some composure. Creator rose from His kneeling position before bending over, hands on His knees, still observing.

"How are you doing?" He asked. No response from Adlai.

Damiel recalled the moment when his own mind stopped fighting the knowledge infilling and simply waited for it to complete. It was only later that he had time to process and work through the thoughts that now lay dormant in his mind.

"Who is that?" asked Adlai abruptly, turning his head and pointing towards Damiel.

Damiel, startled, momentarily forgot that he was visible. The boy's diamond eyes pierced through him.

"He is your mentor, Adlai," said Creator. "One of your mentors, that is. He will help you on your journey."

"One of his mentors?" asked Damiel. "What exactly does that mean?"

Every newly created Host had a mentor. That was standard, but Damiel did not know of any Host with multiple mentors.

"My full plans will be revealed in time, Damiel," said Creator. "Adlai requires the instruction of many."

The purpose of Heilen was straightforward, and Damiel wondered why Creator would train Adlai with multiple Hosts. Creator helped Adlai to his feet, guiding him up the bank.

"Come with Me," said Creator.

Damiel offered to lend a hand at the edge of the bank, although Adlai did not take it, still in a slight daze as his eyes stayed locked on the ground.

"Adlai," said Creator. "I am certain you are overwhelmed with the last few moments, so please, let us find a resting place for a short pause."

Creator led Adlai up a slight rolling hill. Damiel's gaze followed the gentle curvature of the hill to its peak where a single tree stood. It was a familiar tree for Damiel.

The tree emanated the soft, comforting melody that most trees in the Kingdom sang, although he noticed that the typical resonance emitted from the ground was louder here than in the other parts of the Kingdom.

"It's because of the close proximity to the headwaters," said Creator. Damiel enjoyed the rhythmic notes as the tree played on top of the ground's bass tones.

"Please, have a seat," said Creator.

Adlai sat and Creator knelt down while Damiel circled the tree, still taking in the sights of the landscape.

"Amazing," said Adlai. His eyes were fixed in the distance. Damiel turned to follow his gaze. Perfection.

"Adlai, I am so very pleased to finally meet you," said Creator, "and I'm so glad you enjoy it here. I would love for you to get to know Me."

Damiel turned around to rejoin them as Creator stood up, reaching. Both Adlai and Damiel looked up to the broad and outstretched lush arms of the tree. The outermost limbs waved back and forth in the light breeze, perfectly timed to the melody it still hummed.

Creator plucked a softly colored, plump, orange fruit, which shook the branch, sending out a crescendo within the tree's song.

"This tree is the Tree of Goodness," said Creator, "and its fruit is simply divine. Please. Eat."

Creator nodded an invitation, clasping the fruit with both hands and pushed it into Adlai's.

"Fruit from this tree is a staple for us," said Damiel. "Each variety of tree within the Kingdom embodies a different characteristic, detail, or mystery of Creator."

"And to gain its understanding," said Creator, "you must do My favorite part—Eat it!"

Damiel laughed gently. "With each bite, the mysteries of the fruit reveal themselves from within. It won't be long before you are sharing this fruit with the Heirs."

"The Heirs?" asked Adlai.

"Oh yes," said Creator. "You'll get to meet them soon. Maybe you can eat some fruit with them sometime. The Tree of Goodness in particular is planted throughout every neighborhood. Its flavor is, well, good."

Adlai lifted the fruit with both hands to examine it further. His fingers curled around the fruit, his grip hesitant, as he looked to Creator for a final confirmation. As he did, the color shifted from a soft orange to a glowing gold.

A small smile was the only permission Adlai needed to take a juicy bite, the soft flesh easily melting beneath the pressure of his teeth. Adlai let out a grunt of satisfaction, his smile growing. The dribble of the fruit glistened momentarily around his mouth before dissolving. That was certainly one aspect of the Kingdom that Damiel appreciated: no mess. He did not know how the Heirs on Earth put up with it.

"Damiel will be able to introduce you to all of the fruit in this Kingdom," said Creator. "There will be much for you to eat, so I hope you're hungry. Now finish that up. Damiel will be taking you to your Traces ceremony next, and that's where the real fun begins."

2

Adlai's teeth tore through the juicy ripe fruit of the Tree of Goodness. With each bite, knowledge materialized within his mind at a rapid pace, flowing into his very essence. He was becoming the goodness that he ate. The melodious wafts of air from the trees swept around, wrapping him in a comforting garment. He admired Creator without relenting on the fruit. As Adlai ate, he noticed Creator's features softening and morphing, reflecting the growing depth of his own understanding. The momentary peace allowed him to begin sifting through the new memories. A door in his mind creaked open.

"Hello, Adlai," interrupted the other being. "My name is Damiel. It's a pleasure to meet you."

Adlai was unsure of this creature now speaking to him. It stood at a distance, hands clasped. A swirl of colors wrapped around it, looking pleasant enough. Adlai looked back to Creator for affirmation.

"Damiel will do you no harm, Adlai," said Creator. "I created him just as I have created you. He will be helping you complete your training before your missions begin. I have many plans in store for the two of you."

"Mission?" asked Adlai.

He paged through his memories for a contextual meaning of the word. None.

"Purpose," said Damiel. "You have a purpose."

"Now the Orchestra is awaiting your arrival," said Creator. "Damiel has instructions for the ceremony. Once you are done, we'll see how you're feeling. This way, please."

He stretched out His arm to the side, guiding them back down the gentle slope. Adlai struggled to stand, feeling heavy from the weighty fruit.

"Up! Up!" said Creator, reaching down towards him. "Here we go. Let's get you up. You ate that mighty quickly!"

Creator grabbed Adlai's hands, pulling him to his feet. As Adlai stood, he dropped the remaining fruit, watching as it rolled to the foot of the hill, where it slowed and dissolved into the ground. A moment later, a sapling tree burst from the soil surface, sending out a few leaves on its thin trunk.

"Goodness grows very well here," said Creator. "Great ground!"

Adlai looked up at Creator and then back down at the sapling. The trunk twisted skyward, branches and leaves unfolding at a steadily quickening pace. As it reached upwards, the tree sang a high octave melody that harmonized with the chorus of the surrounding trees. Twisting itself higher and higher, glistening orange fruit swelled from the outermost branches. Adlai was enamored with the process.

"Come, Adlai. We have an appointment," said Creator. Adlai tore his gaze from the tree to find Creator beside him, while Damiel stood a few paces above them.

Creator waved His hand towards the horizon, and a doorway appeared at the hill's base by the river's edge.

"Right this way, Adlai," said Damiel.

Adlai glanced to Creator, who nodded with a smile. Damiel walked towards him, passing and continued down the hill. After a brief pause while the request settled, Adlai ran a few steps to catch up, looking up at Damiel and then to the door.

As they walked towards the door, they passed the new tree, which grew to a comparable size to the others nearby. It's trunk still undulated as it shook loose leaves from the branches, pushing them out to fill in the gaps in the foliage. Adlai's eyes widened at the sight of the succulent fruit hanging just out of his reach.

"Don't worry, there will be more," called Creator from behind him. Adlai looked back and smiled.

As they neared the door, its intricate details became clear. The wood appeared as if woven from fabric, with fine gold accents that swam along the trim in time with the background vocals of the meadow. Adlai's eyes traced the path of the gold, spiraling outward before collapsing in an endless, mesmerizing pattern. His vision magnified, focusing on the bonds between the molecules of the stitching. He looked deeper, seeing the sheet music upon which each molecule danced—the song of its creation.

"Even the trim has purpose here, Adlai," said Creator. Adlai looked back as the intricate golden vibrations faded from focus, and the doorway re-emerged into view. The trim continued to swim.

"Where does this go?" asked Adlai.

"This is the entrance to the Ministry of Purpose and Destiny," said Damiel. "It's where you will receive these."

Damiel moved his hand upward, swirling it over his head through the pattern of colors and shapes. "You'll get your Traces."

"You saw the song for the trim," said Creator. "I have a song for you too."

Adlai looked at his hands. His focus did not shift.

"Your depth will come with time," said Creator. "Look at what I sang over Damiel." Creator walked over, swirling His hand through the colorful fabric above Damiel's head.

"These were sung and painted over me on my Creation Day," said Damiel. "I am a member of the Heilen."

"Is that what I'll become?" asked Adlai, glancing over Damiel's Traces with new curiosity.

"Questions can come later," said Creator. "You two have an appointment. Now get on through there!"

Adlai looked back at the door.

"These doorways are our method of transport among the sectors within the Kingdom," said Damiel. "They take us just about everywhere."

3

Damiel approached the dauntingly large, rich brown double doors. He marveled at the ultra-fine gold inlay that wove through the wood, shimmering like stardust. The door peaked in a rounded steeple, with two large pillars rising from each side, the trim intricately carved with swirling geometries and ornamented with iridescent blue that swirled and flowed like the waters of the River of Life. Crown molding adorned the top, resplendent with even more gold.

"You will see this style around here quite a bit," said Damiel. "It is one of Creator's favorites."

Adlai stared blankly, showing no sign of having registered Damiel's words.

"The door," said Damiel, pointing, unsure if Adlai heard him.

Adlai did not answer.

Damiel paused, searching Adlai's face for acknowledgment or understanding. None came. Were all new Hosts like this, or did he just get a particularly unresponsive one? Damiel shifted his attention back to the door. He grasped the vine-engraved handles in both hands and twisted them down. There was a loud metallic *click* as the locks released, and the doors swung open inwardly without effort under his weight.

A rush of warm, honey-scented air welcomed them, mingling with the vibrant symphony of music, colors, and chatter from the beings in the lively foyer. Damiel closed his eyes, inhaling deeply, connecting with the buzz in the room. He turned around to gauge Adlai's reaction to the spectacle now in front of them, but Adlai was nowhere to be seen.

"Adlai!" shouted Damiel over the commotion, spinning around to spot the boy.

Damiel whipped around to see that Adlai had slipped under his arm and was already heading toward the center of the crowded room.

Damiel dodged a variety of beings as he jogged a few paces to catch up to Adlai, briefly admiring the intricate floor tiling beneath him. Each step set off bursts of green light, splashing like liquid across the floor.

"Adlai!" he shouted once more.

The boy seemed oblivious to Damiel's calls, caught up in the moment as he took in the room's activity. Damiel, too, was momentarily overwhelmed by the sights and sounds. As he caught up to Adlai, he slowed his pace, placing his hand on the boy's shoulder to keep track of him. Together, they turned slowly, absorbing the atmosphere.

The room was unexpectedly compact for this realm. The ceilings, visible for once, radiated sunset colors, making the space feel more expansive. The ceiling's colors flowed outwards towards the sides of the room where they melted down the walls in the form of solid pillars of flowing water, which then splashed into the floor. Damiel looked down as he tapped his foot. A small splash of green light glinted before melting back into the ground. Adlai lifted each foot, splashing multiple times and inspecting the reaction.

The anticipation in the room was palpable. Like any moment of great expectation, there was slight trepidation mixed with excitement among the room's occupants.

Hosts of all shapes and sizes were present, some unlike anything Damiel had seen before—large, small, flying, swimming, flaming, bending, glowing. Guides and their new mentees either waited their turn or returned from their session with the Orchestra.

A Host behind Adlai caught Damiel's attention. A member of the Asaad. The Host's lion-like head rested heavily on a solid frame, draped in flowing black and red robes. A wide smile spread across its face. The energy of the room caused the Host's magenta-colored Traces to bounce, spring, and gallop across the room. The colored music notes that whirled around the Host's head melded with a neighbor's, spiraling upwards into a gradient and creating new melodies before dissolving and drifting back down over the heads of their chosen.

Damiel recalled his first time in this room, too overwhelmed back then to appreciate its vibrant energy. *Poor Adlai*, he thought, looking over at the quiet boy.

The swirling colors of the various Hosts' Traces blended together, forming beaming beacons of light throughout the room. Flashes of azure and emerald, ruby and tidras—a dance of hues building to an explosion, each climax met with a triumphant metallic crash and glints of shimmering gold trailing down before dissipating.

"Stunning, isn't it?" said Damiel.

No answer.

Damiel wanted to continue admiring the moment, but he felt the tug of their appointment. He gave a gentle pull with his hand, which still remained on Adlai's shoulder. He turned, searching for some orientation in the room.

"Come, it's time for us to move along," said Damiel.

His eyes landed on a sign near the wall where they had entered. A series of gateway doors rapidly opened and closed as new pairs quietly entered or boisterously left the foyer.

"Over there," he said, pointing to a sign on the right past the doors. "Orchestra entrance is that way."

Set on not losing the boy again, Damiel kept his hand firmly on Adlai's shoulder as the two began to make their way through the crowd.

The fanciful door under the entrance sign resembled the foyer entrance but was a single door this time. As they approached, the door swung open, and they were greeted by a Host dressed in formal wear, his thick black robes draped around him.

"Right on time!" said the Host with flaming hair and scaled silver skin, smiling broadly.

Adlai pulled back in shock, nearly stumbling.

Damiel glanced at the Host's Traces, which now danced around his flaming hair on tempo with the room's ambiance. There was no mistaking this one. There was only one of these in the entire Kingdom.

"Conductor!"

"Welcome Damiel!" said the Conductor. "This must be Adlai," stooping down and placing both hands on his knees.

"How are you holding up, boy?" the Conductor asked, his face at eye level with Adlai.

"Good," said Adlai flatly.

Damiel tilted his head in surprise, finally hearing the boy speak.

"He's still in a bit of shock," said Damiel. "That's the first thing he's said since we arrived."

"Well that won't stop anytime soon," said the Conductor. "Only gets worse from here. In a good way! Poor boy is in for a real treat. Don't worry, Son. They all come in looking like you."

Damiel gave a faint smile.

"Please, come in," said the Conductor. "We've been expecting you."

He stepped to the side and took a deep bow, unfolding his left arm to guide them into the room.

"Please, after you," he said, holding the deep bow.

Damiel noticed the color gradient of the flames in the Conductor's hair, shifting from deep sapphire blue at the roots to nearly transparent at the tips. His Traces continued to bounce in unison with the licks of flame.

Damiel and Adlai entered as the Conductor stood and shut the door behind them. The commotion of the foyer instantly disappeared with the closure of the door. They were in a much smaller room now lit by candlelight. The soft riffs of instruments wafted in from the only other doorway on the opposite side of the room.

"Now you've had a big day already, and it won't stop here," said the Conductor. "Welcome to your Traces anointing, my dear boy!"

The Conductor raised his hand over his head, bringing it down in an overly dramatic swoosh as if the orchestra were already in front of him.

"Now, let's see his papers." The Conductor pinched his fingers together with excited impatience. Damiel reached into his robe to furnish the gold scroll.

"The instructions seemed...peculiar," said Damiel. "I did not understand most of them. I trust it makes more sense to you."

The Conductor's eyes lit up with excitement at the promise of a new challenge. He snatched the scroll and instantly stretched it to the full length, first moving it up towards the ceiling, then down towards the ground. The Conductor tilted his head from side to side, lips moving with only mutterings coming out.

"Hmmmm....Oh? Interesting.... Well, this is different."

The Conductor paused, looking up over the scroll to Damiel.

"Did you know about this?" asked the Conductor.

"I wish I did."

"And Creator gave you…no further instruction?"

The Conductor brought his hands together, folding the scroll in half and gazed at Damiel with a questioning look.

"I am afraid He has not made me privy to the details of Adlai's anointing," said Damiel.

"No matter, no matter," said the Conductor. "This will be a fun one. A first for me!"

The Conductor opened the scroll again, scanned it once more, then began rolling the parchment back up.

"Yes, all seems to be in order. Very good, my dear boy." The Conductor turned and walked through the doorway, speaking over his shoulder. "Now, let's make you an Archangel."

4

Damiel raised his eyebrows, leaning in.

"Archangel?" he questioned. "How can that be?"

Questions swirled through Damiel's mind. Archangels held unique positions in the Kingdom, both acting as Hosts and also holding some of the seats on the Divine Council. They were leaders, and they were doers. No new Archangels had been created since the Foundations.

Damiel looked at Adlai, who now stood next to the side wall, staring at a simple picture with a single spotlight. The Conductor walked back into the room, head buried in the scroll once more.

"Something the matter?" asked Damiel.

"Well, I've never done one of these before. All of the Divine Council were created long before any of us. Creator and Spirit did the anointing Themselves, so I just need to double check a few items here—"

His voice trailed off, still concentrating on the scroll.

"Very good, all ready," said the Conductor. "Come, Adlai."

The boy rejoined the conversation.

"Shall I follow you?" asked Damiel.

"Yes, in just a moment. I'll be taking Adlai to the stage and then will show you to your seat. You are in for quite the show. Please wait here."

The Conductor placed his hand on Adlai's back, and they exited the room. Damiel struggled to understand what exactly was happening. He barely finished his own training, and here he was, a Level 1 Heilen acting as the mentor for a new Archangel. Arch. Angel.

The Conductor reappeared in the doorway.

"Damiel? Please, this way."

The Conductor gestured through the door. His smile was even larger now, and his hair flickered at an accelerated pace. Damiel strode towards the Conductor, passing the painting where Adlai had stood. He paused.

He recognized several of the individuals in the painting, but one caught his eye. Gemstones of every color cascaded like beads of water down the side of his face, across his neck, and down his chest. The golden robes were so vibrant that the rainbow spectrum glinted from the highlights.

"Conductor, is this...?" his voice trailed off before finishing. Damiel raised his hand to point at the individual in the painting.

"Helel?" said the Conductor. "Yes, quite the sight, wasn't he? He certainly does not look like that any longer, but he was quite stunning."

"Did you know him, Conductor?"

"Oh yes, most certainly. He created many of the compositions we use to this day. His voice was unlike any other. I truly miss it. You did not know him?"

"I was still too young when he was cast out. My mentor was devastated when it happened."

"We all were," said the Conductor. "That was the darkest day this place has ever seen. I lost many colleagues."

"Conductor," Damiel paused, "are you concerned that a new Archangel is being created?"

"Certainly not," he said with a confident increase in volume.

"You aren't concerned that this could end up like Helel?"

"Of course not, my friend! You are his mentor," said the Conductor.

"Exactly, Adlai is my first mentee. I have never done this before."

"And apparently, that is exactly what Creator knows to be needed," said the Conductor. "The Divine Council would not accept an addition such as this without careful consideration. Damiel, Creator will reveal His plan. Rest in His perfection, not your own, and enjoy the story that will unfold before you. Now, please, join me. We have an anointing to commence. This way please."

The Conductor extended his arm back out and flicked his hand a few times to have Damiel move along before walking briskly away.

"Please, we are about to begin," shouted the Conductor over his shoulder.

Damiel passed through the door, which led into a dark hallway. Stars of varying sizes sparkled across the walls and ceiling, powdery clouds of green, purple, and red galaxies dotting the vast background. A mineral scent permeated the air. It reminded Damiel of one of his favorite spots on Earth, one of the few where he felt as close to this realm as he could.

Damiel continued to walk as his eyes enjoyed the scene above him. The colors dissipated as another doorway led him into the ground level of the grand orchestra room. He stood staring into the orchestra pit, a dizzying sea of instruments, Hosts, and Traces that extended back as far as he could see, creating a subtle rainbow river of light reaching out into the distance.

To his right, Damiel saw Adlai sitting on a nondescript black stool on the raised darkened stage above the orchestra. A light blue shimmer on the surface of the billowing stage curtains next to him caught his eye, drawing it upward. He could not see the ceiling as the curtains extended beyond the dim light of the room. To his left beyond the orchestra were the audience seats. They too extended higher and higher beyond his sight into the distance. Row after row streaming off into the darkness and vertically towards the back of the room, wherever it may be. Damiel could not see the walls in either direction, only the room from which he just emerged. The space was enormous, and yet, no one was in the audience.

"How many seats are here, Conductor?" asked Damiel.

"As many as we need. This way please."

The Conductor, now moving to Damiel's back, guided him away from the orchestra and to the seating arena, pushing him up the steps a few rows before guiding him into a seat. The seats were identical with the exception of the one he now stood in front of. The back of the seat was wrapped with a simple red ribbon, which read:

Reserved
Damiel

"Here we are," said the Conductor. "Please have a seat and make yourself comfortable."

27

The Conductor smiled and clasped his hands together.

"Can I offer you any food or beverage before we begin?" he asked.

"No, that's quite all right."

"As you wish," said the Conductor. "We will begin momentarily."

The Conductor took a deep bow before skipping down the steps and disappearing behind the stage.

Damiel took his seat. The room was dark and empty with exception of the colored river of orchestra members illuminating the stage in front of Adlai.

The boy rested his feet on the stool's simple cross-support, hands folded in his lap, gaze fixed on the colors before him. The bustle in the orchestra slowly dimmed. Their Traces retreated to a few swirling puffs of multi-colored glow.

A warm sensation stirred within Damiel.

"Is this seat taken?" came a voice beside him. Creator.

Damiel turned his head to see Creator sitting next to him with a large bowl of unknown food and a huge grin.

"Yes, yes, of course," Damiel stuttered. "I mean, 'no.' It's not taken."

"It's a joke, Damiel," said Creator, leaning with His body to nudge him. "Lighten up. Don't worry. We'll talk. Just enjoy the show."

Creator grabbed a handful of the pebble sized food and tossed them all in His mouth. He gestured with His eyes and the box to Damiel.

"No, thank you," said Damiel.

"Come on," said Creator. "I know you want to try one. You haven't had this before."

"What is it?" asked Damiel.

"I am going to call it 'caramel corn.' A real treat. Perfect for the show."

Damiel didn't know what caramel or corn was, but he decided today was a day of new experiences. He grabbed a few morsels. They were rough and hard, but light. He delicately placed one in his mouth. *Crunch.*

The brittle exterior gave way to a soft interior as flavors of butter, vanilla, and toffee swept across his palate.

"Oh, this is nice," said Damiel.

"I thought so too," said Creator. "I can't wait to teach the Heirs. Please, have as much as you like."

Before Damiel could reach for another handful, a new small light appeared in front of the orchestra. The light grew vertically, forming the licking flames of the Conductor's hair as he arose from below the stage. At his pinnacle position, the Conductor stretched out his hands on either side without movement. Damiel noticed Conductor make a quick glance and smile in his direction, surely meant for Creator. Creator waved and dropped a few more kernels in His mouth.

Complete silence in the room. The only sound was the realm's drumbeat, resonating within his heart.

The room members were all motionless, but Damiel suddenly noticed a soft hum, barely audible, reverberating throughout the room. So soft, he wondered if the note had been there all along. A single note hung in the air, growing in intensity.

The show had begun.

A light azure mist began to rise from the instruments, swaying and undulating just above their heads. It billowed up like smoke. Now covering the feet of the Conductor, it slowly cascaded outwards. Then a new major note struck. Then a new cord. The rich mist began to swirl around the front of the stage. Still soft and gentle, the notes caused the mist to gradually move throughout the space, washing it clean. Somehow, the sounds made the room feel more quiet and still. Perfect peace.

Damiel focused on one area of the mist. His eyes drew in as the wave's photons came into view. He observed them, dancing almost. They spun as they vibrated together in a wave. Each shift in note subtly altered the colors' frequency. The waves of blue washed by, then pulled back in perfect synchronization. He refocused to bring the stage back into view.

The mist cascaded over the orchestra area and outwards towards him in the audience, curling up on itself only to fall back down, sending out a white illumination where it struck. Damiel felt a light dampness form on his face as the mist passed by. He looked to Creator, who now had His eyes shut while maintaining an enormous smile.

The gentle music notes continued. Creator's face shifted as He now bit down on His lower lip, body poised on a note, entranced in the moment. Damiel followed suit, closing his eyes and just felt. He felt the music—each note, each vibration. His mind's eye could still see the photon waves cleansing and purging. He felt it synchronizing the energy of the room. He felt the mist continuing to sweep by. He felt the individual particles pass, some momentarily sticking to his face, gently cooling. He opened his mouth ever so slightly so as to taste the blanket of light. A cool breath of peppermint.

The room now smelled distinctly of water. Cleansed and pure. Damiel felt like he could stay in this moment of peace forever.

"Perfect, isn't it?" said Creator.

Damiel made no sound nor opened his eyes, only smiled. He knew Creator could hear his response.

Thrummmmmmm. A new note abruptly appeared. *Thrummmm. Thrummmm.* A gentle beat emerged from the misty breeze. The notes were percussive but passed by Damiel as a wind. They beat in synchronization with his heart. The notes grew gradually louder. Louder and louder. These notes were unmistakable. They were the heartbeat. The heartbeat of this realm. The heartbeat of the Kingdom. Always feeling it internally, the beat took on a new power as he heard them audibly in the room.

As the percussion grew in volume and complexity, Damiel opened his eyes. Adlai still sat dutifully on his stool, eyes locked on the Conductor, who now lightly bounced with each note. The new percussive sounds visualized as teal spikes popping out of blanketing waves that rippled across the stage, orchestra, and audience, chasing out the previous mist, which melted down into the floor.

The volume grew. Damiel could no longer see the Conductor or orchestra. Now enveloping the room, the teal blanket covered the entire space with the exception of Adlai, whose narrow stool and slim body poked up above the surface. He appeared once again as though he were back in the River of Life. The glow of the teal shone upwards on his skin, illuminating him.

While watching the orchestra area, Damiel saw new swirls of color forming below the teal blanket. First pooling, then exploding upwards. New beats building from the base, synchronizing and harmonizing, each jetting up in new color spikes, then falling and washing out through the blanket still covering the room. Reds, greens, blues, every color imaginable spraying and spreading. The aromas shifted rapidly as the colors moved past him. Each breath painted a different scent.

The complexity grew. High notes, low notes, clangs, and clashes. Rapid pitter patter and deep blasts that Damiel could feel in the core of his being.

As the calamity of beauty built to an almost unbearable peak, Damiel hung on the edge of his seat and saw Adlai was doing the same. It was as if Damiel was back on his own Day of Creation. The room was awash with color and sound. Building. Higher and higher. Louder and louder. Aching for the peak.

The pace quickened to a fever pitch, rainbow waves streaming out in every direction.

Then suddenly, silence.

In a deafening moment, the percussion stopped, and the colors vanished in an instant. Damiel drew in a quick deep breath, overwhelmed by the stark transition. But the moment was short-lived.

"That was just the warm-up," said Creator.

The intense percussive notes exploded back into full intensity once more. The colors so strong now began to display emergent colors that Damiel had never seen before. The Conductor, now leaping in place, faced Adlai. The Conductor raised his arms, stretching them toward Adlai, directing the waves of light that poured down. Other streams swept up into the ceiling far beyond where Damiel could see, then crashing down as a waterfall directly on Adlai's head. An electrically colored rainbow waterfall.

Adlai was barely visible underneath the cascade. His hands gripped the sides of the stool and his mouth was open and breathing heavily. He may have been laughing or screaming, but the sound of the orchestra was overwhelmingly loud.

As the colors poured into him from his feet and head, they gushed from him through his chest, bursting out in front of him as a river, pooling onto the floor of the stage before flowing towards the edges of the room.

"We're getting to My favorite part," said Creator. "Here they come."

From behind Adlai, three radiant purple robes flowed into view. Scribes. Their robes were so dark that they reflected the mass of colors that continued to pour down next to them. Their heads were covered by hoods. Damiel could only see their hands.

First, foot stomps in unison with one another and in synchronization with the orchestra. The Scribes brandished slender brushes from the sleeves of their robes with a dramatic flair, one for each hand, and without pause, began to draw. The brushes whipped and slashed, dotted and swiped nearly faster than Damiel could process. As a variety of colors remained in the brush wakes, the wet ink lines dripped like honey in the air. Each hand drawing different symbols at the same time, these were Damiel's first indication of Creator's intention for Adlai. Damiel leaned forward in awe of what he saw.

In rapid succession, the Scribes whipped their brushes in unison with the percussion that overwhelmed the room. Swinging their arms in broad strokes and feet stepping, jumping, and sliding from side to side to draw the massive symbols, the Scribes danced to the beat.

As each Scribe completed a symbol, they leaned in, exhaled deeply with their whole body, and with a quick twirl, sent the symbols crashing into Adlai from all angles as they all called out with cheers of celebration.

With each impact, Adlai shifted in his chair. His looks were now different. Adlai sat for only a few moments, yet he now appeared slightly older to Damiel. His diamond eyes somehow grew in intensity. His Traces matured him. Adlai no longer displayed a look of shock and silenced screaming. Instead, the boy laughed without control. It was a wonder how he even remained on the stool at this point as he continued to be blasted from every side.

As soon as the thought passed through Damiel's mind, Adlai abruptly fell face forward from the stool, landing squarely in the water. Arms and legs outstretched, the rainbow waterfall did not let up, pummeling his body on the ground. Neither the Conductor nor the orchestra seemed concerned. In fact, they each picked up the pace even more. The Scribes, now bouncing higher than before, perhaps jumping more than drawing by now, splashed in the cascading water that flowed from Adlai's body, occasionally kicking the water and sending a spray of color over the orchestra and into the audience seats.

Adlai showed signs of movement as he brought his hands to his sides to push himself up onto his hands and knees. Visibly battling the force of the waterfall, Adlai struggled but successfully made it to his feet. An emotionless face quickly shifting to a grin, Adlai began to bounce, then to hop, then to leap, then to dance with complete abandon underneath the waterfall with the Scribes.

The Scribes retracted their brushes, looking upwards, and began to spin, dancing with Adlai in the cascade. The rainbow waterfall followed Adlai around on the stage, which he now generously utilized.

The group continued to jump, splash, dance, and shout.

In a moment of pure ecstasy, or perhaps exhaustion, Adlai collapsed onto his knees, and all sound and movement precisely stopped.

The room was silent, although the ghostly remnants of the music still resounded in Damiel's ears. The lingering rainbow water fell in a single column before flowing outwards, dissolving, leaving the stage dark once more.

Creator leapt up, clapping with infectious enthusiasm.

"Magnificent!" He exclaimed. "Truly magnificent!"

Creator squeezed past Damiel and ran to the stage. Jumping over the heads of the orchestra and receding colored waters, Creator landed on the Conductor's podium and aggressively embraced him.

"Well done, Conductor!" He said. "Exactly what I had in mind."

"My pleasure, Creator."

The Conductor took a bow, even deeper than his normal deep bow and held it for just a few moments longer. By the time he arose, Creator was gone. He had skipped over to where Adlai remained on his hands and knees and breathing heavily.

"Damiel!" shouted Creator.

Creator waved him over. Damiel was pulled back into the present moment, stuck in his seat and still in shock at what he witnessed. He nearly forgot that the meek looking boy on his knees had just received a declaration never before carried by a Host. Damiel observed the swirling multicolored Traces above Adlai's head. *This changes everything.*

5

Damiel sat motionless. Adlai's Traces pulsed and dazzled, forming their own scenes within the structure.

"Damiel, get up here!" shouted Creator. "You've got to see this!"

Damiel blinked a few times, attempting to reorient his body while still studying the glowing Traces. A specific spiral shape encircled the entirety of the Traces, a very distinct symbol. Adlai was indeed an Archangel. But the majority of the symbols were unique, unlike any seen above any Host. Damiel marveled, sensing the deeper connection of these special Traces.

The Conductor stood below with the Orchestra, covered by a blanket of color as he boisterously greeted and thanked them. With each handshake and hug, a small spurt of color shot up above their heads, intertwining with one another to form a simple melody.

Damiel rose slowly, steadying himself with both hands on the sides of the chair before finding his bearings and walking down the steps of the seating area and joining the celebration.

At the edge of the stage, Creator welcomed Damiel with open arms. "Oh, Damiel! Wasn't that just wonderful? I must say, I knew it would be good, but that was just splendid! What did you think, Damiel?"

The grin on the Creator's face could not have been larger.

"It was...incredible," said Damiel, fumbling for words. "Astounding in fact. I can...barely comprehend the implications. Just look at them."

Damiel's eyes remained fixed on the undulating palette of color above Adlai's head.

"Grand! Isn't it?" said Creator.

"Creator," a soft voice whispered.

Adlai repositioned himself, lifting a leg to balance on and pushing himself back up to a standing position, albeit still wobbly.

"How do you feel?" asked Creator, admiring him as He circled the boy. "You've had quite a bit of excitement for the day."

Creator reached into a fold of His robe.

"Here. Eat this," He said, pulling His hand out to produce a steaming, honey butter biscuit. "It will make you feel better. It's one of My favorites."

Adlai slowly reached out, tenderly gasped the morsel, and took a small bite. His eyes grew wide as he chewed. Damiel's eyes drifted back to the Traces. They shimmered with symbols he barely recognized, intricate shapes that pulsed like living things.

"Creator, surely I am not the one to mentor this boy," said Damiel.

"You are exactly the one to mentor this boy."

"The Traces," said Damiel. "They are…signs I've never seen before. Just look at them. There are signs that I do not possess. Signs that point to something I do not even understand."

"Damiel, if you were not exactly what this boy needed, do you really think I would put him in your care?"

"Of course not, but—"

"You are right, though, Damiel. You don't have all the answers. But that, in fact, is exactly what is needed. So, you are perfect!"

He loves His riddles. Damiel did not respond. Creator maintained the smile.

"Don't you trust Me, Damiel?" asked Creator.

Damiel still had no response.

"I know this is much to handle," said Creator, conceding the silence. "You are right. This is no small task. I have been looking forward to this day forever, and I am so excited that you get to be a part of it. You will have answers soon enough, but for the moment, I think it would be best for you to take Adlai back to the Heilen. Perhaps you will find some answers there."

Damiel felt a tug at his finger. Looking down, he found Adlai maneuvering a hand into his while still tearing through the biscuit with the other. Damiel sighed.

"He's not a Heilen though, is he?"

"In a way, he is, but you don't have to be a Heilen to enjoy their company. You both need some rest."

"Very well, Creator. Come, Adlai. I would like to introduce you to some of my colleagues."

Creator bent down and tousled Adlai's hair.

"You did splendid today, Adlai," He said. "Enjoy your biscuit."

Creator enveloped Damiel in a hug with a sharp inhale and slow, steady exhale. Damiel reciprocated as best he could.

"Carry on," said Creator. "I have an appointment I must be tending to."

Creator strode to the side of the stage, disappearing behind the curtain.

Damiel looked down at Adlai, admiring the shimmering and dancing Traces newly emblazoned above his head. *What am I supposed to do with this? If anyone needed mentoring, it's me.*

"Still here?" asked the disembodied head of the Conductor, floating on the floor of the stage as he peeked from the orchestra pit.

"Yes, we were just leaving," said Damiel.

"Please, let me show you out."

The Conductor hoisted himself up onto the stage, rolling a few times before making it back to his feet and skipping over to meet the pair. He placed a hand each on Adlai and Damiel.

"This has been such a joy, you two!" said the Conductor. "I must say, this may be our best work thus far! Great things are coming."

The Conductor leaned back with a proud smile.

"A masterpiece!" he said. "Please, follow me this way. This has been a true pleasure."

The three of them walked single file through the backstage and returned to the small foyer.

"This changes things, doesn't it, Conductor?" asked Damiel.

The Conductor's eyes sparkled as he replied, "Most certainly. Creator's designs are…always fascinating."

The Conductor opened the door, immediately filling the room with the hustle and bustle of the arriving area.

"Farewell, you two!" said the Conductor.

Damiel and Adlai exited as the Conductor aggressively waved to them. Continuing to walk, they passed a disoriented new Host and her mentor walking the other way.

"Right on time," they heard the Conductor say, followed by the close of the door.

Damiel and Adlai passed through the short hallway, the sounds of the crowd growing louder. As they made their way into the open area, Damiel's pace slowed as wings stilled, whispers spread, and a low hum of energy built as Adlai's presence drew the undivided gaze of the entire room. Damiel felt Adlai squeeze his hand.

Damiel observed the crowd members staring intently at the Traces above Adlai's head. The bright but muddled glow of Traces in the room seemed almost dim compared to what encircled Adlai. Damiel scanned their hearts, looking for any signs of recognition that might help decipher what swirled above Adlai.

The crowd was a mix of smiles and whispers. A large, looming Host approached, crouching down. The being's eye-studded wings wrapped its body but opened as he approached, revealing further layers of eyes across its entire body. All of its eyes looked at Adlai's face, then stepping slightly to the side to look at the Traces while moving around. The Host's wings extended abruptly outward, and it leaned its head back, letting out a thunderous trumpet from its elongated snout as the foyer erupted in a cheer.

Damiel understood the celebration even if he did not understand precisely what was happening. Adlai was quite unique, truly one of a kind. A new Host meant change for the Kingdom, and Creator's changes were always truly spectacular. This time, however, Damiel found himself right in the middle. While he felt the celebration in his heart, Damiel wrestled with his role in this particular grand plan.

Pushing his way through the chanting and celebrating crowd, Damiel led Adlai by the hand to the edge of the room where they could make their escape. As they walked, Hosts brushed their various limbs through Adlai's Traces, sending them whirling around and clanging joyously. Adlai was clearly oblivious, but his Traces were celebrating alongside those in the room, joining together and spiraling upward.

They reached the door for their destination. Opening it, Damiel took one last look at the room. Pure jubilation. He took a breath, exhaling the trepidation and breathing in the excitement for what was coming.

6

Adlai braced himself, tingling as an electric buzz surged through his body. He sensed the energy arcing above him like a charged atmosphere, vibrant and alive. Damiel held his hand as they walked through the dark corridor back into the Conductor's room. Damiel and the Conductor exchanged pleasantries, but Adlai did not listen. He felt them. He felt the exchange interacting with the field of energy around him. Their words came as sensations. He felt the warmth of the Conductor and the shakiness of Damiel. Before he could inspect the pulses further, Damiel led him out the door.

A wave of new noise filled the room. Adlai felt energy approaching. He looked up. Two Hosts. As they passed by, Adlai knew them instantly as if their entire story was dropped into his mind. He felt their energy co-mingle with his for a moment as the fields interacted. His thoughts were still scrambled, but he felt them unfolding like a scroll gradually revealing its secrets.

Adlai followed Damiel's lead as the excitement of the foyer grew. He felt Damiel's uncertainty, the only one in the room. With his eyes on the ground, Adlai saw the ground shift to the shimmering blue and green splashes as he walked into the foyer. A wave of identities flowed through him as the room came to a silent halt. He looked up.

All eyes were on him. A Host approached. The Host's identity appeared in his mind. Salphiraen, a member of the Hasorah tribe. A declarer. The being's face was carried by a feathered, wrapped body. The elongated mouth of the being protruded out, narrowing before flaring at the end.

Adlai felt a probing sensation through his chest. Curiosity. Multiple sets of wings unfolded, stretching back to reveal new eyes all over, each independently inspecting Adlai. He felt the being's energy assessing him. The eyes continued to scan. The being tilted its head back before letting out an abrupt rhythm of blasts from its mouth. Adlai instinctively knew that it was a sound of approval.

The room erupted in a roar as Adlai felt the energy field surge with emotions. He felt each and every one individually and collectively all at the same time. He felt their joy and excitement. He felt their unknowing.

Damiel continued to lead him through the celebratory crowd towards one of the exit doors. Adlai felt serenity on the other side. Damiel opened the door and allowed Adlai to pass through. He took a step through.

Wet. Adlai's feet first touched shallow water, not even reaching halfway up his foot. He took several more steps. As the door closed, the noise shifted from the foyer's cheers to gentle waves and light wind. Adlai turned to see the unsuspecting door perched on a rock pile behind them.

"Welcome to the Hearth of the Heilen," said Damiel, "where those that heal gather."

A small wave lapped at their feet. Adlai felt Damiel's energy tension in his field loosening. The breeze over the water was a welcome sensation. Each lick of the wave also brought a new scent with it, mostly floral.

"Lake," said Adlai.

"Yes, we are at one of the many bodies of water in this realm, the Lake of Restoration. The river that feeds this lake is the River of Life."

"There's no one here," said Adlai, exploring the energy field around them as far as he could reach.

"We are on the outskirts of the land. I wanted to show you this important transition point."

Damiel gestured upriver, which extended up into a forested area.

"These waters flow throughout the Kingdom," said Damiel. "Every land you enter touches these waters. Through every door, each place is connected to this water. It brings and gives life to all. These waters feed the lake as it sinks ever deeper into this place, and it is where we derive the healing powers of our kind before it continues its journey onwards."

Adlai could not see the edge of the lake in front of him as it extended into the horizon. The sun set in the distance, casting a warm glow of flowing reds and pinks across the water. He looked down at the ground. The gently bubbling waters of the river to his left bounced on and around small stones.

"That's where I came from," said Adlai.

He pointed to the water.

"True, indeed. We were in a different part of the Kingdom, but you were plucked from the same river. Allow me to show you around."

Damiel reached his hand towards Adlai, and he took it. Adlai felt warmth with the sensation of lifting. He looked down to see his feet no longer on the ground. He looked up at Damiel to see a set of enormous shimmering blue wings had emerged from Damiel's back, robust feathers overlaid on one another. Their wide breadth rhythmically sweeping through the air, holding the pair aloft. They rose slightly further but still beneath the peaks of the nearby trees. Adlai felt his hand slip as Damiel released him. Adlai's breath leapt in his throat. The shock lasted only a moment as Adlai felt a tug on his back, holding him in place in the air.

"Stunning," said Damiel, staring behind Adlai.

Adlai looked up. Above his whirling Traces stretched a series of multiple wings interwoven across one another, extending beyond his back. They dazzled with an array of rainbow colors, and as they swept to-and-fro, Adlai's Traces zoomed around them, creating a glittering display of light all around him. He examined the wing's covering. The material appeared different than that of Damiel. These looked not only like feathers, but perhaps also swords, or blades of grass, and also arrows all at once.

"This way," said Damiel.

Damiel's wings carried him forward. Adlai instinctively followed without the slightest bit of effort. Damiel rose higher and higher, and Adlai followed suit, passing above the trees. With his new view, Adlai could see the far-reaching areas of the lake and nearby forest. Adlai turned to where the river exited the trees. They followed the River of Life upstream, the thick forest lining the banks.

After a short while, the dense brush gave way to rolling meadows within a valley, decorated with multicolored flowers and a singular line of trees on either side straddling the water, soaking up its life-giving essence. The river widened in parts, appearing almost still, and condensed in others, suddenly picking up its pace and flow. Rolling hills formed microclimate pockets of unique tufts of flowers and vegetation. Adlai enjoyed the rush of energy that he felt as they flew through the air.

As they followed the river through the valley, Adlai admired the varieties of trees densely covering the walls of the mountains. Turning the corner around a sheer rock face, the valley opened up into a wide plain of rolling hills, which had the gentlest of slopes. The river was not singular here. For as far as Adlai could see upstream, the river fractured into many small streams. Each wound around the ridges and valleys of the hills before pooling in various low spots. Each pool shone a vibrant color, sparkling. One caught Adlai's eye that transitioned from crystal-clear to a dark and earthy emerald green. Others bubbled with steam and yet others spouted colored geysers. The pools looked like gemstones scattered across the landscape.

Flowers, grass, a few rocks, and small shrubs dotted the hills in between the pools. Damiel slowed, hovering, and Adlai came to a stop next to him.

Adlai felt echoes returning from within his energy field. There were others here.

"I can feel them," said Adlai. "The Hosts. They feel like you."

"The Heilen are a close-knit Tribe. Powerful beings."

"But I am not like them," said Adlai.

"No, not entirely. But look here."

As they still floated in the air, Damiel swept his hand over Adlai's head, capturing one of the characters.

"This is a symbol of Heilen," said Damiel as he pulled down a series of vertical strokes from Adlai's Traces. "See?"

Damiel swept a hand over his own head, bringing down the same emerald radiant figure before releasing them.

"Healing and restoration is in your nature, Adlai," said Damiel, "But there is clearly much more."

The symbol returned to Adlai's head. He watched as it rejoined, swirling together in excitement.

"Where are the others?" asked Adlai.

"As close to the source as they can be," said Damiel. "Follow me."

Damiel pointed his head towards the ground and flew downwards. Adlai followed. His pace increased. Damiel was headed directly for a deep sapphire blue-colored pool that shot thick geysers into the sky. A powerful spout shot up past Adlai, the waters undulating and swirling every shade of blue and green imaginable. Damiel tightened his posture, sending his body, headfirst into the pool, disappearing.

Adlai leaned in, following behind. The cool water on his face instantly refreshed him, the turbulence tossing him about. The water sparkled, its silky texture brushing his skin. He saw distant rippling figures of other creatures swimming in the pool as well, but his focus was on Damiel. Adlai could see the glow of Damiel's Traces in front of him. They went further downward. Down and down, deeper into the sapphire waters of the pool. Damiel's body shifted direction before disappearing. Adlai moved to the same position and paused before he felt a strong pull upwards. His face broke the surface of a small pool.

"Here you go," said Damiel.

The last time he was pulled from water was with Creator. This new world was just as shocking.

Damiel reached down, grabbed Adlai by the shoulders and pulled him onto the land. Damiel's wings crossed one another, retracting behind him while still dripping water onto the ground before disappearing behind the flow of his robes. Adlai felt movement at his own back, but by the time he looked up, only a dusting of rainbow glitter remained as his wings already disappeared.

The rolling hills above were quite different from where he now found himself. Adlai looked down at the pool he just emerged from. Barely larger than his own frame, the ground around it was smooth slate stone with a dusting of golden dirt and smaller rocks. There were other pools nearby and the overflows of water connected them forming a gentle stream. The outcropping they stood in was framed by massive and dense woods on all sides. The sky was bright. More bright than above, in fact. There was no sign of sunset here. Clouds with a similar variety of color as the pools above hung peacefully in the sky.

Streams of water fell from unseen points in narrow columns interspersed through the landscape. At the streams' points of impact on the ground, a small splash arose but the water disappeared beneath itself into hidden pools. A large school of small birds swam past them, their polished bronze feathers reflecting glints of sunlight. Adlai's eyes followed as the birds left the outcropping through a distinct trail entrance at the edge of the trees.

"Are we underwater?" asked Adlai.

"Precisely. The waters above sink into the ground, permeating the space and giving it life. Above is where we gather strength before missions, but this is where we live."

Adlai did not see any other Hosts, but he still sensed a strong and large presence. The air was filled with vocal calls from a variety of animals, but no Hosts.

"Where are they? I feel them much stronger here," he asked.

Damiel pointed to the trail.

"Just beyond," he said. "There are different entry points here. We could take a door, but I always find the short trip through the pools to be particularly enjoyable."

Damiel began to walk towards the tree's edge. Adlai followed. The entry into the trees was narrow, a tight path flanked on either side with a singular variety of trees that Adlai did not yet know. The bark was white, speckled with brown and black marks that flowed around, creating short stripes. The tops of the trees angled themselves ever so slightly over the path, making a comforting tent structure. The trees were dense, but the sky and light were still visible as they walked.

Thin streams of dripping water intermittently fell in the middle of the path. They first struck Damiel, sending multicolored sprays from his head.

"How long have you lived here?" asked Adlai.

"Since my first day, of course. Once Hosts are given their Traces, they are immediately brought to their native lands to begin training."

"But this is not my land," said Adlai.

"For a time, it will be. I am unsure of what your future holds, but Creator decided that your first home, for a while at least, will be with the Heilen. You are likely to have many homes based on your Traces."

Adlai searched his memories for the Heilen. There were none.

"Why did Creator send me here first?" he asked.

"That's an obvious answer, don't you think?" said a voice in front of them.

A figure appeared in the distance on the path. Adlai perceived the being's warm and fiery energy.

"Asa, my friend, so good to see you again!" said Damiel, jogging quickly to meet the figure. He placed his hand over his heart as he approached. "You will not believe what I have brought back with me."

Adlai walked a distance further, peering from behind Damiel to see Asa, whose wavy emerald hair lifted up and placed itself over her shoulder. Damiel and Asa extended their arms towards one another. Asa's hair sparkled at the touch of their energy fields.

"So good to see you, my friend," said Asa.

"You as well," said Damiel. He lowered his hand and stepped to the side, revealing Adlai in full view. Asa's face shimmered like silver, perfectly smooth and contoured. Her hair, seemingly being controlled by an outside force, once again lifted itself, whirling and waving behind her head as she inspected Adlai. Asa's full identity appeared in Adlai's mind.

"Incredible," she said.

Asa's eyes moved between Adlai's face and his Traces.

"Truly amazing," she said. "A new Archangel. I did not think a day like this would come. What an honor for you, Damiel."

Asa stepped around Adlai, examining him from all angles. Adlai felt her hand on his back. An instant warmth filled his body, swirling inside of him and calming any uncertainty. He let out a gentle sigh.

"Does the boy speak yet?" asked Asa.

"Of course," said Adlai, still enjoying the sensation of the touch.

"What is your name, young one?" she asked, placing her hands on his shoulders and leaning down to his eye level.

"He calls me Adlai."

"Yes, of course He does," she said with a grin. Asa's gaze redirected back to Adlai's Traces.

"Creator said that I am only one of many mentors for Adlai," said Damiel.

"Yes, I see that here," said Asa. "Very complex, in fact. The interactions here are quite unique. See here Damiel?"

Adlai looked up to watch as well. Asa pointed at one of the symbols, following the stroke with her finger as it moved about.

"I have never seen this symbol before," she said. "Yet, it glows emerald as a Heilen symbol would."

"Watch a little longer," said Damiel. The symbol transitioned from green to a vibrant magenta, then a sunset orange, then a cool blue.

"How can this be?" he asked.

"These transition patterns are not standard among Hosts," said Asa, "even among the existing Archangels and other Council members. This little one has quite the unique destiny. Certainly Errapel will have some insight. Come, she is waiting for us."

Damiel turned to Adlai.

"Asa was, in fact, my mentor."

"And a good one at that!" she said. "Let's get you both to the Sanctuary. Errapel has a celebratory feast waiting for you."

Asa turned to face the woods. From the edge of the path, she reached down to a tuft of vegetation. She plucked several handfuls. She placed the greens in a satchel on her waist as she turned back.

"Garnishes," she said. "Errapel requested a few final ingredients."

"Perhaps we can return by doorway?" asked Damiel. "We have been traveling extensively already."

"Of course. Damiel, you know where the entrance is. I want to get another look at these Traces."

Damiel moved his hand to his chin, looking into the woods.

"There," he said. "Follow this way, Adlai."

Damiel walked off the path into the woods, tree limbs parting before him. Adlai and Asa followed.

"I am so honored to finally meet you, Adlai," said Asa. "Creator told us He had something special in store for the Heilen, but I had no idea it would be this grand."

"There is still so much I do not understand," said Adlai.

"More than any of us could possibly imagine," she said. "We will certainly get at least a few answers during the feast."

"Here we are," said Damiel.

There was no door in sight. Instead, Damiel stood in front of a girthy tree with a large gash that opened deep in the trunk. Damiel hunched slightly and walked into the tree, disappearing.

"After you, Adlai," said Asa.

Adlai paused.

"This is your first tree entrance, I imagine?" asked Asa.

"Yes."

"What is a door but only a well decorated tree? We simply take the fuss out of it here."

Adlai smiled and walked into the hallow. No sooner as he entered the tree, the darkness of the trunk disappeared, opening into a vast, festive hall. The area was wide but contained. Adlai stood at the threshold. A rush of mixed energies pushed at him as the room's inhabitants' identities filled his mind, all distinct, but all Heilen. He felt their jovial moods wrapped with anticipation.

The edge of the doorway next to him slithered as branches wrapped and intertwined themselves vertically. Following the edge of the space, the walls were solid, made of tree trunks but constantly moving. The tall trunks drew his eyes upwards towards the tops of the trees where the solid trunks rapidly sent out lush branches that arced up high, bending back over the open area but not quite covering the overhead view. No sky or suns were visible, but lights of various colors and sizes pulsed and twinkled. The branches cast shadows onto Adlai's face as the lights flickered, moving from color to cool darkness, back to light.

Adlai closed his eyes as he felt warmth arise while the different colored lights touched his body.

"Keep moving!" called Asa from behind him.

Adlai stepped to the side to allow Asa to pass. She kept stride, walking into the arena. He and Damiel followed behind her. Asa turned around to face them while walking backwards. Her hair stuck out straight from her head forming a glowing green crown.

"Welcome to the Sanctuary," she said with her hands outstretched.

"This is our main gathering place," said Damiel.

Adlai looked around. Glancing behind him, the doorway was no longer visible. Only vines climbed around the wall near where they entered.

"Exits are all around," said Asa. "Just walk up to the wall when you want to go somewhere. The vines will lead the way."

As they reached further into the Sanctuary, the Hosts became more dense. As each passed, Adlai felt a more focused view of their very being as he perceived their identity. Asa intuitively bobbed and weaved, still backwards, as they made their way through the crowd.

"What exactly do you do at these gatherings?" asked Adlai.

"Anything we want," said Asa.

A sharp wind gust suddenly appeared and blew through the Sanctuary, momentarily forcing Adlai off balance. A pleasant but loud howl arose from the ceiling. As Adlai looked up, the trees around the perimeter of the space began slinging vines from one side to the other, grabbing branches on the opposite end. As contact with one vine was made, others used them as bridges to crawl out and fill in the area above. The vines quickly darkened the overhead light.

"Looks like our meal is ready," said Asa.

The Hosts began clearing the center of the Sanctuary, moving towards the edges of the room. The trio followed.

"What is happening?" asked Adlai.

"Supper is ready," said Damiel.

The whipping noises of the vines throwing themselves quieted. The room was dark, with the exception of the floating halo of glowing Traces around the edges. Adlai noticed the light in the space rise ever so slightly as small twinkling lights appeared in the trees and the new vine-covered ceiling. Glowing orbs within the branches all around lit the space.

The soft and quiet glow was short-lived as cracking and crunching sounds from above brought momentary new light as the vine supports began to lower a circular portion of the ceiling in the exact center of the Sanctuary.

All of the Hosts now paused their conversations to watch the spectacle. A ring of light lit the very tops of the branches, lowering along with the ceiling. Vines flung themselves downward around the perimeter of the ceiling and anchored into the ground. As they pulled, the ceiling continued to lower.

Lofty string music and light from above grew louder and louder. The center ring neared the ground. Adlai was able to see what came along. On top of it, three massive tables were set in the shape of a triangle. A busy set of Hosts that rode the ceiling down moved around the tables, unphased by the descent.

The platform announced its arrival with a triumphant crunch on the ground. At the center of the triangle tables was a raised platform where a Host noticeably larger than the others stood, peacefully observing the bustling activity.

Even considering the stage height, she was at least twice the size of the others. Her deep bronze skin reflected the intensely green Traces above her. They also swept around her body, wrapping it in waves of color. She was clothed in an aquamarine robe that glinted rainbow at its highlights. Her hair was braided silver. Her belt was studded with emeralds. Additional emeralds adorned her face and neck.

Adlai felt the weight of her energy.

"That's Errapel," said Damiel.

"She's so big," said Adlai.

"She is the most senior Host of the Heilen," said Asa. "She guides our entire Tribe."

The Traces that swirled around Errapel's head, even from this distance, were impressive. Every imaginable shade of blue and green presented itself. The core of the Traces whirled in a tight cluster while the edge symbols flowed gently around her body.

"My friends," said Errapel, in a deep but tender voice, "Today is a very special day for us. A day that was destined before time."

Errapel slowly turned on the stage, fingertips touching in a point as she made eye contact with the crowd.

"Our work is critical. Creator is unveiling new plans even as we join here together. Just moments ago, my colleagues of the other Tribes and I were briefed by the Divine Council on this next stage of development. I am sure you will be just as excited as I am to hear the news."

A wave of murmurs swept across the crowd as the color intensities of the observing Hosts brightened at the promise.

"We are joined by a very special guest," said Errapel. "Adlai, please join me."

Errapel turned to face Adlai, her hand outstretched. Adlai felt all eyes of the room move towards him as an audible gasp quieted the crowd.

Adlai felt a nudge.

"Go on, you don't want to keep her waiting," said Asa.

Asa quickly dug into her satchel, revealing the herbs picked from earlier. She eagerly pushed them into his palm and flicked her hands out to get him moving.

"Go on," said Damiel. "She just wants to introduce you."

Adlai slowly started walking towards the stage, looking around at all the eyes on him. The Hosts here had a variety of appearances, but all with one thing in common. Each of them was green in one form or another. Hair, scales, feathers, skin, eyes, lips. As Adlai walked, the sea of greens blurred together to form a waving gradient.

Nearly as soon as Adlai began to walk, clarity returned. He was at the edge of the stage in the center of the room.

"Please, join me here, Adlai," said Errapel, extending her weathered hand downward to assist him onto the stage.

"Allow me to take those," she said, receiving the fragrant herbs with one hand while pulling Adlai onto the stage with the other.

Errapel placed the herbs in a lined basket held by another Host who quickly whisked them away. Errapel smiled at Adlai, pausing for a moment as he saw her eyes scanning his Traces. She returned her gentle gaze to the audience.

"The Heirs are in need of help," she said. "Our help. The Kingdom's help. Our adversary's army maintains its attacks on them in a desperate attempt to undo what Creator already set in motion, but as you can see, there is something new afoot."

Errapel smiled as she looked down on Adlai, waving her hands through his Traces. As her hand touched, a rush of energy flowed through him as the intensity of Errapel's own energy came into focus in his mind. Errapel brought her hands back, cradling Adlai's Traces in front of her in a trembling rainbow gradient. Whispers grew in the crowd.

"Is he a Heilen?" came a shout.

"Yes, of sorts," said Errapel. "But as you can see, there is a bit more to him."

Adlai looked up at Errapel to see her still grinning.

"Here," she said, plucking a few symbols and drawing them upwards.

"Archangel."

Errapel paused.

"We are in need of a new Archangel. This young boy here looks as we all started, but you can see the seed that Creator planted."

Adlai looked between Errapel and the crowd, trying to make sense of the statements. She plucked another.

"Justice is here. Justice is what Creator is bringing to the world of the Heirs. Justice is what Earth needs to settle the balances upset by Helel's forces. He has already taken so much from the Heirs and only plans for more destruction. We cannot stand for such acts."

Errapel paused, scanning the room.

"Justice does not fight against wickedness. Justice only fights for a purpose. Adlai, the hand of Justice of the Lord Almighty, will lead that charge in favor of the Heirs."

"Why is he here?" asked another Host from the crowd. "Shouldn't he be with one of the typical Guardian Tribes?"

"At some point, yes, he will be," said Errapel. "But for the moment, Creator stated that his initial training be with the Heilen. Adlai represents a new kind. One that crosses Tribes and Orders."

Whispers arose once again in the crowd.

"Damiel, will you join me here?" said Errapel.

By the time Adlai turned his head to look at Damiel and Asa, Damiel was already taking a step onto the stage.

"My friends," said Errapel. Join me in blessing this pair as they set forth to do incredible works yet unseen by the eyes of Host or Heir.

A Host appeared from behind Adlai with an emerald studded silver goblet, firmly placing it in his hand.

Errapel raised an even larger goblet. "To the joy of the Lord. His work shall be done!"

A loud but brief vocalization erupted throughout the room as Adlai saw the other Hosts drinking and figured he should do as much. He took a sip of the golden nectar, the sweet taste of honey moving from his mouth throughout his whole body.

"Now please, enjoy the incredible feast that our Hosts have prepared," said Errapel.

Adlai heard a pop from the tables below. Foods of every kind appeared. Stews and porridge, greens and meats, every imaginable food appeared on the tables as the room of Hosts greeted one another as they sat themselves. Platter after platter mounded with the most succulent food filled the tables leaving nearly no room for the Hosts to even sit.

Errapel leaned down to Damiel and Adlai.

"Now for you, please will the two of you join me in my quarters?"

"Do you have room for a third?" asked Asa, stepping onto the stage with a grin.

"Certainly, my dear Asa. Come. We have much to discuss."

7

Errapel stepped off the stage into the center of the arranged tables as Hosts streamed in from all sides of the Sanctuary to take seats. She extended her arms, reaching for Adlai and moved him from the stage to the ground as Damiel and Asa stepped down. This was the closest he had ever been by her. Even off the stage, Errapel's height was dominant in the room, and she walked with confidence as steadfast as the trees that lined the perimeter.

Errapel was created nearly at the very beginning. She had seen much and experienced even more. This was Damiel's first time accompanying Errapel to her chambers, and he looked forward to seeing what awaited them.

Errapel turned to face Adlai as they exited the seating area.

"I sense you are hungry, Adlai," said Errapel. "Not to worry. We will have our own feast of sorts."

With a smile, she turned back and continued to walk to the edge of the Sanctuary. As the group approached, the swaying walls pinched and parted themselves as a curtain, branching out to the sides to create a space to walk. The area on the other side was dark, but Damiel immediately heard the sounds of trickling water.

As he followed the group through the dark passage, a cool blue light grew, illuminating the space, opening up into a lightly wooded area with a shallow area of the River of Life. While there were many rivers throughout the Kingdom, only one looked and sounded like this river. The notes that it played against the stones brought a sense of peace and stillness.

"Please, refresh yourselves," said Errapel.

She hopped over a few rocks with surprising grace to the middle of the river where she lowered herself, the ends of her robes dipping into the flowing stream. She scooped water into her hand, bringing it to her mouth to drink. The river's tell-tale rainbow glint shone from the water falling off her hand.

Adlai eagerly hopped onto his own stone, crouching down, and followed suit.

"You seem to be getting the hang of things," said Damiel.

Adlai smiled through the hand in front of his mouth.

"Shall we have a snack?" asked Asa.

She stepped directly through the river, sending rhythmic chimes into the air.

"Right this way," said Errapel.

Errapel arose methodically, her robes momentarily shining gold where they touched the water. She walked over a few more stones with her long legs to the path on the other side of the river. Damiel, Asa, and Adlai followed. Adlai ran forward and grabbed Errapel's hand while Damiel walked alongside Asa.

"You've got your hands full with this one," said Asa.

"I don't really know what to do," said Damiel, shaking his head.

"Sometimes not having all the answers is for the better. You know how Creator loves His scavenger hunts."

"Truly."

"If I might make a suggestion," said Asa, "simply start from the beginning. You remember what your time was like after creation. The memories were happening everywhere all at once. He has no context for nearly any of this world and certainly any of our work with the Heirs."

"That's true," said Damiel. "But, he seems to be adjusting well."

"Do you remember the first thing we did after your anointing ceremony?" asked Asa.

"Eating," he said with a grin. "So much eating."

"Naturally," said Asa with a chuckle. "You had a lot to learn!"

Damiel recalled his own first bite of the Tree of Goodness. The way the fruit absorbed into his body and instantly manifested knowledge in his mind.

"Damiel, you are over-thinking your responsibilities here," said

Asa, snapping Damiel back into the moment. "This is your first assignment. Everyone feels a little overwhelmed with their first. But despite Adlai's Traces, he is still a boy that needs to learn and grow."

"I'm just worried that I will make a mistake," said Damiel.

"Damiel, your only task is to be present," said Asa, placing a comforting hand on his shoulder. "Creator is with you always. Simply tap into His heart to know what you are supposed to do next. This is also a part of your own maturing process. This isn't only for Adlai's benefit. Creator has special plans for you and needs to ensure you are prepared as well."

"Thank you, Asa. That makes me feel a bit better."

"Goodness!" shouted Adlai, pointing to a tree near the path.

Damiel felt a swell of warmth watching Adlai's excitement. The glistening orange fruit was unmistakable.

"Yes, very good," said Errapel. "I see Damiel has already begun your lessons."

"Wish I could take credit for that one, but that was Creator," said Damiel.

"Well you'll have plenty of time for fruits," said Errapel. "How about this one?"

She walked to the other side of the path, beckoning with her hands towards Adlai. He ran over to her, and she effortlessly lifted him onto her shoulders.

"Steady now. Grab one!" she said.

Adlai balanced on top of Errapel and reached for a satin purple fruit with golden sparkles.

"That's one of my favorites," said Damiel, joining them beneath the tree.

Errapel lowered Adlai back down as he clutched the fruit with both hands. The points where his fingers contacted intensified the gold color.

"What is it?" asked Adlai, his eyes widening.

"How about we save that for the feast?" said Errapel. "Here, put it in my satchel for safe keeping." She pulled open the small pouch that slung across her chest. Adlai carefully lowered the fruit inside, seemingly to already sense its level of preciousness.

A small group of Hosts appeared from the forest on either side of the road.

"We are ready for you, Your Honor," said one of the stoic assistants. Whenever Damiel saw Errapel, her assistants were always nearby. Errapel's distinguished nature meant she was no longer on the front lines of battle but provided guidance for the Heilen.

"Please, let us escort the guests in," said Errapel. "We have esteemed colleagues and several guests of honor with us today. You all remember dear Asa."

Asa placed her hand over her heart and nodded.

"Today will be Damiel's first visit to my quarters," said Errapel. "I am truly excited to finally have time with you, Damiel, now that your initial graduate level studies are complete."

"The honor is mine, Your Honor," said Damiel.

"This is a day of firsts for many of us," said Errapel. She turned to Adlai. "Our protocols normally would not allow us to gather."

"But you sure are special, Adlai," said Asa. "Most of us don't get to meet Errapel like this until after our training studies."

"How come?" asked Adlai.

A sweet smile formed on Errapel's face.

"You will see there are many levels of glory in this Kingdom and on Earth. Creator is acutely aware of each individual's ability to hold, protect, and steward. We are all on a journey of growth, so our protocols are a method of protection."

"You're special, Kid," said Asa. "Somehow they painted you with some wild Traces."

Asa thrashed her hand about, pointing above Adlai's head.

"You're on the fast track," she said. Adlai's face lit up, delighted by the praise.

"I have been watching your progress, Damiel," said Errapel. "And I am quite impressed. It is no wonder Creator chose you for this important mission with Adlai."

"Thank you, Your Honor," said Damiel. "It is a pleasure to be invited and share this time with you."

"I'm hungry," said Adlai, drawing the attention of the group.

"I bet you are," said Errapel. "The boy gets a taste of what's coming and won't stop until we run out of food! Thankfully for you, that won't ever happen."

Errapel turned back to her assistants.

"Would you please open the gateway for our guests and show them to their seats?" she asked. "I will join the group in just a moment."

"Certainly, Your Honor." The assistant bowed. Damiel observed the appearances of Errapel's assistants. Each one looked quite similar to Errapel, but with a distinct characteristic exaggerated. This one had ecstatically thick silver hair.

"Your Excellencies and Distinguished guests," said the assistant with an arm extended to the side. "Please, follow me this way."

The assistant walked off the path into the dense, unmarked forest. His hair floated ahead, casting a glowing beacon amid the brush. As he approached vines or branches, they bent and moved out of his way, forming a tunnel of sorts through the forest for Damiel and the others to walk through. As the group continued down the vegetative hallway, the density of the surrounding brush grew, slowly dimming the light around them. Soon, the path was only lit by the group's Traces and the assistant's glowing silver hair, which cast dancing light on the sides of the brush tunnel. The glow stopped moving, and the assistant turned to face the group, his face lit.

"Your Excellencies, I am pleased to welcome you to the Chamber of Errapel, Ruler of the Tribe of the Heilen."

The assistant bowed, facing the line of those following, then paused, staring into the distance behind them. No one spoke.

A light floral scent filled the tight space as the sound of rain appeared but without any actual rain. A single strand of purple vined flowers descended from above, glowing and illuminating the faces of the group. The flower's petals spiraled, wrapping shades of purple on itself, revealing a shimmering silver center at the top. Sparkles of silver scent overflowed from the flower's center as a mist, disappearing below the glow.

As the strand continued to slowly descend, those nearby parted as the group stared at the stunning flowers. Damiel observed the silver flecks wafting to the noses of the group members, including himself, as the scent intensified.

As the strand came to a stop, another began to descend. Then another. And another, all around the group. The space that was once dark became increasingly bright, fragrance growing. Soon, the space was awash with bright purple. The flower's fragrance was so strong that the silver flecks began to form vibrating sheets as they fell to the ground, emitting a delicate melody.

Suddenly, the densely packed cascade parted in half along with the brush, opening a doorway behind the assistant, whose emotionless face had shifted to a large grin.

"Please, be our guest," said the assistant.

Stepping to the side and extending an arm to welcome the group into yet another garden area, the assistant lowered his head as the group passed by. The brightness from above was intense, causing Damiel to momentarily squint as his eyes adjusted to the sight in front of him. The space was small and intimate. The same purple flowers from the tunnel twirled and dropped from a pergola above stretching over the well-manicured courtyard. Even with the shade, the light was still quite bright. At the edge of the courtyard stood a small, neatly decorated table. Adlai ran towards it, which now materialized a variety of appetizers onto the surface.

"We'll eat in just a second, little one!" said Damiel. "How about a different snack first? Did you see what's over here?"

Adlai's eyes followed Damiel's point to the edge of the courtyard. Errapel's court was lined with a wide variety of different fruit trees. Damiel walked towards the orchard.

"You've had some Goodness, but how about this one?" asked Damiel.

He reached up and plucked a swollen bulbous fruit with both hands. The skin was plump but gave under the weight of the fruit as Damiel held it. The skin swirled different shades and sounds of red.

"Any guesses what this one could be?" asked Damiel.

Adlai shrugged.

"Mercy," said Damiel.

He knelt down with the fruit, gently setting it on the ground, being mindful of the tender flesh. He stuck both thumbs into the top and pulled it apart, spilling a rainbow of kernels held within.

"Amazing!" said Adlai.

"I'll take some of that too!" said Asa, walking over to them. "Open your hand, Boy."

Asa strutted over and took a fist full of the kernels from the center of the fruit and sprinkled them into Adlai's cupped hands.

"Eat them all at once or one at a time," she said.

Adlai ate face-first into his hands, multicolored juice immediately flowing through his fingers.

"Easy there," said Damiel. "There's a lot to take in with this one. Very complex flavor."

Damiel more delicately scooped up a small handful of kernels and began popping them into his mouth one at a time. With each bite, Damiel felt a streak of warmth run through a different part of his mind and body, wrapping it in a comforting blanket.

Adlai raised his head, the rainbow of colored juices dissolving off his face as he stared into the distance, eyes darting from side to side.

"How does it feel?" asked Asa.

"Perfect," said Adlai.

"My friends!" said a strong voice from behind the group. Damiel turned.

Creator entered the courtyard from a tunnel opposite them.

"Good to see you all again," said Creator. "I see you are settling in quite well, Adlai."

Adlai nodded eagerly.

"I hope you all are hungry," said Creator. "I've been working very hard on today's feast."

As He spoke, vines began to arise from the ground, curling around themselves to form four stumps before grasping one another and filling in with dense foliage for the top. A large, intertwined table of green sprouted up, taking form as it pushed through the ground.

As the twisting and growing slowed, foods popped out of the table's surface. First, three silver bowls followed by the fruit exploding up in unison from the cavities and landing back inside. Foods continued to pop up sporadically around the table. Damiel recognized a few staple dishes, but others were new to him. Creator stepped up to the table as Damiel and the others followed.

"I thought it would be fitting to choose some of My favorite foods from the test kitchen. That one," pointed Creator, "is simply divine."

"What is it?" asked Damiel. "I've never even seen it before?"

"Pudding," said Creator, rubbing His hands together. "It's one of My favorites. I think it's a real winner."

He thumped His chest with His fist. The food concluded with the simultaneous appearance of all the silverware at once, leaving the space with a clean ringing harmony as the pieces landed on the table.

"Fantastic!" said Creator, clapping.

The trees behind Creator parted once again as Errapel flowed into the courtyard with her remaining assistants.

"Welcome, Creator," she said. "Thank You for preparing and joining us for this feast."

"The pleasure is Mine. Please everyone, let us eat. Damiel and Adlai, I would love for you to sit next to Me."

Damiel walked with Adlai to the head of the table, sitting him on one side of Creator and Damiel taking the other seat. Adlai eyed the table up and down. The boy had quite the appetite.

"Please begin everyone," said Creator with welcoming open arms.

Adlai did not hesitate spooning food from every dish within his reach. Creator leaned into him.

"I saw you were enjoying some of the mercy fruit earlier," said Creator.

Adlai nodded eagerly as he simultaneously chewed food while spooning more onto his plate.

"Mercy is one of the bedrocks of the Kingdom," said Errapel. "It is quite simple, but you will see once your interactions with the Heirs begin, it can become quite complicated."

"I look forward to you meeting them," said Creator. "They are quite special. Just as you are quite special, Adlai."

"I remember the first time I saw an Heir," said Asa. "My mentor and I went on an observation mission. I was surprised to find how much they looked like us. Smaller, a little more delicate. Outwardly a simple version of us. After hearing about them for so long, I thought they would be taller and a bit brighter. But it was as if someone took a Host and washed off the color. That's what they look like."

Creator laughed. "That is a fairly good description, Asa. Most Hosts take a bit of time to get used to interacting with such powerful spirits in physical form. They may look meek, but I have made them so incredibly powerful."

"Why aren't they here with us?" asked Adlai. "I remember so much cruelty in my memories, yet I see none of it here."

"You're more like the humans than you know, Kid," said Asa. "Therein lies one of the biggest questions all of the Heirs ask at one point or another."

"That is why I wanted you to begin your journey with the Heilen," said Creator. "The Heilen are reconcilers. They are the rebuilders of the connection between this Kingdom and that of the Heir's, allowing the many good things from this realm to spill over. Healing is one, but connection is the most important. The Heirs are able to partially see through the veil to this realm, but there must be separation now.

"Wouldn't it be easier to simply remove this veil?" asked Adlai.

"You ask exactly the right questions, Adlai," said Errapel. "This process for the Heirs is similar to the process you are on now. You are learning, growing, and strengthening. The Heirs, on Earth, are doing the same. Learning, growing, and strengthening their ability to love."

"Couldn't they just do that here?" asked Adlai.

"Certainly not," said Errapel. "Struggle brings strength and growth in ways that they cannot receive here. The Heirs exist here before they exist on Earth."

Adlai's chewing slowed.

Creator placed His hand over His heart.

"They are all here," He said. "Each and every one, individually unique live right here with Me as My perfect seeds."

"Perhaps it would be easier for You to show him?" asked Damiel.

Creator placed a second hand over His heart before separating His arms. A small speck of light remained in front of His chest, and in the moment of expanding His arms, the light exploded into blinding white rays around the table as Creator did what only Creator can do. He transported the table and its guests.

Instead of forest, Damiel and the others at the table were enveloped by swirling streaks of light. As his eyes adjusted, Damiel followed the synchronized twisting and turning of the light, as if Conductor were back orchestrating its dance. The streaks, the bodies, moved in unison, creating an intricate ballet of silvery reflections that danced in the glow of the room. The mass seemed to breathe as one, expanding and contracting fluidly, flowing like a living tapestry. With each subtle shift in direction, the whole entity transformed, forming delicate patterns that appeared and vanished in an instant.

Glistening and morphing hues of color whirled around the space as the spirits of the Heirs spun with excitement and cheered with glee. The harmonizing chorus of notes from around the room flowed together as a coherent song.

"We are ready!" they sang together. "Send us!"

"These are all of My children," said Creator, "perfectly formed and ready for growth. The spirit of every Heir that will ever enter a womb on Earth is right here."

Creator gazed upwards, admiring the Heirs as they zoomed around Him. Adlai moved his head around, trying to track some of the lights.

"The Heirs I see in my memories don't look like these," said Adlai.

"Adlai," said Creator. "I am love, and I only want love to grow. The only way for that to happen is to grow Myself. Children are how that is done."

Creator stretched His arms out, standing and turning as He smiled.

"My seeds — My children — are how Love grows. The expanse of My love is unlimited because of them."

Creator slowly walked around the table.

"They know love here. My love. But to learn to love others, there is only one way for them to grow and expand, and that is through the human experience. Do you hear them calling?"

The room was awash with noise coming from the Heir spirits. Adlai nodded.

"They want the human experience," said Creator. "They want to grow and expand. They want these things because that is what I am like, and I am their parent."

Adlai furrowed his brow.

"But the Heirs I have seen are so cruel," said Adlai.

"I understand your confusion," said Errapel.

"Unimaginable evil," said Adlai.

"To be bound to a physical form and born into Earth," said Errapel, "the Heirs are unable to retain the knowledge of this place. They must find the way for themselves."

"Even if it means they choose evil?" asked Adlai.

"Even if it means they choose evil," said Creator. "My children here are like Me in every way. Love is not controlling, which means I do not control the choices of My children. Some will find and grow in the path of love, and some will choose otherwise. I only want them to choose good, and as you will see, I do everything in My strength to help guide them through the challenges of human life. For those spirits here that choose to become human, I want to be reunited with each and every one. It is never My desire to see them do harm to themselves or others. Love is a choice, and that is the ultimate goal of the human experience. To learn to choose love. Without that, they are lost."

"And that is precisely why you are here, Adlai," said Errapel.

"Me?" said Adlai sheepishly.

"Yes," said Creator. "I do everything in My power to be reunited with My children. Those beings led by Helel that were banished from this Kingdom and chose a path of wickedness, are increasing their attacks on the Heirs. They are jealous, coveting the space I hold for the Heirs for themselves. If only they realized that the love that the Heirs develop is the same love that the Fallen covet and also reject."

"Why do they fight against the Heirs?" asked Adlai.

"The human life of the Heirs was not meant to be wicked," said Creator. "But the Fallen are vindictive, only wishing to attempt to harm Me and those that I love. They exert their influence on anyone and anything in order to build themselves. Helel has already recruited some of My Sons in addition to the Fallen. He knows I long for all My children, no matter the form. Helel and his followers will do everything in their power to skew the human experience to inject pain, suffering, loss, and tragedy. These are and were never My intention."

"Why not just prevent the bad things from ever happening?" asked Adlai.

"The Fallen are fighting against the foundational principles of existence for any creature. They will ultimately lose. In their naivety, they expect that the evil they cause will diminish My light and purpose. What they do not realize, or rather, have rejected, is that no amount of evil can deter Me. Love will always conquer and no matter the level of evil, I will repay it many times with good. You are here, Adlai, because I do take action. You, Adlai, are My hand of Justice. Some of the spirits you see here will be Heirs that you will help in the future."

"I feel so inadequate for such a mission, Creator," said Adlai.

"That is why I have given you Damiel."

Creator turned towards Damiel with a smile.

"Don't worry, Damiel," said Creator. "I know how you feel about that."

Damiel's smile was tight, his lips pressed thin, reluctant but respectful.

"Part of every creation's journey, whether Heir or Host, is trust," said Creator. "Love is trust and part of learning love is learning trust. All of My creations are forever on a learning journey. Even Errapel here is still learning."

Errapel raised her eyebrows and nodded slowly with a tilted head.

"Growth requires challenge," said Creator. "No one can grow without a challenge that exceeds their current abilities. The Heirs are being challenged uniquely on Earth and all of My Hosts here are being uniquely challenged based on their individual needs."

"You'll get it, Kid," said Asa. "Don't worry. Now how about that food? Can we finish the conversation back where we've got something to chew on? All this discussion made me even hungrier."

"Certainly," said Creator with a smile of agreement.

He raised His arm, sweeping His forearm down in a fluid motion. The lights and singing faded as lush trees popped up from the ground and Errapel's courtyard came back into view. The table guests remained silent. Creator took His seat.

Errapel leaned in.

"Adlai, I cannot count the number of times I have had the privilege of seeing and hearing what you just witnessed, but I can tell you that it never becomes less impressive. The world that you are in now has many things for you to learn, and even in your entire existence, there will still be secrets to be discovered. Please, do not be overwhelmed by what we discuss here. You will be well taken care of. For the time being, please eat. This is one of the fastest ways to learn some of the basics."

Adlai's grin widened, and he dove back into the feast without another word.

"Creator," said Damiel, "may I ask why I was chosen for such an assignment? I do not see any special characters in my Traces nor the experience to guide an Archangel. Why not Errapel or another leader for this training?"

Creator shifted in His seat.

"Damiel, innocence is a trait that cannot be learned. I have chosen you for this purpose. The work I am doing through Adlai is unique and special. He represents a new tactic not yet seen. How then, could I have someone with established knowledge teach him things they do not even know?"

"Wouldn't their skills allow them to adapt faster than I?" asked Damiel.

"Perhaps, but this isn't just about Adlai," said Creator. "The journey belongs to both of you, Damiel, as you each discover the treasures I have set before you. My plans are far greater than any individual, whether Host or Heir, and there are plans being knit together as we speak that no one is yet aware of."

Damiel spooned some food into his mouth.

"Where do we start?"

8

"I thought you would never ask." Creator smiled. "Naturally, Adlai will receive the standard training, but in his case, I would also like for him to be exposed earlier to the work of the Heilen."

Creator turned to Adlai. "How is your food?"

Adlai's mouth was full. Damiel was unsure if the boy was even taking breaths in between bites.

Creator laughed. "I thought you might enjoy that."

Adlai eagerly nodded his head.

Creator continued to admire Adlai as the boy devoured the food before him.

"But while this is a perfect moment," said Creator, "We must remember why we are here and what is at hand. Helel is attempting to undermine everyone in My Kingdom and create his own kingdom in the process. I was grieved to see Hadad and Molech both defected from the Council during the Fall with the promise from Helel of new levels of power, Princes in their own kingdom."

"Yes, we have seen his positioning," said Asa. "We await Your word to overthrow them."

Creator gave Asa a patient smile. "The wait will be longer than you might expect, dear Asa."

"Why would You not want to remove them?" asked Damiel. "They were Your own Council members, your Sons. They have betrayed us. Betrayed You."

"A King is bound by His word," Creator explained, voice steady. "I gave My full authority to the Heirs. When they handed it over to Helel, he thought it meant I would be powerless to alter the course he's now steering."

"I don't understand," said Damiel. "You are just letting him win?"

"Sometimes the only way to conquer is to be defeated, at least in the eyes of your enemy," said Creator.

"I don't understand," said Damiel.

"Helel rejected the perfect unity here for his own sake," said Creator. "He was driven by his jealousy when I banished him, but now he is still blinded by his own worship of himself. Helel thinks he can sustain perfection outside its source. He believes he can rally My other Sons, inspiring them to turn against the Kingdom for his own. But he is blind to the futility of this path."

Creator smiled. "I didn't answer your question."

"You only can lose a battle if you fight the battle," He continued. "Helel believes he can be the antithesis of My existence, My perfect and opposite equal. Or rather, My superior even! The only problem with that is he is wrong. There is no battle here."

"Helel expects that we will mount a counter of some kind," said Errapel, "exactly as you might suggest, Asa."

"He expects that we will storm his gates," said Creator, "because that is what he would do. He still sees himself as My equal and expects that I will challenge him head on. The issue is that Helel is only a king of his own realm. His defeat will not come by My hand, at least, not My hand alone. His defeat will come at the hands of those he attempts to control."

"The Heirs," said Errapel.

"Those he hates," said Asa.

"Precisely," said Creator.

"But he will destroy so many in the process," said Damiel.

"Were I to intervene in the way Helel wants me to, it would mean the destruction of all," said Creator. "For me to intervene would render My Word void. A King is only as good as his Word, and if My Word is invalid, then so am I. Should I intervene, it would mean I would be taking control over authority that I already yielded."

"And Helel knows this," said Errapel.

"Certainly," said Creator. "I spent immeasurable time with Helel. He understands the foundations of the Kingdom perhaps better than anyone. But he expects that I hold the same pride and jealousy that now consumes him. And here, he is wrong."

"I'm still not sure how we defeat him," said Damiel.

"Battles are defined in the arena that they are fought," said Creator. "Helel is the king of the Earth because the Heirs yielded their authority to him. We do not have authority on Earth to fight Helel's army. The Heirs are the only ones that can defeat him."

"But the Heirs seem so...frail," said Damiel. "How could they possibly challenge Helel, not to mention Hadad and Molech? They were the most powerful of the Council."

"In the Heir's perceived weakness, they are strong," said Creator. "As you saw, there is a piece of Me in each one of them, which means there is an unbreakable bond between the Heirs and Us. They have the opportunity to tap into My power and this is something that Helel does not understand because it is outside of his entire experience of Me. He assumes that he knows everything about Me, but time will show that this pride of his will lead to his downfall."

Creator nonchalantly scooped some red noodles onto His plate.

"Helel believes I am prideful because he sees the Heirs exhibit those characteristics. He attributes their behavior to their nature. His own pridefulness blinds him to the truths that he in fact knows but fails to acknowledge. Helel expects that we will challenge him because he is unable to comprehend My ability to use all situations for good."

Creator spun some of the noodles onto a fork and ate them. "Oh, this is good. Did you try some?"

No one responded. Creator set His fork down. "A paradox, isn't it? Suffering that leads to love growing. No suffering, no growth. When I cast out Helel and those that he took with him, he started a strategy to go after My children—any that contained divine seed, whether here or on Earth. He was able to convince two of My Sons to abandon their positions on the Council and partner with him."

"What is the Council?" asked Adlai.

"The Council is the governing authority of all Kingdoms," said Errapel. "They are highly specialized beings, each distinct and unique. Some are Sons, others are not. We will certainly introduce you to them when the time is right."

Adlai's head tilted as he slowly chewed on a piece of bread, clearly pondering what he just heard.

"Helel was on the Council too," said Adlai.

"You're picking up quickly, My dear boy," said Creator. "Helel was indeed on the Council. He sat closest to My throne. But now, he only tempts and lies to hurt Me and usurp power."

"So he's provoking you," said Adlai.

"Most certainly," said Creator. "If I dominate My Sons and violate My Word, then I have become no better than Helel. In fact, if I were to do so, I would yield My authority within the Council as King and take up the Office of Controller. In that moment, Helel could petition for the throne. What horror these realms would face if that happened."

"So, what are we going to do about it?" asked Asa. "The Heirs are already emboldening Hadad and Molech. Idols are already being built. They walk embodied in flesh among the Heirs as gods and give them knowledge that they are not yet ready to carry."

"Helel lured some of My Sons away from me," said Creator, "teaching them to redirect the praise of the Heirs to themselves to gain power. He believes he can redirect enough strength to vanquish Me. He will try. He will succeed with some."

"What are we to do about it?" asked Damiel.

"My full plan will be a story for the generations. It will be revealed in time. For now, I believe it best for you to see what My Sons are doing as we speak."

Creator manifested a scroll from within a fold of His robe, gesturing with it across the table.

"Errapel, please escort our guests to the Courts of Baal Hadad. Issue him this decree."

"Certainly Creator," said Errapel.

"Request an escort from Michael's personal forces," said Creator.

"Of course."

Errapel rose, retrieving the scroll. She lightly bowed and turned to face Adlai.

"No slow moving for you, Adlai," said Errapel.

She glanced at his Traces.

"You are on the fast track. Come, we will go to the transit station," said Errapel, turning back to the group.

"Asa," said Errapel, "please send a request to Michael's office for the escort to meet us prior to departure. We will meet you there."

Asa nodded, rising quickly to exit the feast hall, disappearing through the winding vines, her wild hair vanishing into the thicket.

9

Damiel stepped out of the darkness of the tree. He turned to see the Gates behind him and the transit station ahead of him.

"Prior to the rebellion," said Errapel, "this station was located within the Gates, but the actions of Helel required that they be moved outside."

Damiel looked around the platform. It was clean and orderly but lacked the luster it once had. Where once ruby-encrusted walls gleamed, only smooth stone stood now, cold and lifeless—a pale imitation of the Kingdom. Instead, it looked like Earth.

"Is this where the Heirs live?" asked Adlai.

"Not quite," said Errapel. "This is the spiritual jurisdiction for Earth's governance. The Princes that you heard Creator speak of, Hadad and Molech. This is a separate realm that they control."

"But they have been violating their orders under the encouragement of Helel," said Asa. "He has convinced them along with many Hosts to join his rebellion. Where Hadad and Molech once held some of the highest positions in the Divine Council, they now only rule as a facade."

"Why have so many rebelled against Creator?" asked Adlai. "I can't imagine turning against the love and connection I feel."

Damiel stepped towards Adlai. "When love is perverted, disaster arises. Helel redirected love towards himself instead of Creator. Hadad and Molech too are following the same path, causing them to seek after power to support their own pride. Helel is attempting to create his own governing council with the Princes that he convinced to abandon their duties."

"What is so special about the Heirs?" asked Adlai. "Creator says they are powerful, and He is a part of them, but my memories show much weakness. Why does Helel seek after them?"

"As the Princes and their lesser orders intimidate and deceive the Heirs, the Heirs redirect their praise from Creator to the Princes, boosting the Princes' authority and strength on Earth," said Asa.

"And that's what Creator meant when He said that He would not intervene?" asked Adlai.

"Precisely," said Errapel.

"So what are we going to be doing there?" said Adlai.

"Creator will always follow the structure," said Errapel. "It is a part of His nature. Even in their rebellion, the Princes are treated in accordance with the Kingdom's righteousness."

"I see," said Adlai. "Is Helel one of the Princes?"

"No, Helel was not one of the Children," said Errapel sternly. "He was created as a Seraphim, the most beautiful and powerful in the Kingdom. He did hold a position on the Council, but he was not a Prince."

"To work with humans means to work with, or rather against, what the Princes are attempting to impose on the Heirs," said Asa. "Much of what we see in the behavior of the humans is rooted in manipulation by the Princes and their minions."

"Most Hosts do not ever directly encounter one of the Princes," said Damiel, "so this is highly unusual, especially the rank of Hadad."

"He is the most powerful of the Princes, even among those that remain, and he knows it," said Asa. "Before his rebellion, Hadad oversaw the Kingdom's treasury. He held much power and responsibility, and Helel went after him immediately. Helel spends much of his time with Hadad to ensure their plans are coming to pass."

Adlai eyed Michael's soldier that stood motionless next to them.

"And you think he will harm us?" asked Adlai.

"Unlikely," said Errapel. "Even in his rebellion, Hadad knows the repercussions of such an attack. Helel and Hadad are on guard to ensure they don't return the authority that they have been granted. Such a choice at this stage would be devastating for their plot."

"You ready?" asked Asa. "I hear our ride."

Adlai shrugged his shoulders. A transit vehicle streaked by them, slowing to a stop as unremarkable doors opened in unison along the length of the vehicle.

"Come, it is time," said Errapel.

The group sat down as the doors closed, and the vehicle accelerated. As soon as it began, the train began to slow, stopping. The doors opened. The group exited. The landscape before them now was still well manicured but noticeably desolate. The space was filled with doors of differing sizes and shapes. Errapel walked towards the most ornate door and gestured to the guard, who opened it in front of them, a twisted golden calf's body adorning the top frame. He entered. Errapel held the door to allow the rest of the group to enter. Damiel examined the detailed engravings and precious gem insertions throughout the door. He had never seen nor met Hadad before, but he already sensed what was coming. Errapel followed Damiel in, shutting the door behind.

"This looks like our Kingdom," said Damiel, seeing the gold flanked walls and floor. Gemstones studded accent points on the statues and walls, sparkling, but with an unusual glint.

"What you see here is purely manufactured," said Errapel. "Inspect further."

Damiel focused on a large ruby inset in the eye of one of the statues. The glowing red faded as his focus drew in. Red to brown. Brown to gray. Gray to black. There was nothing inside. Damiel withdrew his focus.

"It's a facade."

"Nothing below the surface," said Errapel. "Everything you see here is a counterfeit, only valuable to the eyes of those who wish it had value. Hadad exploits the everyday of our Kingdom because he knows he can impress the Heirs. He is attempting to convince the Heirs that he is the source of prosperity, and he wants to look the part. You will find no humbleness here."

Two stoic guards approached the group, clad in gold. Errapel turned to face them.

"We have an appointment," she said.

"His Highness has been expecting you," said one of the guards with a voice of disdain, eying the group. "This way."

The guard turned, continuing to walk down the lustrous hallway.

Damiel observed the scenes of the golden reliefs on the walls. Each one showed a grandiose Hadad towering over crowds of worshiping Heirs with a thunderbolt in hand. The clunk of a door lock echoed down the hall. Damiel turned to see the guards opening large double doors. The guard's hand gripped the door handle, a writhing calf statuette. Damiel made eye contact with the sparkling silver eyes. The extravagant carvings continued into a foyer, which opened up into a larger area.

"My friends, what a pleasant surprise it is to see you," echoed a deep voice through the chambers. Adlai stepped behind Damiel as Hadad arose from a throne at the very far end of the expansive space. As he approached, Damiel saw lightning sparks streak around him at varying intervals. He wore a golden tunic, surprisingly simple given the self-aggrandizing room, and his hands were adorned with a rainbow of large gemstone rings. A silver mantle hung over his shoulders, a counterfeit of what he once wore along side the other Sons.

Errapel stepped forward in front of the group, not acknowledging his statement. She unrolled the scroll. "Hadad, by the order of the Utmost High, you are hereby notified to be in violation of the natural law due to your incitement of worship. Do you understand this order as I have read it to you?"

"Most certainly," said Hadad, with an almost cheerful tone. "Anything else?"

Errapel rolled the scroll. Her body position loosened into a more casual stance.

"Hadad, you still have a choice. Helel knows only lies and deception. He will not protect you when the time comes. You are an Elohim. There is no higher position. You already ruled over this region."

Hadad lowered his head, clasping his hands in front of him. He let out a gentle set of "tsks."

"My Father has kept much from us, Errapel," said Hadad. "It was only with Helel's illumination that I now see our true destiny, what we truly have the capacity to do. You were not on the Council, so I understand how difficult it might be for you to understand such things."

"This is not wise, Hadad," said Errapel, holding her ground.

"Do you really wish to be on the side of these Heirs?" asked Hadad, lowering his voice and stepping even closer to Errapel, causing the security escort to step towards him. "Of all the creation across all of the galaxies, this is the one He calls His joy? Then what are we, Errapel? What am I? I am called a Son, but I am not like Him."

"It is not our role to question His decisions," said Errapel.

"It is precisely our role to question His decisions," said Hadad with a condescending chuckle. "Why else have a Council, Errapel? Why even create us if we were not needed?"

Hadad turned his back to the group, taking a few steps away in frustration before turning around.

"Look at them, Errapel," he said. "Feeble and simple. They don't even realize what is at stake. They simply wander around aimlessly. Do you realize how easy it is to impress them? I make one tree grow, and they bow down to worship me. But they are right, I am a god here. My strength grows by the day."

"Your attempts at a coup are futile, Hadad. Surely you must recognize that?" said Errapel.

"Do you really believe these 'Heirs' are the missing piece?" asked Hadad. "What we have waited for? Just look at how easily they stray. But I must say, for as weak as they are, the energy of their worship is quite impressive. I have never felt as strong as I do now."

"Your deception of Cain will forever be remembered as your act of betrayal against us," said Errapel.

"There was no deception. I told him exactly what I could offer and what I needed."

"You knew the implications of redirecting his offerings," said Errapel.

"Our Father feasts on the worship of the Kingdom, leaving the scraps for us," said Hadad. "What kind of father is that? I did what I was permitted to do, so how could it be wrong? Even now, where is He? He sends you do to His work for Him. These supposed beloved Heirs feel all but forgotten by Him. We are the only ones even helping—"

"Manipulating—" interjected Errapel.

"Them."

"And yet, Cain still returned to the Father," said Errapel.

"It will take some effort to break those instincts," said Hadad, wafting his hand, unimpressed, "but it won't be hard. Just look at their Traces. They were made so…open. Truly bizarre. Now that Father has banished Cain, I am the only one that Cain has. Don't worry. I will treat him very well. Far better than our Father ever could. We will bless his family."

"'We?' You're the one bestowing blessings now?" Errapel's tone was thick with disdain. "And you still believe you understand Creator's plans."

"Who better, indeed? Between Helel and I, Cain's family will flourish. That is, as long as it serves our purpose. Helel will impart to his family the most glorious songs, and I will bless his ability to yield from the land. His family will be famous for many generations. All those that see his family will want to know where he gets his strength and prosperity."

Hadad took a deep bow as Errapel shook her head.

"You are deceived by your own pride," she said.

"You have a choice too, Errapel," said Hadad. "Imagine your strength multiplied a thousand-fold. Father prevents you from becoming stronger because He is afraid of what you could do, but I'm not. He has always been afraid of what His creations could become. Why do you think Helel was banished? For rebellion? No, Father was afraid that Helel would reveal our true natures, and we would overtake Him."

"Your perceived successes are merely short term, Hadad. Your actions will lead to your own destruction and the destruction of so many others."

"How can our Father be perfect when these creatures created in His image are so flawed? Either He is not perfect, or His design is broken. It's time we leave our Father's house and make our own family."

"You will be destroyed, Hadad," said Errapel.

"Soon they will forget our Father as God. His memory will fade as we rise."

"You think Creator will simply allow you to go through with this plan?" said Errapel.

"He must," said Hadad. "My power no longer comes from Him. It comes from the Heirs, who He foolishly gave His power to. As long as I have their praise, He knows that He cannot do anything. He will be forced to simply start over in another set of dimensions. He knows this one is lost, but He is the one too prideful to recognize it. Until that day comes that He simply wipes them from existence, we have an endless source of power. We no longer need to grovel for it at His feet like animals. We can earn it ourselves."

"Your resolve is clear, and your heart is black," said Errapel. "You are deceived beyond what I imagined."

"And I wouldn't have it any other way."

"As you wish, Hadad," said Errapel.

"Your statements have been heard," he said. "You may depart."

"Very well."

Errapel stepped aside to turn around.

"Stop," said Hadad, with an elevated tone.

Damiel saw that Adlai was now exposed to Hadad's view.

"We seem to have a special visitor, Errapel. You weren't thinking of leaving without introducing us, now, were you?"

Hadad strode closer to the group, his golden robes flowing like water as he stepped.

"That's close enough," said the escort, metallic clinking from his armor echoing through the chamber.

"What a strange creation to be accompanying a group of Heilen," said Hadad.

He studied Adlai's swirling Traces.

"I don't think he needs any introduction, do you?" said Errapel.

"No, perhaps not."

"Does this change your response?"

"No, but it does make things more...interesting. Is Helel aware of this...boy?"

"Perhaps you should organize a discussion to inform him," said Errapel.

"Oh yes, I most certainly will," said Hadad, tilting his head as his eyes remained locked on Adlai's Traces. Hadad pulled back.

"You could join my battalion, Errapel," he said. "I have the most power. Imagine what your skills would be able to do with the Heirs."

"Power is not what I seek, Hadad. We are done here."

Errapel turned to lead the group away.

"I look forward to our interactions, Boy," called Hadad. "What is your name?"

"Adlai," he said proudly.

Hadad smirked. "Very well, then. My brother will be very interested to learn more about you. Are you sure you do not wish to stay for a tour of my kingdom?"

"Come, Adlai," said Damiel. "We are finished here."

Damiel put his arm on Adlai's shoulder to lead him away with Errapel.

"We'll be seeing you soon, I hope," called Hadad as the group departed. None responded.

Damiel passed each of the ruby-studded columns, catching his reflection in a kaleidoscope array. The hallway seemed longer on the return. No one in the group spoke. He saw the transit station guards approaching at long last. Errapel furnished papers.

"By order of the King," she said.

The guards parted, and Errapel stepped to the side.

"So he is the one we are fighting?" said Adlai.

"He is one Prince on Earth," said Errapel. "But no, we are not fighting him. We do not fight in this realm. Please, no more words until we have returned."

The guard stood watch as the group passed through the doorway. The group made their way in silence to the transit station and onto a vehicle back into the Kingdom. Once on the other side, Errapel moved swiftly back through the gates before speaking.

"Come, Creator is awaiting us."

Errapel stuck her hand like an arrow into the greenery of the wall. The vines cracked and crunched, splitting themselves into a makeshift doorway. Damiel recognized the view from the other side.

"Quickly, we have an appointment, and He is expecting us," she said.

Damiel gave Adlai a pat on the back for encouragement to move through the doorway. The entrance grounds dissolved back into Errapel's private quarters. Creator stood solely in the center of the courtyard in front of the vine-wrapped table from their feast.

"Welcome back," He said with a smile. "Uneventful travel, I hope?"

PART TWO

10

Acantha stepped into the child's cramped room, the portal snapping shut behind her. She took in the surroundings, adjusting the zeyrith-colored silk sash around her waist, its shadowy violet and sapphire undertones glistening in the dim light. Everything here felt dull, uninspired, and unimpressive. She ran her hands down her coarse dark torso-length hair, smoothing it after the rough journey. Travel to Earth was always jarring, such a fitting entry to this dismal world.

Tick...tick...tick. The child's clock echoed from the nightstand, its uneven rhythm grating in her ears. "Good enough" seemed to be a moniker for the humans, something Acantha could not understand. They seemed to settle so easily for mediocre lives.

The boy, called Liam by his foolish parents, lay before her. What a wretched little creature. He was only nine Earth orbits old, yet his Traces were clear and surprisingly well-formed given the absolute mess of a household that he was raised in. He was a gatherer and uniter of humans and posed a threat if left unchecked. That much was obvious.

Acantha took two steps to his bed where the boy lay asleep, his foul breath polluting the air. She bent down, eying him from head to feet. *Filthy beast.* She inspected his lightly glowing Traces, part of the protocol for each visit to assess any growth or change. The width of several symbols was thicker. *Interesting.*

Each human's Traces looked different, corrupting alongside their pitiful lives. A spark of resentment flickered within her as she recalled the day her own Traces were torn away.

Acantha did not understand why the Creator did not enable the vast majority of humans to be able to see Traces. Those that could, only saw in simple terms—a glowing color. The human mystics were so entranced by their "auras," oblivious to what they were actually sensing. The Creator seemed to wire the humans for failure from the start, enabling them to wander the Earth with no sense of purpose but with an ability to hide their motives from one another. Such rudimentary feeble creatures.

In the rare instance that her missions faltered, the Traces would defiantly grow. Thankfully, that did not happen often. Acantha took pride in ensuring those symbols dimmed, each mark on a human's spirit as a testament to her mastery. Typically, the Traces would darken or shrink as the humans turned their backs on their defined natures. Humans gave up so easily. The melodies and symbols of the Traces never changed, however. Those were given by the Creator and could not be changed regardless of the humans' choices, but Acantha would do anything to smother them.

Humans puzzled Acantha. They seemed to be set on their own destruction, unable to be happy without others being sad or hurt. They were a strange race. Frail, disorganized, messy, short-sighted. It was a wonder how the Creator imagined they could possibly represent Him, especially after already ruling over the galaxies with His Council. Acantha was embarrassed on His behalf.

She longed to be reunited with the Creator, like how the Kingdom was before He created the humans. She was saddened at the separation, but knew the work that she was doing would bring them back together, someday. Surely the Creator could see how disappointing these creatures were. He destroyed them before, and she knew He would do it again. It was only a matter of time before He would give up on this grand prideful experiment of His. Regardless of His actions, the humans always found a way to sabotage Him.

Their pitiful future lay bare in these parents, indulging the child's every whim, excusing every fault. They coddled him, oblivious to the festering ruin beneath their pathetic attempts at love. No discipline. No order. If humans were made in His image, Acantha should not be surprised to know that the Creator was just as indulgent. Of course He would give them chance after chance even though they throw their lives away. These human parents did the same thing.

She, and the others like her, believed in Superior's mission. They knew that the Creator became too prideful in His plan for human creation, unable to acknowledge His own mistakes. He would keep fighting, challenging, pushing them to be something greater than they were or could ever become.

The Creator faulted Superior and his followers for the faltering of the humans, but that was not true. Superior only exposed the broken faults in their hearts. Once he could show the Creator that there was no hope for these humans, Superior was certain that he and the others would be welcomed back to the Creator's Kingdom and rightfully placed in the positions of honor and power they once held and deserved.

How could the Creator call these humans "Heirs?" They squander resources, act in their own self-interest, and destroy the beautiful planet they were once given, spreading their filth. They did not deserve the authority of that world.

Acantha hated being in their presence. Their imperfection only reminded her of the glory she once lost. But this was important work. Essential for the Opposition to restore order throughout the Kingdom.

Acantha stared at the boy for another moment. *You will be destroyed.* She looked forward to this day ever since it was conceived in the war rooms. Today was finally the day. It was time for the anointing.

She lifted her arm, grabbing a black strap connected to the flask that rested on her side. The anointing oil inside of the flask was special, a gift from Superior. It had the ability to accentuate the frailties of these human bodies and minds. Pulling the flask around to her front, she clasped it with both hands.

The flask was ornate. Fashioned from the molten ore of a dying planet, the color was most similar to what the imperceptive humans would call blue. Acantha pitied the humans. The few times her missions required embodying a human flesh carcass, she disgusted herself. They were unable to see and experience the true world all around them, only having a muted lens giving them a small sliver of reality. No wonder they sought pleasure. Their mere existence was so devoid of any awareness of what surrounded them at all times.

Acantha leaned over the sleeping boy once more, inspecting him more closely. The melody of his Traces was entrancing. What had this boy done to deserve such a connection with the Creator's heart? Nothing. Acantha and the Opposition were the only ones fighting for unity, not this beast.

The melody was very familiar to Acantha. It was one she sang and painted many times as a Scribe. Before the Divide, Acantha fashioned that same melody over countless Hosts, binding their calling with their spirit. Not all Hosts were called to unity, but the song was one of Acantha's favorites to sing. It had been millennia since she last painted that melody over any Host. Many of those same Hosts were the ones she now fought against.

War had never been in her nature. She was once called to nurture, a truth that disgusted her now. Her former Traces were a dead relic, replaced by a higher mission of which Superior had deemed her worthy.

Acantha could remember the moment of her creation. That beautiful moment in the River of Life when she was plucked from nothingness. "Zareo" was her given name, her dead name. An identity she no longer wanted or could associate with. She could not bear to hear it since the Divide. Superior had renamed her now that she had a new mission. Superior was bringing her into her true calling, something the Creator resisted.

Acantha stared at the helpless boy. He has no idea what is about to be planted. Nothing tears apart a family quite like problems with a child. There were no Guardians in sight on this evening, just as the authorities stated. They were probably bound in the chains of words released by those they were here to protect. It was clear that humans had no understanding of the power of their words.

Thankfully, there would be no need to fight in Liam's room tonight. The Creator assigned Liam and every other human Guardians, yet the tireless squabbling, insulting, and cursing by the humans with one another rendered most of the Guardians powerless. Such strong beings on the side of the humans. Beings that Acantha once called associates. Beings that failed to open their eyes to the failures of their Creator.

Superior rarely needed to send warriors to fight. The humans bound their protectors almost willingly. The humans gladly handed over the authority of their minds and bodies to Superior. Simpletons. They were such easy targets.

Acantha could not understand how the Creator failed so badly with this creation after making the beautiful heavenly realm Acantha once called home. How could He stand by and continue to let them wreak havoc everywhere they went?

Worst of all, humans looked at their own iniquities and tragic conditions and blamed the Creator, as if the destruction of their families, jobs, and planet were His desire. Humans were living in a world directly resulting from the tragic flaws of their own decisions and looking for anything other than themselves to blame.

The Order of Guardians were led by a general named Marius, a fierce warrior who directly reported to Archangel Michael. Guardians were warring angels, specifically designed to fight on behalf of the purposes of the Creator. Before the Divide and the creation of humans, Guardians were protectors of heavenly assets, although they never had a challenger. Acantha always found it odd that a realm with no enemy would need protection. It was as if the Creator knew they would be needed one day.

After the Divide, Acantha began to see the former Guardian patrols demoted, tasked with the responsibility of protecting humans. Humans were weak, so it was not surprising the Creator would give them added protection, although the Guardians often fought against the desires of other humans just as much as against Superior's influence.

That was not a worry of hers tonight. She was thankful to be able to complete her mission uninhibited and undisrupted. The little beast's parents, the ones supposed to watch over him, were the ones that bound the only real protection that could stop her.

Acantha placed her index and middle finger over the lip of the flask, tilting it upside down to draw out the thick oil. Flipping it back over, she withdrew her hand, rubbing her thumb and two fingers together in the thick oxblood-colored oil.

Acantha began to trace an elaborate set of symbols on the boy's bare chest. She would normally not be able to touch the boy in this fashion, but Liam's protections were removed. He was hers. The boy's mother and father were relentless squabblers, nitpicking and tearing each other down. Their comments were driven by their own selfishness. The mother's aunt recently died, thanks be to Superior, leaving the entire family in an emotionally vulnerable state. Superior was so wise to choose this time to initiate the boy's intervention.

Humans had a predictable pattern of self-sabotage that Superior was able to consistently initiate. It was a wonder that humans could not recognize it. Then again, humans were self-absorbed and lacked nuance.

The pattern was pitifully predictable. Their hearts, bloated with pride and ignorance, reflected their Creator's own blind arrogance. Pride was the seed, already planted.

Alongside pride, humans paradoxically filled their minds with a lack of self-worth. If only they actually knew just how powerful the Creator intended them up to be, they might have a fighting chance. False identity was the water.

At this point, humans were already teetering on the edge of an emotional cliff. It would not take much to push them over the edge. It only took a simple nudge to convince any of them that they were being left out, put down, or ignored by another. The hurt was the fertilizer, allowing the weed in their hearts to grow large and strong.

The rays of self-pity shone bright causing the weed to grow even larger and prompting reproduction, choking out what little hope remained. The human would then continue to make a series of choices that reaffirmed the hurt, plucking the seeds off the weed and continuing to plant them in their heart's garden bed. But humans love sharing misery, so they often lashed out, causing a cascading reaction in those around them. This method was modeled like a human virus. One that humans could not cure on their own.

Liam's family was no different. His mother, Rebecca, a dreadful wench, felt obligated to care for her ailing aunt after Rebecca did not receive any meaningful connection with her own perverse mother, the result of another one of Superior's brilliantly laid generational plans. Rebecca felt ignored and unloved by her mother, and she was willing to sacrifice anything to feel that love from her aunt, even if it meant sacrificing a relationship with her own family. Rebecca's husband, of course, felt left out and ignored. It was a source of constant strife between the two. It only took one curse exchanged in a heated moment for chains to be placed on the family's Guardians, leaving them open to Superior's influence.

With tensions high, it was the perfect time to anoint Liam with a new seed. This would not be a natural disaster, broken bone, or accidental death. That would be too sudden. This was one that would grow much more slowly. Like a thorn slowly digging itself deeper into flesh, Acantha knew this particular tactic would be unbearable for the boy's family.

Acantha finished tracing the symbols and smeared the remnants onto her lips. The thick musky scent of the oil lingered, filling her with satisfaction as she sealed the boy's fate. The moonlight glinted off the wet oil on the boy's chest. She repositioned directly in front of his head, leaned over, and pressed her lips against his. The contract was sealed and bound to the boy's flesh. She saw from the corner of her eye as the oil dissolved into his skin. She arose to admire her work. It was good.

Neither Liam, nor his parents, would notice any difference, at least for a while. They would be given time to grieve and heal just enough so that Acantha's actions would be felt that much stronger.

Liam's family was a perfect specimen for this application, and Acantha looked forward to seeing how the seed would grow. Acantha heard muted voices coming from the direction of Liam's parents' room. She would not visit them tonight. Tonight was about Liam, and her work here was done, at least for this evening. She would continue to monitor the family to ensure the seed grew well. Acantha did not want to disappoint Superior, particularly on a case like this.

The General would be expecting a full report on the mission and an updated strategy brief for ensuring mission success with Liam and his family.

With a flick of her hand, a portal tore through the air behind her. She cast a final glance at the boy, already envisioning the slow unraveling of his life. It brought a rare smile to her face. Acantha took a step backward into the portal and disappeared.

11

The soft glow of the gooseneck fixture above the unassuming wooden door was oddly welcoming despite the otherwise unnerving darkness. The grass beneath Harriet's bare feet was cool. She clenched her toes in an attempt to anchor herself to the moment, but she knew the door was meant for her.

Harriet released Aleifr's hand and cautiously approached the door, walking towards it to inspect from all sides. The wooden door frame, weathered yet well-maintained, seemed unremarkable.

She peaked around the other side. There was nothing behind it, simply another identical frame with another light fixture. She looked down. The dim light barely reached the ground where she saw a doormat atop grass that read, "Welcome Home." Harriet pursed her lips and furrowed her brow as she looked back at Aleifr.

"He thinks it's funny," said Aleifr.

"Who thinks it's funny?" she asked.

"You will meet Him soon enough."

Harriet let her eyes wander, attempting to identify anything else that might bring clarity to her situation. *The afterlife wasn't supposed to look like this. No clouds, no cherubs. Not even a bowl of grapes!* Just a door in the middle of nowhere. If she was wrong about that, what else was she wrong about? Harriet returned her eyes to the door, knowing that she would need to step through.

"He is inside waiting for your appointment," said Aleifr.

"Who is this He?" she asked.

Aleifr did not answer.

Harriet stepped around the door one more time, looking for any final clue about this world. There was none. The door was plain and insignificant, perhaps taken off of a mountain cabin.

Harriet stood on the doormat, its coarse bristles pressing into her feet. She looked back at Aleifr.

"Do I just walk in?" she asked.

Aleifr stood in silence, only his glow visible at the outer ring of the porch light. Harriet turned back around.

"He calls himself my Guardian angel and can't even answer my questions," she muttered under her breath.

Harriet mustered what little courage she had, raising her arm with a fist to knock on the door. She swung her arm down, but just before making contact, the door opened, sending her off balance.

"Woooahhh," dodged the figure in the door as Harriet's hand dropped through the threshold, sending her off balance. The figure stood back up, blocking the entryway. "Did you just try to hit me?" he asked sternly.

"I'm so sorry!" Harriet exclaimed. "I was just trying to knock to let you know I was here." Harriet was mortified. She was already second guessing all of her beliefs, and now she nearly hit this man, or maybe angel, or maybe spiritual creature that looks like a man. He stared at her for a moment, rugged, emotionless, dressed in a simple tan tunic. His appearance was oddly human compared to Aleifr.

"It's OK," said the man, tossing his hand. "I knew you were here. I was just joking. I'm fine. Please come in!"

The man waved over Harriet's shoulder. "Thanks, Aleifr. I've got it from here."

Harriet's mouth hung open as she tried to process the bizarre interaction. The man stepped aside as she walked over the threshold and into the room, her feet touching soft carpet. She looked around. It was her living room.

"Please, have a seat," said the man, closing the door.

"Forgive me," said Harriet, "sir, ma'am, angel? I'm sorry. What are you?"

"You can call me Manny," he said with a smile.

"Excuse me, Manny? That's your name? I'm sorry, this is all so confusing. I guess that I was expecting a little more formality in the afterlife."

The man stared at Harriet with a playful smile, one she knew well as a parent when her son tried to correct her.

"I'm Harriet, but you probably already knew that," she said, breaking the silence.

Manny smiled. "Now, you must have a list of questions for what is going on here, and I assure you that they will all be answered in time. But first, we have one very important matter to discuss."

He paused, clasping his hands together.

"Would you like some tea?" he asked. "I have some of your favorite here."

He turned around, approaching a beautiful buffet against the wall. Harriet was not sure if this moment could get any stranger, but the thought of tea actually did sound nice. She had not even thought about food or drink since this whirlwind began. She nodded to the offer, if only to give herself a few more moments to take in her surroundings and this Manny fellow. Harriet was, however, pleased to find that there was more in the afterlife than just grapes.

"Two scoops of sugar, please," she said as her eyes wandered around the room.

"I know," said Manny without turning around.

Harriet walked deeper into the room as Manny prepared tea in the corner, the sounds of a spoon clinking around in the glass in an oddly satisfying harmony. Her eyes slowly took in the familiar room. At the far end were the white linen curtains that she had hated cleaning. They looked nice here, perfect even. There was no light visible from behind them.

Flanking the window was a seating area where she spent many evenings crocheting scarves for her neighborhood church outreach programs. The repetitive motion was soothing for her, and she liked the idea of bringing comfort to those in need. She stopped after arthritis devastated her hands. She walked over and sat down. It was far more comfortable than she remembered.

The couch adjacent to her on the left looked newer than she had ever seen. After Harriet's husband George passed, her income was limited to the meager government paychecks, barely able to keep the lights on and food on the table most nights. The two of them spent many days sitting on that couch watching reruns. Harriet smiled at the memories.

"Do you like it?" asked Manny.

"Pardon?"

"The room. I thought this would make you feel a bit more comfortable."

Harriet looked around.

"I lived a lot of life in this room. A lot of spilled food, arguments, makeups, parties, cleaning. Never-ending cleaning. Those kids never did pick up their toys."

As Harriet glanced back towards Manny, her eye caught the gaze of a portrait of a woman on the other side of the room. She was the most beautiful woman Harriet had ever seen. Glowing ebony skin and perfectly placed hair. Stunning. The portrait moved.

"Good Lord! That's me!" she exclaimed.

Harriet leapt out of her chair and dashed to the wall where her mother's heirloom mirror hung. She turned her head from side to side, not breaking eye contact with the woman in the mirror. Harriet inspected the face staring at her, placing both hands on her cheeks and pulling down in disbelief of the reflection. The woman staring back at her was not the frail, old, wrinkled geriatric. No sunken eyes or tired skin. No thinning hair or glasses. Glasses! Harriet had not even realized she was able to see perfectly without any glasses.

"I look 30! Holy moly, I look good! Ooo wee!"

She made eye contact with Manny's reflection as he walked over to her smiling, teacup in hand. "You do look amazing," he said.

"Will I always look like this in Heaven?"

"Oh, this isn't Heaven," he said, still with a smile on his face.

"Your mind will need to get used to your new spiritual body," said Manny. "I'm sorry your body failed you in your latter years. That is not something you need to worry about here. Please, sit. I've been waiting a long time to talk to you like this."

Harriet stepped backwards through the room, still not breaking eye contact with her new reflection. She sat on the couch.

"Do you know where you are?" asked Manny.

Harriet looked at him.

"Not the foggiest idea," she said. "Why are you the one asking questions? You live here. Where exactly are we if this isn't Heaven? Is this...you know. The Bad Place?"

She timidly pointed downward.

"Do you work for...him?" she asked.

"This is a secret place in my father's heart," said Manny before blowing over the top of his teacup. "It's a place of comfort and peace. I like meeting new arrivals here because of that. I know your journey was rather overwhelming, and you could use a little break."

"Your father's heart?" she asked, eyebrows knitting as she leaned back in her seat. "Am I going to get some straight answers? What on Earth does that mean?"

"Well, we aren't on Earth, so no," said Manny, lightly taking another slurp of tea. "Oh, this is tasty."

Harriet's mind raced with questions. Maybe this was the Bad Place. After all, these questions and nonsense talk from Manny felt like torture.

"Harriet," said Manny, causing her mind to instantly snap back to the present moment. "Do you know who I Am?"

Harriet's eyes reflexively closed under an immense weight that instantly fell on her consciousness. A flood of knowledge and understanding rushed into her mind, swimming through the entirety of her body. As soon as it began, the rush evaporated, leaving an imprint of wet ink on her mind.

Harriet's chest tightened. Her breath hitched. Her hands shook slightly as she stammered. She knew exactly who this man was. This was no angel or spiritual creature or divine tea preparer, although the tea was exquisite. The veil was lifted. This was Jesus. The Son of God.

Harriet stumbled over her words as every corner of her mind rushed a question to her mouth. Was this the moment of judgment? Harriet's nerves began to stir further, still not knowing what exactly she was experiencing.

"There is no need for fear here, Harriet," said Manny. "I simply want to talk with you."

His voice deepened and softened. His words soothed and pierced her concern.

"Is this where I get judged?" she asked. "I'm sorry, I know I wasn't perfect. Lord knows, I wasn't even close to perfect but—"

"No, Harriet. Judgment is not My role. I just want to talk."

Harriet pleaded to talk with God throughout her whole life. Through the struggles, the pain, the hurts, the losses, the betrayals. All she wanted was to hear the voice of God. She wanted guidance, condolences, confirmations. She begged for just a single word to know that He was there; that she was on the right track; that He cared for her. But those words never came. Yet, here she was, face to face with Jesus, and now all of a sudden, He wants to talk over a cup of tea?

"Harriet, how are you feeling? Take a sip," He said, gesturing with an encouraging hand.

"Overwhelmed and confused," she said, lifting the cup to her lips.

"That's understandable. How can I help you?"

Harriet found it strange that the creator of the universe had so many questions.

"What is this all about?" she asked. "You told me that I'm not being judged. We aren't in Heaven. You just keep asking questions, but You certainly must already know the answers. So, what are we doing here?"

"Do you love Me, Harriet?" He asked abruptly.

Harriet exhaled sharply, hearing Him avoid a response yet again, but she pondered the question for a moment. The word "love" seemed to take on a presence as He said it. It was common for her to say that she loved God in church, but that felt very different now that Jesus was right in front of her, sitting just a few meters away. He was a being that she did not see, touch, or experience while on Earth. How could she have loved that?

She thought about what love actually meant. She had experienced many different kinds of love. The romantic love for her husband. The protecting love for her children.

"What did you do with My love, Harriet?" asked Manny, interrupting her train of thought. "Do you choose Me?"

"That's a silly question. Why would I not choose You?"

"Embarrassment, pride, shame. Those feelings disconnect Me from My people, and they are unable to receive My love."

"I might be embarrassed of parts of my life, but yes, I choose You," she said.

He smiled.

"These conversations don't always end like this. My people don't always choose Me, and that breaks My heart. Thank you for choosing Me, Harriet. Now please finish your tea. I would love to introduce you to Father. I have been talking to Him about you for a very long time, and I know He is very eager to meet you."

Harriet did not particularly understand what happened. Each

statement out of Manny's mouth raised dozens more questions.

"I have to ask," paused Harriet. "Why food?"

Manny laughed.

"Now there is a good question. Harriet, you must remember that you are not a physical being anymore. In fact, you never were. Your spirit was knitted to your flesh. You lived in a physical world with physical rules. The spirit realm, the only true realm, has rules too, just different. It will take some getting used to, but I think you will find the differences to be quite agreeable. The world you lived in was merely a faint shadow of My Kingdom. There are endless experiences here for you to explore. What you knew on Earth as eating for nourishment is actually quite the same here, but nourishment is not simply physical energy. It is so much more. When you eat, the food you consume becomes a part of you. Your journey continues as you are constantly shaped and grown by what you eat."

Harriet heard Manny's words, but they were difficult to process as she sat in her tiny living room. The idea of the afterlife was not new to her, but she knew the world that now awaited her was very different from what she grew up learning.

"Do you mind if I call you Hattie?" asked Manny, interrupting her moment of contemplation.

"That's what my mother called me. I was only Harriet when I was in trouble." She smiled. "I would love that. Now, what exactly should I call You? You don't really want to be called 'Manny,' do you?"

"You will find that I go by many names, including Manny. Well, that's short for Emmanuel. You may choose any of My names. Many in this realm use Creator, but that is only one part of Me. You will see Us as many others over time."

Harriet realized the cryptic verses she read in her Bible really were from God. This was no easier to understand. Creator lowered His tone.

"I take great care in My Words, Hattie. They are not meant to hide and conceal truths but rather to plant and grow them. Now come, Father is waiting for us."

Creator outstretched His hand, rising, taking Hattie's and walked back to the front door. He smiled and looked at her as He placed His hand on the knob.

"Are you ready?" He asked.

Harriet let out a nervous laugh. "Would anyone be?"

"No, but that's part of the fun," He said.

Creator opened the door, stepping back to allow Hattie to enter first. Hattie expected to see the dark where Aleifr would be waiting, but what she saw confirmed Creator's words. This world was unlike anything she could imagine.

12

Had she been on Earth, Hattie certainly would be blinded by the light that now enveloped her entire field of vision. The light blanketed her senses with a quiet peace, soft and sweet on her tongue. Butterscotch. That was new. She could hear it, feel it, and taste it. A low, single note held perfectly in her ears. A distinctly cool breeze on her skin.

Her senses harmonized with one another, at least that was the only way Hattie could describe the feelings swirling through her very being. While the light shone bright, the normal reflex to turn away did not trigger. Instead, she was drawn closer. Hattie took a few steps, feeling the texture of the floor change as she stepped over the threshold of her living room that was no longer visible. Linoleum gave way to something much more solid. She looked down. The material was distinctly gold, yet translucent. There was movement below it, like watching a river flow beneath a frozen ice cap. She stared for a moment, trying to comprehend what she was even looking at.

"Harriet!" shouted a voice. Her heart leapt in recognition before her mind fully comprehended.

"Harriet!"

She looked up just in time to see the flash of her husband George's face in front of her before his body barreled into hers with a hug so grand it instantly brought tears to her eyes. At the moment of embrace, she tasted peach.

Hattie pulled her body back for a moment just to look at George again.

"Look at you!" she shouted. "Would you look at you! George, you look like a kid again!"

George laughed before pulling her back in. The feeble old man that Hattie watched wither away in bed was long gone.

"Prime time, baby," he said. "I've been waiting so long for this."

"This is unbelievable," said Hattie. "I never thought I'd be so happy to be dead. My God!"

"Yes?" said Creator, stepping into view on her right. Hattie paused.

"Did you need something?" He asked.

Hattie stuttered.

"It's a joke, Hattie," said Creator. "You're really going to need to loosen up a little."

"Hattie?" said George. "Is that what we are calling you now?"

"Oh yes, that's my name here."

"Well then 'Hattie' it is," said George.

"You two will have plenty of time later," said Creator. "But first, we have an appointment."

Hattie struggled to pull her gaze away from George as she turned towards Creator while keeping a death grip on George's hand.

"Life grip," corrected Creator.

"Right," she said.

"Death has no strength here, so a 'death grip' is quite weak actually," said Creator.

George smiled at her before giving her hand another squeeze.

"Now if you'll follow Me this way," said Creator.

He held out His hand, palm up to invite them along as another door appeared amidst the light. It's sparkling diamond frame appearing out of the ground, the movement below flowing upward and materializing the crystalline structures. Hattie stood in awe of the sparkle.

"This...might be a little overwhelming," said George.

"What do you mean?" she said.

Before George could respond, Creator twisted the solid emerald doorknob, clinking the lock open and leaned forward, opening the door in front of them.

The moment a sliver of intense red light from the other side became visible, Hattie's legs instantly buckled as the rays burst through the door and landed on her with a crushing weight unlike anything she had felt before. She dropped to her knees at the threshold as Creator stepped through the door, disappearing through the curtain of light that now enveloped the room, wrapping her in an intense embrace of warmth. The sounds of thunderous, roaring drums filled Hattie's ears.

"Just relax," she barely heard George say as she stared at the ground, attempting to steady herself. She leaned back onto her feet, bringing the door back into view. The rays of light licked about the room, sweeping around Hattie and George, who seemed unaffected by the sensations.

As she watched, the light seemed to transition back and forth into visible and audible sound waves, plucked by an unseen force. With each strum, a fresh wave washed over Hattie, feeling the note hit to her very being. An intense pleasure and sense of belonging now exploded outward from her core as she felt the surge through her body. Her senses were on fire. The musical notes that she now watched and heard simultaneously resonated in her chest and from within her. She now recognized the melody of the light not as instruments. It was voices. An incredible range of vocals harmonizing atop the intense drumbeats. She was captivated, pushing herself to her feet and reaching for George. While she still felt the weight around her, her body allowed her to move once again.

The ruby rays drew her in as she put her hand out in front of her, stepping into the billowing red ocean of light. As she passed over the threshold, her other hand holding that of George's behind her, Hattie's vision was momentarily, completely flooded by the red light.

"Keep going," said George, his voice also harmonizing with the others beyond the door.

Hattie took a few more steps, the vocals and drums growing. The light was still present, but the intensity seemed to part, allowing her vision to return. After a few more steps, she could finally see the new room, if you could even call it that since there were no visible walls or ceiling. Creator stood with His back to her as He stared at a mesmerizing white exploding orb of light visible in the distance, resembling the sun she once knew.

The light was so bright that Hattie could not accurately judge the size or her distance from it. The orb spewed bursts of multicolored light that flowed like lava, exploding, then running down the sides of the orb before dropping to the ground, momentarily flashing and then dissolving away.

Hattie felt the deep bass drums hitting her body with force. Above the orb, she saw massive creatures floating. As her eyes adjusted, she saw that the multi-layered wings of the creatures were generating the relentless drumming, a thunderous wave reverberating through the room with each beat of their wings. The beings emanated a different frequency of light that burned hot, glowing. Hattie's pulse quickened as she stared at the creatures, her heart feeling as if it might burst with fear and awe.

"What are those?" she asked.

"Seraphim," said George. "They are the angels closest to the Father, never leaving His side. They create the atmosphere."

Hattie didn't understand anything George was saying, but the mesmerizing view captivated her regardless. Her line of sight dropped below the light to a mass of people all around the exploding star, and she saw that sheets of red vocals were arising from the crowd, spiraling upward and around the glowing orb before washing outward. She felt George's hand on her shoulder.

"Who are they?" she asked.

"Not who. What," said George.

Hattie stared further when suddenly the nearest but still distant figure came into perfect focus. As she scanned the outskirts of the crowd, creatures walked, trotted, soared, and swam. Sparkles wafted out of the creatures' mouths as they sang. Some creatures appeared human, but most did not.

"What is this place?" asked Hattie.

"Can you taste it?" said George.

Hattie smacked her lips, her heart still racing, and breathed in the light.

"Honey," she said. "The good kind too. Not that stuff we used to get from the store."

"We love honey," said Creator, turning back to face them. "Welcome to the Throne Room, Hattie. Please, this way."

He held out His hand.

"George, would you mind waiting here while Hattie receives her judgment?"

Hattie's head snapped back to look at George.

"Of course," he said.

Hattie glared before whipping her head towards Creator, who now took her by the hand.

95

Mentally unwilling but physically unable to resist, Hattie took a few steps forward while looking back at George. He waved. As she turned around, those two steps that should have only been a meter or two brought her deep into the crowd, seemingly many kilometers. There were no people here. Only creatures, but unlike those she had ever seen. They had eyes, heads, and limbs all over. She made eye contact with a large, looming creature, its shape bulbous but unrecognizable, only to realize that the creature was covered in eyes, some focusing on the orb and others examining her from every angle. The eyes shifted like that of a chameleon. The intensity of the faces, or at least the areas of their bodies that looked like they might be faces, was stern.

"I don't think I like this," said Hattie.

"Your judgment will only take a moment," said Creator.

Hattie's racing heart surged even further. He led her a few more steps. As she walked, light streaked by, and the creatures blurred. He stopped. She stopped, the light streaks around her slowing. They now stood directly in front of, or perhaps inside, the exploding star of light, colored lava popping and splattering around them with the clashing sound of cymbals as it hit the ground. The core was clearly still more intense, yet she saw explosions around them.

Creator stood staring directly into the center of the light. Hattie looked behind her to see a boundary of creatures. She and Creator were now at the center of the crowd in the light.

"Father," said Creator, "I am pleased to introduce You to Our daughter, Hattie. She traveled a long way and is ready for her judgment."

"No I'm not! I'm not ready!" said Hattie reflexively.

"Harriet," boomed a voice that sounded like a waterfall, echoing in the deepest parts of her core. The voice was stern, but soft, warm, and smelled like forest. She felt exposed but protected.

"I have been waiting for you, Harriet," thundered the voice, shaking loose more lava.

Hattie did not know how to respond, but as she opened her mouth, she felt a rush flow out of her heart as a stream of lights and sounds exploded from her chest, swirling around her like a tornado. She could not see, but she felt. It was her life. Not sequentially like in the movies. No, all at once and in every direction. She could see the external influences leading to her life circumstances, not only her own choices, but the consequences of those for others. As the light encircled her, each memory hit like a shockwave, the joys as piercing as the regrets. Small gestures of kindness and careless words, the happy laughter of children, and the strained silences long forgotten.

Harriet stuttered out all she could.

"I'm so sorry. I didn't mean to—"

"Did you love well?" gushed the voice as the whirlwind dissipated, allowing Hattie to catch her breath. The weight of the images still felt thick.

"There were things that—"

"Did you love Me well?" repeated the thunderclap.

The question echoed, and Hattie felt the rawness of it sink in, as if it reached into the deepest, most hidden parts of her. She struggled to answer, her voice barely a whisper, trembling beneath the weight of all her faults and failures. But before she could speak, Creator spoke over her.

"Yes, she did Father," He said. "She chose Us."

"Very good," declared the voice, silencing the remaining echoes in Hattie's heart. "You have been deemed righteous and holy. Welcome home, Harriet. I am so glad to have you here, My daughter."

An uproarious wave of cheer swept across the crowd as a shower of golden sparks fell around Hattie. The cheers transitioned seamlessly back into the polyrhythmic orchestra of sounds and instruments that should have sounded chaotic but somehow blended perfectly. Harriet stood motionless, letting the waves of light and sound wash over her.

Creator slowly approached, taking her hand in His.

"How are you feeling?" He asked.

"That's it?" said Harriet.

"Certainly. Did you really think you would be in the Throne Room without already being cleansed."

"This is the Throne Room of God? *The* Throne Room of God?" she said in disbelief.

"This is merely a formality," said Creator. "You were deemed righteous and holy as soon as you chose Me. Everyone gets the choice, but not everyone will choose Me, and that breaks My heart. This is the public declaration for all to see and know that you are Ours and We are Yours. Us are We."

Hattie paused, attempting to sort through the rush of memories and connections that still hung like a massive spiderweb in her mind.

"I have so many questions," she said, shaking her head.

"And you will get answers," boomed the voice of the Father. "There is an eternity for answers. But now is a time for celebration. I'm so glad you came home, My daughter."

Harriet looked back into the glow. The blinding light that only moments ago looked like the surface of the sun now gave way to a visible structure. A massive golden pillar sat directly at the core of the light. Her eyes followed it upward. The structure was dauntingly large, but it was not a pillar. It was the golden leg of a throne. The reverberations of the Father's voice caused the massive pillars of the throne to tremble.

Hattie stood in awe, watching the swirling waves of rainbow colors that condensed and dropped as the colorful lava melted into the crystal-clear floor.

Creator placed a hand on Hattie's shoulder to turn her back towards the crowd. A path parted. A few steps later, the crowd blurred for a moment, and she was once again back with George on the outskirts of the room.

"You'll get used to travel here," he said. "It just takes a little bit."

"That seems to be a theme," said Hattie.

"Very good," said Creator. "I will leave you with George to take you to your new home. We have a few more surprises waiting for you there. I can't wait for you to see."

"You aren't coming with us?" asked Hattie.

"I'm always with you, but this time is for you two. Now hurry along. You don't want to be late for this party."

Creator gestured upwards and another glistening crystal door with an emerald doorknob appeared right in front of them. Creator grasped George's hand, transferring Hattie to him.

"You can take the scenic route," said Creator. "George can show you around a little bit."

Hattie did not know what new environments and creatures awaited, but with George, she was ready for anything. Creator opened the door. This time, the interior of the frame swirled like an oil spill on vertical water. She could not see through to the other side. Hattie paused.

"Go on," said George. "You'll like it. Trust me."

Hattie stepped forward to the spinning colors. She closed her eyes and instinctively held her breath. She felt a cooling breeze on her face. As Hattie dramatically leaned back to steady herself, she lifted and arched one leg. Hattie kicked her leg through, her foot landing with a distinct loud crunch, unmistakably the feeling of snow.

Hattie leaned forward, pulling George through the doorway, her other arm stretched out to her side to steady her as she looked around at the winter wonderland that she now found herself standing in. The thundering drumbeats of the seraphim's wings ceased in an instant as she heard the door shut.

"Do you like it?" asked George.

"This is unbelievable."

Hattie turned her body to look around, her bare feet not moving. Despite the calf-deep snow that she now found herself in, the ambient temperature was no different than a typical home. They stood in an outcropping of trees dusted with fresh snow, the forest all around them extending into the distance. She huffed.

"I can see my breath!" she said.

"Of course you can."

"But it isn't cold."

Hattie lifted up one foot.

"It's not even wet."

"This realm is full of the best experiences without any of the down sides," said George. "I thought you might like to see some snow.

His eyes glimmered. "Do you remember?"

"How could I forget that vacation?" she said.

Hattie grew up in the South, never seeing snow. For their tenth anniversary, the family took a trip together to stay in a snowy, mountain log cabin in the woods. It was magical.

Hattie felt a chilly prick on her cheek. She positioned her hands upward as snowflakes began to descend. She gazed upward, opening her mouth to catch a few. Her head jolted back towards George.

"This tastes like rainbow sherbet!" she said.

"Oh, that is a good one. What else did you get?"

"More flavors?"

"You didn't think the snow only came in one flavor, did you?"

She quickly tilted her head back, mouth catching more flakes.

"Cornbread...Strawberry...I don't even know what this is, but it's really good," said Hattie.

"Infinite flavors. Remember in school when the teacher would say that every snowflake has a unique pattern? Turns out, in the *real* world, they have unique flavors too."

"So it's like Heaven's version of a snow cone," she said.

"Not quite," said George. "This is the original. *That* was the copycat. For every good entrepreneur on Earth, there's a great heavenly inspiration."

Hattie smiled and closed her eyes, tongue back out.

"We do need to get going," said George. "This was just a taste of what's to come, you could say."

"Go? I don't even know where we are right now."

"This is the Tundra of Taste," said George.

Hattie scowled.

"That's a ridiculous name."

"That won't be the last pun you hear. Creator has a strange sense of humor and has a particular fondness of alliteration."

God is funny? Humor was a difficult character trait of God to grasp. She was used to the sermons about wrath and suffering at church. Never one about humor. The thought left a smile lingering on her face.

"Very well," said Hattie. "Where are we off to next? The Auditorium of Apples?"

"Not today, but I think you would like that place too."

"You're kidding, right?" asked Hattie in disbelief.

George was straight faced.

"Not at all. If you can imagine it, it exists here. Do you think your mind has more creativity than the Creator of the universe? Before we were here, our minds were already connected to this place. We just didn't know it. We called it 'intuition,' 'creativity,' and 'inspiration.' All good things come from this place. Now, we get to experience it without the veil in between."

Hattie remained quiet. George was not what she would describe as a Bible thumper, yet his words struck her stronger than any sermon she heard on Earth.

"So Creator made this place?"

"No ma'am," said a soft feminine voice. "I did."

Hattie turned towards the voice.

"Yoshiko, so good to see you again!" said George, hopping through a few meters of snow to hug the woman who wore a flowing purple satin tunic.

"I'd like to introduce you to my wife, Hattie."

Yoshiko stepped forward and abruptly wrapped her arms around Hattie with a tight hug.

"Oh!" said Hattie with surprise.

"It's a pleasure to finally meet you. George has spoken to me so much of you."

"Yoshiko's family and mine go way back, apparently," said George. "We met when I first arrived, and she introduced me to her amazing creation."

"You made this?" asked Hattie.

"Yes, of course," said Yoshiko. "I love eating, and I love snow, so I dreamed this place with Creator centuries ago. We brought it to life, together."

The soft skin on Yoshiko's face did not look a day over twenty-five.

"Amazing," said Hattie.

"Peach?" Yoshiko reached down and scooped up a handful of snow, offering the clump to Hattie with a smile.

"No, thank you."

Yoshiko took a bite before dropping the snow, the remnants on her hand disappearing.

"Does that mean Heaven was incomplete before you made this place?" asked Hattie.

"Not at all," said Yoshiko. "This place always existed in the mind of Creator."

"But if it wasn't built, then it didn't exist, right?" asked Hattie.

"Quite the contrary," said Yoshiko. "Here, there is no separation between imagination and being. We may go through the act of creating a space or tool or a technique, but all things have already been imagined. We simply partner with Creator to pull it into being. Does that make sense?"

"Not really."

"Hattie has not received any assignments yet," said George.

He turned to her.

"Don't worry dear, you'll—"

"Get answers in time," interrupted Hattie. "I know. I know. Now I have homework too? Great."

"Hattie, what gives you passion?" asked Yoshiko. "What fulfilled you beyond your wildest imagination in your earthly lifetime? What surprised you more than anything?"

Hattie didn't hesitate.

"My children. I miss them so much."

George and Hattie grew distant from their adult son, Ryan, as he removed them from his life. Hattie held onto the good memories of him. It was at least more than she had with her daughter. She would have given anything for just another day with her. Her son could not even be bothered to be with her during the surgery that ultimately took her earthly life.

"Oh, I see," said Yoshiko, strangely staring above Hattie's head into the distance. "I know exactly where you'll be placed."

"Don't spoil the surprise," said George.

Hattie's eyes darted back and forth between George and Yoshiko to see them both with knowing smiles. George reached his hand out. No sense in asking. She already knew what they would say.

"Ready?" asked George.

"Please, I'll show you to the door," said Yoshiko.

Hattie took his hand.

"We're off to see the Institute of Ice Cream," said Hattie.

"Oh! That's one of my favorites!" exclaimed Yoshiko.

Hattie laughed and shook her head.

"You weren't kidding, were you, George?" said Hattie.

"Can't lie here," he said. "Actually, we're heading to your new home for the welcome party."

"Oh, so you have just arrived!" said Yoshiko. "How magnificent. Please, take some caramelized tangerine frosted carrot cake."

Yoshiko scooped up a large armful of snow.

"Please, it's quite all right," said Hattie. "I don't—"

As she stood, the snow morphed, and colorized, forming a beautiful teal and orange layered cake perched atop a silver pedestal. Yoshiko plopped it into Hattie's unwilling arms.

"How did you do that?" asked Hattie, staring at the luxurious dessert.

"Easy. I had all the ingredients right here." Yoshiko swirled her finger towards the ground. "It was really no trouble at all. It would be my honor for you to serve it at your party."

Hattie looked at George, then the cake, then to Yoshiko. Snowflakes still fell from the sky.

"It would be my pleasure," said Hattie.

Yoshiko walked them a short ways to the edge of the forest that encircled the snowy embankment where an ornate red door stood, engraved with gold and studded with rubies and diamonds.

"Back to The Center, you go," she said. "It has truly been a treat, Hattie. I look forward to getting to know you more."

"This has been quite the experience," said Hattie. "Thank you for the cake."

She lifted the dense cake and gave a modest nod since it was the only movement she could muster. The cake was enormous.

"See you next time, Yoshiko," said George. "We have to taste that one flavor again."

"Christmas Morning?" said Yoshiko. "Another all-time-favorite. Farewell, and welcome home, Hattie."

"Thank you."

Yoshiko opened the door. This time the other side was quite clear. George put his hand on her back as they walked through to the other side.

13

Hattie hadn't known there could be a perfect height for grass, yet here it was. Manicured, lush, and soft under her feet. The lawn stretched out like a deep green carpet, inviting and endless.

"Welcome to The Center," said George.

"No funny name, this time? It looks like a park." asked Hattie.

"It's technically called The Central's Centered Center, but we just say, "The Center" so we don't get confused with The Central's Left Center and The Central's Right Center."

"There's more than one center? How can you have more than one center?"

George smiled.

"Let me guess," said Hattie, interrupting herself. "Space behaves differently here and don't worry Hattie, there's plenty of time for answers. Did I get it?"

"Exactly!"

Hattie looked around. The grounds were immaculate. A series of paths interwove across the flat land connecting to a variety of doors that extended out into the distance. The paths looked more like shallow creeks as she saw colored spray kick back behind one of the people walking. The doors displayed multiple styles. Different colors, textures, and heights. Trees dotted the landscape, some bearing heavy colored fruit.

"How far are we going?" asked Hattie. "And what do I do with this cake?"

"Please allow me," said a dwarfed creature, appearing at Hattie's feet. "I shall deliver it to your party."

The creature looked as though a whimsical artist had mashed together an owl's sleek body, a giraffe's spindly legs, and the muscular arms of a gorilla. Hattie felt her jaw drop.

"Thank you, Transport," said George.

Hattie stared at the peculiar creature. As it turned around, cake in hand, Hattie also spotted a small pair of wings that flapped on its back, seeming to defy its bulky proportions. As soon as it turned, the Transport disappeared with a bolt of lightning into the distance.

Hattie looked back at George.

"Transport," he said as if nothing were out of the ordinary.

"That was a strange looking angel."

"Not all creatures here are angels," said George. "Transports are a type of Messenger and report to Gabriel's organization, but they aren't angels. They don't work with the humans on Earth."

George pointed across the vast lawn to a massive onyx and gold door.

"Actually, there's his door right there," he said.

"Archangel Gabriel," said Hattie in disbelief. "*The* Archangel Gabriel just has a front door in the middle of a park?"

"Yes, of course," said George. "I'll introduce you to him some time. Nice fellow. Throws great parties."

"I guess I would think his door would be up on a mountain or something," she said.

"His door is actually not normally here. He must be hosting an event at his palace."

Hattie continued to scan the beings in the landscape. Some looked like people. They wore the same white tunic that Hattie wore. Some of the creatures looked familiar, reminiscent of Aleifr, although they sported a wide variety of clothing, hair, and skin colors. One angel caught her eye as the light shimmered off its faceted aquamarine-colored skin, sending flashes around The Center like a disco ball.

There were creatures whose forms were an unpredictable mix of legs, wings, and limbs in an array of colored feathers, scales, fur, and other unknown materials. It was as though each being had borrowed elements, creating a living tapestry of life in all forms imaginable. They moved methodically in and out of doors.

"How do you find a door if it's not here?" asked Hattie.

"The Kingdom's resources are organized on need," said George. "If you need something, it's right there. There tends to be a lot of need for government buildings or access to the university, so the doors to those communities are almost always visible here."

George pointed to a set of doors through the trees.

"University classes are over there."

He gestured to a scholarly looking double door that could have been removed from a British boarding school.

"School, my favorite," said Hattie.

"You said you wanted answers, didn't you?" said George.

Hattie shot him a tough glance.

"Remember, what we experienced on Earth is merely a shadow of what the real thing is. This university is about unlocking mysteries and understanding all aspects of the universe. Where do you think it got its name? If you want to know about a subject, there are classes here. If you can imagine it, that knowledge is held right behind those doors. Humans, angels, and creatures alike attend classes, so you may be sitting next to a Thorabeen or Badgocite while chatting away with a Guardian. Great place to meet folks."

"You are taking classes then, I assume?" asked Hattie.

"I'm on sabbatical, but I will be going back soon for a course on Sub-Saharan leaf patterns."

"The mysteries of the universe are held in leaf patterns?" asked Hattie.

"Oh yes. One of the best ways to understand Heaven is studying Earth's patterns first. Creator was clever. He placed heavenly patterns all over right in front of our eyes. We were just too blind to see the obvious design in front of us, so it makes it a little easier to understand for us here."

"How many classes are there?"

"Infinite. Most classes are taught by leaders from the respective Authorities or Council members, but Creator likes to guest lecture quite a bit."

George raised his hand, pointing past her face behind her.

"Government agencies are through that door."

He pointed to a thick gold door studded with every imaginable colored gemstone creating a blaze of rainbow around it.

"This is one of the key hubs of Heaven," said George. "When you want to go somewhere, The Center is the place to start. The door to your neighborhood is over there."

"I thought we were going to *our* home."

"Yes and no," said George, bobbing his head. "Neighborhoods are connected linearly through family lines but also circularly through those we met, befriended, and loved through our lives."

Hattie responded with a blank stare.

"It's easier to show you. This way," said George.

He grabbed Hattie's hand and started walking down the path that led away from Yoshiko's door. With each step, the watery material on the path let out a soft instrumental sound, like millions of tiny harp cords were being plucked.

Hattie further examined the people and creatures that passed them.

"That fish is flying," she said, turning her head to watch a blue tinted feathery fish swim by her in the middle of the air.

"Oh yes, that's normal. Fish fly, and birds swim here. Another one of Creator's jokes. He was particularly amused at Himself for making a flying fish on Earth. Have Him tell you the story sometime. It's actually quite funny."

George led Hattie down a series of splits and merges in paths, eventually leading to an unassuming door with painted white wood trim around glass panels with minor detailing.

"Is this it?" asked Hattie, with a twinge of disappointment.

"Yep, are you ready?"

Hattie inspected the door.

"But it's so...basic," she said. "There's no markings on it. How do you even know this is the right one?"

"Feel it."

Hattie reached out and placed her palm on the door. George laughed.

"No, *feel* it. Go deeper."

"I don't understand what you are saying," said Hattie.

"Don't touch it with your hand. Touch it with your heart and see what it feels like."

Hattie waited for further explanation, but none came. She turned to face the door and stared at it. *Feel with my heart. What does that even mean?* She stared further.

"Just wait, it will come," said George in a soft voice.

Hattie waited. And waited. As she stared, she did notice a slight warmth in her chest. Her eyes changed focus, zooming in on the door past the wood bits. As she focused on the feeling, the sensation grew. As she focused, the door transformed into a mosaic of her life's memories, each moment alive with warmth and color. Scenes from childhood with her parents, holidays, and adventures with George and Ryan wove together like an intricate tapestry. Each touch, each laugh, each love was knit together in a perfect, pulsating fabric. As she scanned the different images, the full memories felt as though they were projected into her heart. Wrestling with her siblings. A church recital. Ryan's first day of school. Her eyes froze on a family picture.

"See it?" asked George.

Hattie's eyes refocused to bring the door back into view.

"Yeah, what is that?"

"We have new senses here. Remember that whole Earth being a shadow of Heaven? All of our senses were shadows. Every part of our body is meant to connect. From the top of our head to the bottom of our feet and everything inside. All have different receptors."

"Incredible."

"I learned that one in class," said George.

"Of course you did."

"The Father is all about family and our connections with one another," said George. "We recognize each other not just based on sight but based on heart. We see people with our heart here. You are feeling what is behind this door, Hattie. That is how you know it's yours. This is your family's neighborhood. Are you ready?"

Hattie smiled and grabbed the doorknob. She was not sure what exactly to expect, but this was Heaven after all. She thrust the door open. The smell of vanilla hit her palate.

"Surprise!" echoed a joyful chorus. Hattie's heart raced as she took in the sea of beloved faces. Her eyes landed on one figure, and she felt her breath catch. She let go of George's hand and stepped forward, her heart soaring as she crossed the threshold, feeling the past and present merge in this precious moment.

14

Hattie leapt through the door, landing on a glistening white wooden house porch. The crowd surrounded her, spilling down the steps and out into the yard. She was focused solely on one face, gently smiling and with loving eyes that Hattie longed to see.

Hattie's heart raced, her hands trembling as she whispered, "Momma," barely able to get the word out.

"My dear," said her mother, wearing her favorite floral dress.

Tears welled in Hattie's eyes as she raised her arms to embrace. Hattie's mother was her rock. From childhood to adulthood, she was steadfast. Always present and always providing. Hattie was devastated when her mother was diagnosed with cancer shortly after marrying George, only to watch her waste away in a slow and painful death. That was the year she swore off God. That is, until she had children of her own.

Hattie pulled back slightly to look her mother in the eyes, now youthful and full of life. Hattie tried to speak, but all of the unsaid words of the last several decades all rushed to her mouth at once. The cheer of the crowd around her was deafening. Before she could get any words out, Hattie found herself spun around, people left and right with enormous smiles, hugging and cheering with her. There was one small face she looked for in the crowd but everyone blurred together. Whistles and cheers, whooping and hollering. The faces were a blur. An aunt, an uncle, her best friends from school. She lost sight of her mother. The crowd seemed to grow. Hattie barely had time to process each face before the next was in front of her with pure jubilation.

George was nowhere in sight, but she could still feel him there. Somewhere in the crowd. Suddenly her gaze stopped once more. Her eyes locked on a new but familiar face.

"Pop."

She froze, unsure of what his reaction might be.

"I've waited a long time to see you, Harriet," he said with a grieved voice, stepping towards her.

Hattie did not have the best relationship growing up with her father. He tried his best, but it was rarely enough. The missed birthdays and endless lectures on right and wrong were exhausting. Hattie left home as soon as she could to try and escape. She maintained contact with her mother but kept relationship with her father only to formalities. It was the only way she could maintain any sense of emotional stability.

"I'm sorry, Harriet," he said, tears forming in his eyes.

He looked different here. Pure. He felt different too. Hattie let her focus on him expand to examine his heart as if he were an unknown door. He was whole, but she could see what was left of his earthly life. They appeared as golden scars on his inside. She pulled her focus back as her father stood before her. He reached for her hand and moved it over his heart.

"I'm so sorry, Harriet. I was not the best father I could have been. You deserved so much more, and I'm sorry that I was not there for you in the way that you needed. I did my best, but it wasn't enough. I see that now. I am truly sorry. I hope you can forgive me."

Hattie choked back tears. These were words Hattie waited a lifetime to hear. Parenting was not easy. She knew that. But she wanted some acknowledgment of what happened. She never got it. She built an emotional fortress between her and her father, and it stood firm. Until now.

His words were genuine. On Earth, these words would never be found on his lips, but she could feel his intentions here in a way that she never could on Earth. She could feel the struggles he had and how he tried his best to overcome them. In a moment, she received new perspective on his actions. Her walls came crumbling down.

"I forgive you, Poppa," she said through tears.

"I hope we can get to know each other here," he said. "The way it should have been."

She embraced him, head pressed against his chest. A fresh wave of tears flowed down her cheek. Tears of joy. Upon entering Heaven, she felt whole, yet with each experience here, she felt even more wholly whole, or perhaps it was just holy whole.

She felt a hand on her back.

"Welcome home, my sweet."

The voice of her mother embraced them both. Hattie stayed in this moment for an eternity before pulling back. A flash of yellow caught her eye. As she looked down, she saw flowers sprouting from where her tears struck the ground. Daffodils, her favorite. The remainder on her face dissolved as she caught flecks of glitter shimmering out of the corner of her eye.

With one hand on Poppa and one on Mamma, she looked around. The crowd enveloped her on all sides. She scanned the group, seeing just how large it was. Movement on the side caught her attention as George pushed his way to the center to be with her.

"Welcome home, Hattie," said George.

"I could get used to Heaven," she said with a laugh.

"No, I mean HOME home. This is your home. Your forever home."

In the overwhelm of the crowd, Hattie forgot the destination. She opened her eyes wider, slowly spinning to get a full view of the house and land. The covered porch she stood on was enormous as was the double door entrance to the house. She ran her fingers over the railing, marveling at the delicate carved vines twisting along its length, each leaf catching the golden light. The crowd parted as she descended down the steps to the base of the house, turning back to see it all at once. Her hands involuntarily moved their way to her mouth.

"It's beautiful," she said. "Stunning. Absolutely stunning." She shook her head in disbelief.

She turned and gasped at the sight before her. Rising above her, the house stretched three stories high, every window glimmering like polished jewels set into cream-colored walls. Dark sapphire shutters framed each window, and at the very top, a magnificent stained-glass window reflected the sunlight in shimmering hues. The scent of magnolias drifted around the wraparound porch, mingling with the subtle warmth that radiated from the mother of pearl columns. Her favorite.

"It's perfect in every way," she said.

"Isn't it grand?" said a voice.

Creator appeared from the crowd.

"I knew you would like it," He said. "The porch came out absolutely exquisite."

The golden light of Heaven reflected off the mother of pearl in a way that it looked like milky metallic liquid swirling inside the solid structure. Colors that Hattie did not recognize emerged.

"I could look at this forever," she said, entranced in the flow of color.

"Good, because you are," said Creator. "But first, I want to introduce you to someone."

Creator grabbed her hand and pulled her back up excitedly onto the porch where a woman stood, set apart from the crowd. Hattie could feel the connection to the woman even before Creator spoke.

"This is your Great Great Great Great Great Grandmother. She was the first of your lineage in America, brought as a slave to South Carolina. She was an artist, just like you. In fact, she was so talented that the slave owner's wife took notice and had her give the children art lessons. It was her kindness that ultimately led to the owners releasing her as a free woman."

The reality of being a Black woman in America was certainly not new, but Hattie never imagined that she would meet those that actually went through slavery. She could only imagine the horrors this woman experienced through in her lifetime. But here, she just smiled.

"I am so glad to meet you, Hattie," said the woman. "I have been so blessed watching my line grow and blossom. From the seed I planted, such beautiful fruit now flourishes. You are incredible, Hattie. I am so proud of you."

"I look forward to you uncovering the story of your family line, Hattie," said Creator. "It's a story for the Ages! Trust me."

Hattie hugged the woman. Hattie hugged everyone. Her ability to heart-sense grew as she could feel the individuals of the crowd, even without needing to focus. The love she felt intensified. She did not need Creator to introduce her to anyone. She felt each of their spirits. She felt their stories. She felt her impact on their lives and theirs on hers.

A friend of her son that she took in, who considered Hattie his real mom.

A stranger from an elevator on the verge of suicide encouraged by a simple compliment and smile one day.

The people that stranger saved after becoming a nurse. All were connected to Hattie, and the love she felt was enveloping. Hundreds, no thousands, if not more, stories surrounded her. She was brought to her knees on the porch at the feet of her Grandmother. Hattie never knew the ripples she left behind.

"I felt so insignificant for so many years," she said through a fresh round of tears. "I was just a mom."

Creator and George lifted her up.

"Mothers are incredible in their own right," said Creator, "but now you see the full picture. Our actions lead to impacts around the world. The people here are only a fraction of those that were blessed through you. On Earth, humans are short sighted. Buying a cup of coffee for a stranger or a gentle smile to someone on the street may seem insignificant, but those things impact the universe forever, and they are all seen here. There are people here directly linked to a set of actions set in motion by what you did for others. You are a blessing, Hattie."

Hattie stood in a growing bouquet of daffodils as she continued to weep. On Earth, she was so fixated on what she was doing wrong, and there certainly was plenty of that. But here, she could see the truth. Even the smallest of actions were remembered in the Kingdom. There were people around her that she never met that were brought to Heaven because of the way she loved. Despite always feeling insufficient, she gave what she could. And now, she could see the result.

"This moment...," she said. "This moment is perfect. I wish I could have seen this before."

"If people could only feel this single moment, they would know the hard work of life is worth it," said George. "Even in the darkest times, we matter. Our smallest actions change the course of humanity forever. We were so concerned with our bad decisions that we never realized what a little love could do."

"It is love that transforms everything, quite literally," said Creator, arms outstretched, spinning.

George pulled Hattie in, hugging her from behind.

Hattie continued to sense the crowd, wave after wave of impacts hitting her. A murmur began to grow in the crowd. Then moans, then grunts, then cheers, shouts, and screams.

"I think they're ready for the party," said Creator. "Are you?"

"I never thought Heaven would be a party."

"Well, you would be wrong then," He said. "We have every resource at our disposal, and you think humans invented parties?"

"I guess I never thought of it like that," said Hattie.

The crowd's shrieks reached a new high level exploding into a thunderous roar. Creator took her hand, leading her forward through the crowd. The murmurs softened as they neared the sapphire-studded doorway, and Hattie stepped inside, her breath catching at the sight before her.

Her new home. As she crossed the threshold, a soft warmth enveloped her. The light poured in through floor-to-ceiling windows, illuminating the rich, mahogany floors and the delicate iridescent inlays that traced the borders of the entryway.

"Oh, just look at all these books!" said Hattie, skipping over to the right and running her hand across the ornate covers of stories she did not recognize.

"Well I will let you two explore the house," said Creator. "I'm going to go get something to eat." He exited abruptly through a door to the left, leaving Hattie and George standing in the foyer.

It was familiar, but new. With sounds of music and laughter as her guests entered behind her, they streamed into different doors on either side of the foyer.

"They seem to know where they are going," said Hattie.

"I would hope so. They helped build this place," said George.

Hattie and George both looked around, spotting the meticulously placed treasures all around.

"My mother's mirror!" exclaimed Hattie, spotting the family heirloom on the wall of the foyer.

Hattie walked to it, placing both hands on its sides to inspect it. The material was fresh and alive. Imperfections and cracks sealed with precious metals.

"It's beautiful," she said.

In the reflection, Hattie's eye caught a familiar color. She turned. Meticulously placed on the edge of the couch lay a quilt she'd made as a young bride.

"Did you see that chair over here?" asked George from behind her.

Hattie turned towards the living room to see the most beautiful wingback chair, its grand arms welcoming them as they walked into the bright new room.

"We never had a chair like this," said Hattie.

"But you always wanted one," said George. "The details of this house will always be emerging."

Hattie walked over and brushed her hand along the chair's tightly bound fabric, soft beyond any silk. Hattie looked around.

"This place is enormous!" she said.

Hattie scanned the living room and adjacent spaces. The inside was decorated in a classic Southern style, Hattie's favorite. Only it was done in a way beyond perfection. It made those designer magazines look like child's play. Clean and warm but filled with eclectic lovely items that connected directly to Hattie. Some were exact items from her life. Others were new and exciting, clearly tailored just for her taste. Gone were the secondhand chairs and beat up carpet. This house was pristine.

"You gotta see this," said George, his voice wandering to another room.

Hattie followed the sound of his voice. Turning the corner, she found herself in the kitchen where many of her guests now stood. Hattie's eyes widened.

Every possible favorite food of Hattie was there. Salads, brownies, her mother's baked Brussels sprouts, cornbread, meats of every kind. She even spotted Yoshiko's cake on the buffet.

"Is that peach cobbler?" she asked, pointing to the mass of food.

"It most certainly is," said George.

Every flat surface of the kitchen was neatly stacked with mouthwatering food.

"I've never seen so much food in my life!" exclaimed Hattie.

"Just wait until you taste it," said George.

Hattie was not hungry. She was not sure when the last time she ate was. But the biscuits smelled divine. She observed a pattern of peach-colored steam rising from the basket. She walked over to uncover the heavenly delights. Her approaching hand sensed the warmth emanating from the basket.

"Still hot," she said, looking up at George.

Unwrapping the cloth, there were seven perfectly shaped and browned biscuits, sliced in half. Hattie saw the melted butter and touch of honey dribbling from the cut, just the way she preferred. She grabbed one and took a bite. Her eyes instinctively closed, and she let out a deep grunt. George laughed.

"Pretty good, huh?" he asked.

"Do you know when you haven't eaten all day, and you take that first bite of food? It's like that times a million."

The flavors harmonized in her mouth unlike on Earth. The flavors resonated audibly in her ears and visually with colors. She took another bite before setting the biscuit down. It disappeared.

"I wasn't done with that!" she Hattie.

"It's OK, grab another," said George. "They're all just made of light. No dishes or cleanup here."

Hattie threw back the towel over the basket once again. Seven biscuits still remained. She picked one up. Almost instantaneously, another pushed up from the bottom, shifting the others in the basket.

"No shortage here," said George.

Time blurred in this boundless joy. How long did the party last? Minutes, hours, or years. The moment felt like one continuous heartbeat. Hattie was home. She met loved ones, friends, and strangers, at least they were strangers on Earth. They were all connected through her. Everyone was connected. Between the hugs, the laughs, and the endless food and peach tea, Hattie felt more alive than ever. If the events since her passing were any indication of what was to come, she knew Heaven would be nothing short of the time of her life. Or rather, the time of her eternity. No cherubs and grapes, although she was sure there was probably a room with that too. Fulfillment like she had never experienced. The things she longed for on Earth were here. She knew it. And she could not wait to discover more.

15

Rebecca sighed, hands resting heavily on the dresser, head bowed. She straightened up, slipping into her black dress, her gaze fixed on the floor.

"I still can't believe it," she said. "Aunt Hat was such a big part of our lives."

"Yeah, I know," said Frank, his voice flat.

Rebecca's shoulders tensed.

"Can you not use that fucking tone right now, Frank?" she said, turning to face him with a glare. "We're about to leave for the goddamn funeral, and you can't even show a little respect?"

"Ree," he paused. "I'm agreeing with you. She's family, but it's been a lot of work."

Frank buttoned his shirt, avoiding even the slightest possibility of eye contact. Rebecca turned away. She loved her aunt, but caring for her the last few years was hard on her and even harder on her marriage. Lost date nights, missed cues, drained finances. Frank didn't just hint at his resentment. He told her regularly. But Aunt Hat was family, and she had no one.

I'm family too, he would tell her. But this was different. This was blood. This was not a choice. This was family. Frank broke the silence.

"What are you going to do if your mom shows?" he asked.

"Same thing I always do. Ignore her."

"I really don't feel comfortable being around her, especially with Liam there," he said.

"You've never even met her."

"Really? That's where you want to take this? Ree, she's dangerous."

"She's not going to do anything at a damn funeral," scoffed Rebecca.

"You don't know," he paused, voice hardening, "what that monster is capable of."

"She's not a monster."

"If that isn't a monster, I don't know what the hell you are thinking," said Frank. "God help our son if that's your attitude about it."

"Don't bring him into this. I would never let anything happen to Liam."

"You have to be around to let something happen," said Frank under his breath.

"Excuse me?"

"Oh, was I unclear? You haven't even been around to let something happen. I've been the one taking care of him while you waited around for Hat to die."

Rebecca shook her head and didn't engage, instead redirecting her focus to the mascara that she was surely about to ruin.

"Unbelievable," she muttered, her hand shaking as she finished applying it.

She watched Frank in the mirror as he turned and left the room with a door slam. Rebecca let out a sigh in an attempt to steady her hand as she leaned into the mirror.

"Come on, Mom! We're ready!" Liam's voice cut through her haze. She took a steadying breath, smoothing her dress.

Just keep it together. She can't do anything.

16

Hattie waved to the last of the guests as they left, their boisterous laughter fading down the steps of her porch. She closed the door and turned to face George.

"I should be exhausted," she said, as she walked briskly from the foyer and plopped onto the gray satin couch in the living room. "I have never felt this kind of energy before. How long was that party?"

"As long as you want it to be," he said, smirking. "Time is only relative to those around you. In this realm, behind each door, you can live eternities, but when you walk back out, not a moment has passed. Time is multidimensional."

"This sounds like a CS Lewis novel."

"Where do you think he got the idea?" said George.

Hattie eyed the room where only moments ago hundreds, if not thousands, of people wandered around. Any remaining food, cups, and plates already dissolved. The house was impeccable.

"No mess. I could *really* get used to that," she said. "How does that work?"

"This place is a Kingdom of light and everything within it is light, so it's just light being absorbed."

"I don't understand anything you just said, so I guess I will wait for the school lesson on that one too."

George smiled.

"Well," he said, slapping his thighs and slowly rising to his feet. "It's time for me to go."

The last time George "left," it was the most heart-wrenching feeling.

But here, the feeling was quite different. She was completely fulfilled. No fear of separation or distance. Only a knowing connection.

"Are you going to your home now?" asked Hattie.

"Yes, but I won't be far."

Hattie rose and began walking to the door.

"I must say, this is beyond anything I could imagi—" she stopped short, realizing George was not beside her. She turned.

"What are you doing?" she asked.

"That's not how I get home," he said with another knowing smile. "Follow me."

George welcomed her to him with an outstretched hand and turned to lead Hattie up the cascading staircase to the second level. In the hustle and bustle of the party, she did not even take a moment to venture upstairs. Sapphire studded onyx railings lined the staircase. Family pictures dotted the walls all the way up. One caught her eye, and she stopped to look. Her wedding day. She smiled as the memory reran through her mind when suddenly the frozen moment between her and George started to move.

"Oh!" she exclaimed.

The image of her and George leapt to life from the portrait in front of them, showing an almost holographic view of the moment they were pronounced husband and wife before dissolving back into the frames. She looked at George.

"Why didn't you warn me?" she asked with a playful scolding.

"I thought you would like the surprise. Come on, you'll have time later to relive all of those memories."

They reached the landing where a long hallway stretched before them. Hattie looked around to see this floor as immaculately decorated as the first. It was shaped like an arc with multiple hallways extending off like a hub and spoke.

"If you ever need me," said George. "I'm right through here."

George took Hattie by the hand and led her down the hallway directly in front of the landing. He stopped at the first door on the right.

"This is where you live?" she asked. "In the spare bedroom?"

The door looked like that of a kid's clubhouse. The only thing missing was a messily painted "No girls allowed" sign hanging off-center. George opened it without answering.

She heard the distant caws and chirps of birds. The quaint Southern house of Hattie opened up into what appeared to be a tree house.

"What is this place?" she asked.

"I always loved the outdoors."

"I never knew that."

"I didn't even really know myself," said George. "I remember as a kid playing in the forest, but growing up, that faded into only a memory. But now that I'm here, I couldn't imagine a more perfect space."

He smiled proudly. "Please, come in."

The two stepped over the threshold, entering George's otherworldly estate. The floor was a solid deep colored wood with golden grain lines that moved through each plank like water. A spiral staircase on their right led to an upper floor. A stream of water in a shallow gutter flanked each side of the staircase, corkscrewing down from the ceiling and into the floor to at least one level below. Plants hung from the ceiling, walls, and supports. Plants filled every corner, each one alive with movement as vines crept and bloomed across the space. Hattie watched them, exploding open with a rainbow of colors and metallic sparkles like fireworks. Fruits expanded out of the centers of some of the flowers, and their colors transitioned to show ripeness. The space was alive.

"George, this is beautiful," she said, taking a few steps towards a particularly brilliant yellow flower, whose center glowed with spinning fire.

There was so much to see that Hattie's eyes darted back and forth. There were no walls, only support posts open to the outside. Beyond the edge of the expansive flat was jungle. Hattie ran to the edge to look.

"Incredible," she said.

Forest for as far as the eye could see. She looked down. They were elevated off the ground and perched on the side of a gentle hill sitting in the valley of a steep mountain range. Trees speckled the area directly around the house before becoming dense in the forest beyond. A gentle mist blended in the distance, masking the size of the forest. A flash of color swooshed past, stopping in the tree immediately in front of Hattie.

"Is that a toucan?" she asked.

"What else would I be?" said the bird with a surprisingly gruff voice.

"Excuse me?" said Hattie.

"Don't mind him," said George, waving his hand at the bird.

"You didn't tell me the animals talk here," she said.

"One detail at a time, Dear."

The bird darted off without another word. Hattie admired the jungle view, taking in the chirps and clicks of birds, insects, and other forest critters just beyond the tree line. Looking down, she saw at least two more levels and a stream running alongside the house. Looking up, another cantilevered level extended out beyond the edge where she now stood.

"Here, hold this," said George, pulling a stick from the ceiling somewhere, and it floated above their heads. Hattie grabbed it, unsure of its purpose.

"Hold on!" he shouted.

Before Hattie could ask a question, George gave her a firm shove off the edge of the landing, and she gave him a loud scream.

"Zip line!" she heard him shout.

Before she knew what was even happening, Hattie's feet were off the solid floor and now swung seemingly autonomously in shock as she accelerated through the jungle, suspended by a stick. No line above, no harness. Just forest. She could not contain her screams. The trees and birds screamed in chorus with her as she passed.

After the initial moment of shock wore off, Hattie was surprised to find the moment exhilarating. Trees whipped and slapped around her. Birds dive bombed the path, pulling back just in time before a collision. Hattie's screams turned to laughter. She felt light. She certainly was not carrying her own weight on that stick.

"Let go!" she heard George shout from behind her.

Hattie spun herself slightly to look behind her. She was stunned to see George on the same path, arms outstretched beneath the stick, flapping.

"You don't need to hold on. Let go!" he said.

Hattie had no fear here, so she did just that. Upon letting go, she was flying. Actually flying, but the course she was on no longer sloped downwards. As the mountain range opposite George's estate approached, her body dipped before forcefully moving upward along the slope of the mountain. She could hear George hollering behind her in pure ecstasy.

She zigged left, then right, up, then down. She had no control over where she was going, and she was loving it. A small flock of parrot-looking birds flew alongside her in unison for a moment. Their feathers were crystal and see-through. Their beaks solid gold and their eyes blazed as a red ruby. They disappeared into the forest as quickly as they appeared.

As Hattie passed each tree, she felt an echo of its essence. Each one was a joyous memory from George's life. Hattie was amazed that the memories appeared in her mind in an instant, all at once, but just as soon as she recognized one, another pushed its way into her mind as she watched the highlights of George's life and interactions with those around him. As she swooped through the forest, she was overwhelmed with the joy she had for her earthly husband.

"Almost there!" shouted George.

The path took a sharp upward turn, nearly vertical moving up the steepest part of the mountainside. As her path took her above the treeline, she entered a misty cloud, momentarily losing sight of the forest before exploding out the top into sunshine, pulling a billowy tuft with her into the clear sky. Her body slowed before gently depositing itself on a flat but colorful meadow atop the mountain. She heard George's laughs growing in volume as she turned to see him burst into view and land beside her. He had the biggest grin on his face.

"You could have just told me what to do," said Hattie. "You didn't have to push me."

"Where's the fun in that?"

Hattie paused.

Her scowl turned to a smile. "It was really fun actually."

Fun. There it was again. Fun. She was actually enjoying herself here in Heaven. It was nothing like the stuffy church services, so why was this place so fun?

"Do you remember the first vacation we took with the kids?" asked George.

"Oh do I ever. We spent weeks planning that thing."

"And everything we did was meticulously scheduled and thought out just so the kids could enjoy themselves. Our joy came from seeing their joy."

"I never thought about it like that," said Hattie.

"This realm is fun because Creator delights in His kids having fun. It brings Him joy when we are joyful."

Being a parent brought Hattie some of her greatest joys and deepest sorrows.

"We felt what He feels," said George.

"What do you mean?"

"Earth was architected as a sliver of reality. The things we experienced and felt were merely a training ground for what was to come. Why bother needing to create children? They're loud, messy, expensive. There really is no point when you think about it. Other than the fact that we were given a glimpse of the Father's experience. There would be no other way for us to get that here."

"I never thought about it like that either."

Hattie's eyes traced the green ground that dipped off the edge into the lake of clouds.

"The more time you spend here, the more the mystery unravels and the deeper the understanding. What seemed trivial or unnecessary on Earth suddenly became immensely important from our perspective here."

"Do you come here often?" she asked.

"It's my thinking spot, and I do like to think."

Hattie let her mind wander, flashing through different life moments and wondering what the deeper meaning was.

"All will be revealed in time," said George.

Hattie nodded, understandingly.

"But for now, I will leave you to your house to explore."

George jogged a few paces through the flowers and touched a rock on the ground. A Southern style door clad with silver rose up from the dirt, soil and greenery perched on the top door frame while a few dirt clods fell to the ground as it rose.

"This will take you back home," said George.

Hattie did not feel the need to say goodbye. She did not feel any sorrow, anxiousness, or longing. She knew that beyond that door, she was more connected to George than she ever had been.

"I'll see you soon, Honey," said Hattie, stepping forward to embrace George.

"Very soon, my dear."

They both paused in the embrace for a moment, connected in a way unlike before. Hattie pulled back and gave a soft wave as she turned to open the door. She stepped over the threshold back into her familiar space. She turned to wave at George once more in his mountaintop meadow. He smiled and gave her an exaggerated wave back. As Hattie closed the door, she saw him turn and leap off the ground, soaring back into the air.

As the door closed, the jungle vanished.

17

A chorus of crickets greeted Hattie as she closed the door behind her. They sounded exactly like on Earth.

"Welcome back, Hattie," said Aleifr, his looming figure standing at the top of the staircase. His once glowing presence that was blinding on Earth was barely noticeable here.

"I didn't think I would see you again," said Hattie.

"My role did not end with your earthly end. That was merely the beginning."

Aleifr's onyx-colored face was soft here, happy even. The stern eyebrows and terrifying glare were gone. He seemed at peace.

"I trust you had a good time enjoying George's estate?" he asked.

"I don't even know what to think about all of that," she said. "It was exhilarating, and I just felt so...so—"

"Connected," said Aleifr.

"Yes, exactly. Connected. But connected to what?"

"You are all connected to the source," said Aleifr. "Your presence here in this realm connects you in a way that was masked while on Earth. You're connected to Creator, the Father, and Their Spirit. That connection links you to George too, as it does to everyone in the Kingdom."

"Spirit," Hattie repeated. As the words rolled off her lips, they took on a weighty presence.

"Please, let me take you to your room."

Aleifr led her further down the hall. The more they walked, the longer the hall grew. They passed door after door. Some seemed to fit the house. Others seemed to come from different places or times, blending their own character with the house's timeless design. She passed a beautiful golden door with diamonds intricately placed in a floral pattern around the edges. Hattie stopped.

"Where do all of these go?" she asked.

"That is for you to explore," said Aleifr. "Creator made this place exactly to your needs. Any want, need, or desire, can be found in this house. Somewhere."

"I just walk through them unannounced?"

"That's how doors work, yes," said Aleifr. "You can knock if you want, but it is unnecessary. Please, this way. We are nearly at your room."

Hattie began to follow once again, trying to assess each door and what wonders might be behind it.

"You are my Guardian angel, right?" she asked. "What do I need guarding from here?"

"On Earth, we are Guardians of your physical growth and being. Here, we are Guardians of your spiritual growth and being."

"So you're my teacher," said Hattie.

"Only in this simplest of descriptions," said Aleifr. "Here we are."

Double doors towered at the end of the hall, solid gold stamped with inlays of sapphire scrollwork. Aleifr waved a hand, and they clicked, opening gently.

"After you," he said.

Hattie took in a sharp breath as she saw inside. She stepped into her room, met immediately with the comforting scent of lavender and jasmine. The room was adorned with the finest decor. Stepping in, her feet felt massaged by a plush carpet that shifted with a rhythmic pulse, like ocean tides lapping on a beach. Every step seemed to settle into the floor, only to rise again in soft waves of blue and gold. Above her, the ceiling arched like the sky itself, lit with soft, glowing clouds that drifted leisurely across a navy-blue expanse. Faint pinpoints of light twinkled. Aleifr stepped to the side, making his way to a small seating area just inside the doors.

"Tea?" he asked, walking past the Victorian mansion-style furniture, gilded and gold clad.

"Yes, please," she said while wandering further into the room.

The walls seemed alive, a muted glow radiating softly in shades that shifted as she moved—mossy greens, deep blues, and the occasional soft blush of rose. The light wasn't cast by any visible source but felt as if it radiated from the room itself. She watched, entranced.

"George mentioned a university," said Hattie. "Is that where you teach me?"

"Yes, that is one component. We will select your coursework depending on your assignment. There will be other teachers as well."

"I never liked school," she said. "Never found it interesting. After third grade, no one ever asked me what the state bird was or how to do long division."

Aleifr smiled.

"But strangely enough, school actually sounds exciting. I assumed going to Heaven meant instant knowledge and understanding. That happened a bit, but I still have so many questions."

"Every question has an answer," said Aleifr. "Some are obvious. Others will take time. Still others take eternity."

"What happens next?" asked Hattie.

"How do you mean?"

"I mean, we're here for eternity. I know there isn't the whole cherub and grape thing here, but what exactly is the purpose now? School forever? Church forever? Parties forever?"

"Hattie, you must remember that Earth was a shadow of this place. The patterns you saw on Earth were foreshadowing for what you would experience here."

Aleifr lifted the glass of tea and drew her back to the seating area.

"Thank you," she said, taking a sip. Perfect temperature, of course.

"You have a purpose, Hattie. Not just an earthy purpose. An eternity purpose. A destiny. An assignment."

"Yoshiko mentioned an assignment. What does that mean? I need to get a job here?"

"None of your experiences were by chance, Hattie. They were only the beginning of your true destiny."

"So, what is my destiny?"

Aleifr leaned in, lightly blowing into Harriet's face. His breath smelled of rain. His hand passed in front of her eyes, and she closed them. A silent moment stood.

"Open them," he said.

Hattie slowly opened her eyes, and she saw him staring intently at her with his burning gaze, his face close. She looked up, a colorful flick catching her attention. A dancing abstract painting spun over Aleifr's head. Her head tilted as she stared.

"Those are my Traces, my destiny. We all have one, including myself," said Aleifr. "Our Traces are known before the beginning of the world."

Aleifr gestured with his hand before raising it, twisting above his head, wrapping the colors around it and pulling the fluid painting down to present to Hattie. She stared. There were distinct colored symbols, but they were not like any she had seen before. Complex line strokes, and not just two dimensional. They had depth and were undulating, growing and shrinking in fluid unison. Ribbons of misty colors weaved their way through the symbols, seemingly to tie them together.

"Guardian," she said, surprising herself. "It says 'Guardian.' I can feel it."

"Precisely. Traces are tied to your existence. When you connect with others, you feel these as well."

"Why couldn't I see your Traces before?"

"The sensations of this realm can be rather overwhelming as your spirit readjusts to being home. More will be revealed in time. But these? Every being has one, including you."

Aleifr directed his gaze above Hattie. She looked up to see different colored ribbons threading through one another and gently throbbing above her head. She recognized a few symbols from Aleifr. A color like red but simultaneously gold shimmered. It was the predominant color. Hattie reached up and waved her hand through the painting. The colors and patterns swirled around before drawing back together with magnetic attraction.

"Comfort," she said.

"Yes."

"I don't understand. What does that mean, my purpose is comfort?"

"Before you were born, you existed here," said Aleifr. "You are and were an infinite spirit that existed within the Father's heart. He anointed you with this trait, which is one of His traits."

"Isn't that a little generic?" asked Hattie.

"Yes, by design. The same free will that humans have on Earth is here. You will have your own choice of your final assignment.

Naturally, you will be drawn to areas that align with your destiny."

Hattie chuckled at the word.

"Destiny?"

"Destiny does not end on Earth, Hattie. This is only the beginning. You were trained on Earth. Now is when you get to truly step into what you were always meant to do. Only here will you finally fully see how all the pieces begin to fit together. These pieces will be revealed in time, of course."

"Of course," said Hattie, taking a playfully serious tone.

As Hattie looked back up at her Traces, memories flashed through her mind. Her daughter with a bruised knee. A friend that lost her parent. George when he was fired. Her greatest joys came from caring for others in their sorrow. Paradoxically, she felt most fulfilled when she was giving parts of herself to others. The memories were different now. Her Traces grew brighter in each memory, the colors pulsing, reaching out to embrace those she comforted. The moments took from her but also grew her.

"This has always been your destiny," said Aleifr, "from the very creation of the universe."

"But there is no suffering here. What is there to comfort?" asked Hattie.

"There are those that still need care. Creator made us and this place so there is no limit to comfort and love. Comfort becomes a joy, not a necessity for survival. Your human body had many limitations. Those do not exist here."

Hattie paused to think.

"Kids," she said. "I really like kids. I want to help them."

Hattie had yet to see any children.

"Rest assured, they are here," said Aleifr. "I will take you to them soon. But it is first important for you to understand yourself first. Look around you, Hattie. This place was created exactly to specifications that even you yourself would not be able to define. Take this time to explore the house and learn about who you are and who Creator made you to be. Only then can you care for others once you know yourself."

Hattie set down her tea.

"Where do I start?"

"Right here, of course," said Aleifr, opening his palms. "This room represents your deepest feelings and identity."

"I thought you brought me here to sleep."

"There is no sleeping here. No exhaustion, no tiredness. You are constantly fed energy and sustenance by merely existing. Remember, Earth is a shadow of Heaven. Your bedroom previously was a space for regaining energy, healing, and rest. Those same things happen here, but they look different."

Hattie looked around. The space looked like a bedroom. Certainly no ordinary bedroom but still a bedroom, nonetheless.

"So that isn't for sleeping."

"That is for you to discover, Hattie," said Aleifr. "I must leave you now. Explore. Creator has hidden many secrets in this home for you. An eternity's worth of secrets."

"When will you be coming back?" asked Hattie.

"When it is time," he said.

Aleifr stood and walked to the double door, waving his arm, and the doors opened once more in unison. He walked through, raising a hand, and the doors shut. Hattie had more questions. She jumped up to follow him, opening the doors, but he was gone. Only the long hallway remained. And the melodious sounds of the heavenly crickets.

18

"In time, of course," Hattie mimicked, rolling her eyes. "What's a girl got to do to get some answers around here?"

Hattie shut the doors and turned to face the bedroom. She crossed her arms and looked around.

"My adventure awaits."

Hattie's frame of reference struggled to judge the size of the room. As she stared at each private corner or display, it seemed to grow. The room simultaneously felt like a cozy cottage and an elaborate day spa.

Hattie moved back to the couch and sat down, picking up her tea to consider what was next. This was the first time she found herself alone, giving her a moment to simply feel. Aleifr was right. She wasn't tired. She glanced at the bed. It was far too inviting, billowing upwards like a fluffy marshmallow that could swallow her whole, the soft peach-colored linens perfectly made. She couldn't resist.

Hattie walked over to the bed, running her hand along the intricate quilt that lay immaculately on top. The detailed golden filigree spun itself across the quilt, slowly moving like a line of hardworking ants. As she ran her hands across the design, the little gold ants scattered around her finger before reforming and continuing on their mission.

Hattie pushed on the bed. Soft, as expected. Really soft.

"Why not?"

Hattie turned around, looking over her shoulder to line up, squatted, then launched herself backwards into the air, arms outstretched. The moment of free-fall quickly brought back her time in the jungle until her body made contact with the top of the fluff. She felt

132

the lush and luxurious cushion, so soft like a hug. It was so soft she could barely feel any resistance on her body. She descended further. She tried gripping the bed to slow her sinking body, but her hands melted beneath the linens. Suddenly, she began to accelerate downwards, the bed swallowing her whole as the soft silk sheets swept across her face, her view of the ceiling disappearing beneath the underside of the quilt.

Her legs dropped faster, orienting her body in a downward slide. She saw a path before her as she slid down a golden chute. Perhaps George was playing another joke on her, except this time, no anxiousness followed. Only laughter.

The slide swept left, then right, dropping down and doing loopty-loops. Streaks of rainbow light flashed above, casting warm glows on her skin as she sped down the chute. She laid back. The slide was soft like the marshmallow mattress, but somehow still smooth and accelerated her faster and faster.

The top of the slide opened up as Hattie looked around to see a grand room before...PLOOF! Hattie slid directly into the biggest colored ball pit she'd ever seen, sending her several meters below the surface.

Fully submerged beneath the sea of colored balls, this ball pit actually felt like she was in water. She stretched her arms out in front of her, pulling them back in the best stroke that she could muster.

"Everything OK down there?" she heard a voice call out from above.

She felt the spirit's identity before rising to the surface. As she emerged, now floating buoyantly on top of the sea of balls, Creator leaned against the far edge of the pit with a grin. He waved.

"Oh, everything is good, all right," she said.

"I thought you'd enjoy the surprise."

Tears began to well in Hattie's eyes as she recalled Ryan's joyful laughter, the memory crystal-clear even after all this time.

"Come on, Mom! Come in!" shouted Ryan, waving eagerly from the center of the ball pit.

"I don't know about that. I might be too big," said Harriet.

"Just come in already. It's fun."

The boy scooped a handful of balls and tossed them in the air, laughing.

Harriet sighed, unable to withhold herself from her son.

"All right, all right. Just give me a minute," she said.

Harriet eyed the edges of the pit to find the best entry point. She sat on the ledge and swung her legs over, hopping in with a little crunch from the balls that only reached her knees.

"See, I told you," said Ryan. "I told you you'd like it. Come try to get me!"

Harriet snapped back into the moment, bobbing in the pool of balls.

"I thought you might like to have one of these in your room," said Creator.

Hattie swam towards Him, gazing at the vast room, which resembled the inside of a circus tent. Colorful streams of fabric flowed down from a centerpiece in the ceiling to the outward walls. Playful lights twinkled and spun on every surface and some even levitated. Carnival game booths with attention-grabbing colors and flashes extended line after line. This place was a little kid's dreamland.

Hattie reached the edge of the ball pit where Creator had a waiting extended hand.

"I actually quite like it in here if You don't mind me staying for a moment," said Hattie.

"Not at all. I would hope this would bring back some good memories."

She grasped the edge as the balls ebbed against the wall. He was right. When Hattie raised her kids, they didn't have much extra money. Their family treat was a visit to the local fast-food spot. A burger and playtime in the jungle gym and, of course, the ball pit. The ball pit was Ryan's favorite. Her daughter was never big enough to join him.

"Do you miss him?" asked Creator, looking down with a tender smile.

"Ye—." She paused, stopping her instinctive response.

"It's different here," she said, staring off into a distant corner of the room as she reflected. "I can sense the separation, but I feel connected at the same time as if there is no distance between us. Same for George and Rebecca. They all feel so close."

"On Earth, our connections were limited by time, space, and even forgetful memories. But here, there is no separation. This realm is vast and small at the same time. We can be separated but right next to one another at the same time."

"That doesn't make any sense," said Hattie.

"It will with time. The paradox of this realm expands what is possible beyond your imagination."

"Ah yes, the theme of Heaven," said Hattie. She laughed to herself just thinking about how many times she was told "in time." Creator let the silence settle, as if waiting for her thoughts to catch up.

"I do wonder what he's doing," she said. "I don't even know how long I've been here. I don't have any sense of time."

"Time works a little differently here, but I'm sure you're used to hearing that by now."

"If I had a nickel," said Hattie.

"We have time and seasons just as on Earth, but they are multidimensional. On Earth, time was actually quite abstract even though it felt very real. At the size and speeds that humanity operated at, time essentially felt the same. The physicists are finally scratching the surface of the plans I laid. They are really trying their best, those sweet creations. I must say that I'm really enjoying them starting to sound more like religious scholars than cold-hearted skeptics. They are in for a real surprise."

"Why do you do that?" asked Hattie.

"Do what?" He said grinning.

"That! You pretend to not know things and be surprised. You're GOD. How can You be surprised at anything?"

"I simply choose to be."

Hattie huffed.

"I know," said Creator, "I'm probably making this much more difficult than you are wanting it to be."

He laughed.

"Do you think humans invented surprise?" He asked.

"I don't even know where to begin with that question."

"Do you think humans invented surprise? It's a simple question."

Hattie didn't respond.

"Humans are modeled after My being. A simplified version, yes, but still in My image. Humans feel surprise because I can feel surprised. The only difference is that I choose to be surprised."

"That didn't help," said Hattie. "How can an all-knowing, all-powerful being experience surprise?"

"You said it yourself. All powerful. I choose to be surprised. I can hold knowledge and choose to be surprised when that knowledge is presented to Me."

"Why would you do that?" asked Hattie.

"Life is much more fun that way, don't you think?"

"I guess so," said Hattie.

"Where would the sense of adventure and excitement be if I simply sat around in the clouds with grapes as you humans so like to portray, just 'knowing?'"

"I suppose that doesn't sound very enjoyable," said Hattie. "Does that mean all the bad stuff that humans do is inside of You too?"

"I, just like you, have free will. But My will is guided by perfect love. All good traits that I possess have an opposite. Since humans have the capacity for those good traits but do not live out of perfect love, My adversary and his followers are able to create scenarios on Earth that warp those traits for evil."

Hattie needed an extra moment to ponder that one.

"When I raised my kids," she finally said, "I did everything I could to prevent them from getting hurt or being taken advantage of. Why do You let bad things happened? Every single person in the world asks this question, and so many turn from You because they don't get an answer."

"Frustrating, isn't it?" said Creator. "Did you ever deliberately put your children in harm's way, Hattie?"

"No, of course not."

"But bad things still happened to them, yes?"

"Unfortunately, yes."

"And what did you do when those bad things happened?"

"I was just there for them. If I could help, I would, but it was usually just helping them emotionally work through whatever the problem was."

"Very good," said Creator. "You, as the parent, had no ill wishes towards your kids. You did everything you could to protect them. Yet, when bad things inevitably happened, you took the situation and gave them a wider context. You taught them why certain people act or behave in a certain way. You taught them empathy and the ability to understand different perspectives. You had them inspect their own feelings and better understand what was going on in their own heart.

And herein lies a cosmic paradigm."

"You use things for good," said Hattie, feeling a weight settle in her chest.

"Precisely. Just as a human parent teaches their children and helps them become more resilient through difficult times, this is also what I do. I do not wish ill on My children. I do not cause injuries or sickness or death. But they still happen. In fact, they are a requirement for a world where free choice exists. My adversary, in his flawed view of humanity, believes the more harm he can cause, the greater a wedge he drives between Myself and My children. But the exact opposite is true. These challenges, hurts, pains, and griefs, are what I use to strengthen My children and their resulting capacity for love is greater than if no challenge ever faced them."

Hattie put both hands on her head.

"Sorry, this is hard to wrap my mind around. How can You not want to cause pain but be happy when something bad happens? Why don't You just put a stop to all of this pain and suffering?"

"That's simple," He said. "If I remove pain, I remove choice. If I remove choice, love can no longer expand. If love no longer expands, then we have collectively reached the maximum potential."

Hattie followed the logic, but the paradox of pain and resilience still did not sit well with her.

"But so many go to their graves thinking You abandoned them," she said. "Can't you just remove Your adversary and let us make choices after that?"

"It is true that My adversary will be removed. For the lifespan of a human, it can be difficult to understand why his existence is permitted. Across the full life of humanity, his attempts at distracting destiny only cause the tree of humanity to be pruned and fertilized. With the raging wind he sends, the trunk strengthens. With the shaking of the ground, he creates deeper pathways for the roots to sink further in."

"Why didn't you put that in the Bible? It makes so much more sense."

"I hide Myself not because I don't want to be found. I hide Myself to increase the joy of the reveal. I do not wish pain on My children, but I am far more interested in raising children that have immense capacities for love and those that can exist in this realm without choosing darkness. Someday, all on Earth will have this understanding before re-entering this realm."

"I begged my whole life to have conversations like these," said Hattie. "If only I had known, I would—"

"Would have what, Hattie?" said Creator, abruptly. His interruption startled her.

"I have existed with My people at many times. I have appeared to them in the flesh. I have sent My Hosts. I have performed incredible miracles. And what do they do? They still reject Me."

"I wouldn't reject you," said Hattie sheepishly.

Creator laughed, "I'm sure you wouldn't, Hattie. The reality is that humans, like Me, are built for mystery and uncovering truth. Living and engaging with humans as I did previously was only meant for a season to ensure My tree sprouted. But to grow? That needed a different type of care."

"But some people don't learn and reject You," said Hattie. "Not all of Your children are here. I know there's no way my sister would end up here."

"My time with your sister has not yet arrived. You would be surprised by who did and did not choose Me, Hattie, but I wish for all of My children to be here. Each one is so unique and represents a different part of My own spirit. My adversary is able to convince some of My children that they are not worth My love or worthy of their own inheritance. They reject Me even in My final pleas to be reunited. If only they understood that just like any parent, I do not look for perfection, only participation."

Hattie felt a twinge of sadness strike her heart.

"My child rejected me too," she said. Creator lowered the volume of His voice.

"Hurts, doesn't it?" He said. "You only want love for them, but in their own choices, they choose to not accept you. Despite the hurt, even in your final breaths, wouldn't you take them into your arms?"

"Without question," said Hattie, breathlessly. "I would do anything for Ryan. I would do anything for my little girl."

Creator tapped the edge of the ball pit.

"See, you're more like Me than you realize," He said. "There are far greater powers at work than the singular lives of humans. One side of humanity's history has been one of death, war, and struggle. My adversary would have everyone believe that is My nature and the peak of humanity. Instead, I have been growing a family tree of love. One whose roots run deep, whose branches reach wide. The fruit harvested from that tree is the sweetest and tastiest of all."

"I wish I could see my boy again," said Hattie. "Is there a room in the house for that? Can You take me to see him?"

"I thought you'd never ask," said Creator.

He extended a hand to assist. Hattie pulled herself out of the ball pit.

"So do I become a ghost?" asked Hattie.

Creator laughed.

"Ghosts, as the humans like to call them, are anomalies between the spirit and physical realms. Earth is here, and We are there. Spiritual and physical realms are intertwined. It's easier for some to believe that ghosts exist more than My existence, but that's not something for you to worry about at the moment. We won't physically be returning to Earth."

"Then how will I see him?" said Hattie.

"As I said, these realms are connected. There are different methods of connections for communications, transport, or other interactions. The one I am taking you to is certain to become a favorite."

Creator walked her past the line of carnival games.

"Don't worry," He said. "You'll have plenty of time to come back and enjoy the other festivities of the room."

They reached the edge of the room where a circular door awaited them, although there was no actual door, simply the framing. It was an antique gold with oxidized greenish copper-colored feathering. The center of the door looked like melting metallic seafoam paint dripping from top to bottom but also from bottom to top. There was a flowing curtain effect about it.

Creator stepped through the door, disappearing.

Hattie wasn't sure if she would ever get used to walking into a seemingly solid surface, but she accepted the invitation with a step containing as much confidence as she could muster.

19

A thin sliver of light forced its way through a crack in the curtains, piercing the room's darkness.

"Oh good, cereal again. My favorite," said Ryan, dropping a spoon into the bland colored cereal bowl. "It's the same damned thing every day," he said, shoveling a spoonful of the mush into his mouth.

Ryan sat at his table in the only spot that did not have a pile of something on it. The kitchen looked especially filthy today, evidence of a good weekend. The dishes were piled in the sink, and the trash stank. Vomit mostly, but he still didn't care to take it out. This was just life. Worthless, fucking life.

Cereal was maybe the only stable thing he had. The cold milk, the crunch, the metronome of the spoon hitting the bowl punctuated with a slurp. Today was a puffed rice day. It was a good day.

The months since his mother's passing had not brought the closure he expected. He didn't go to the funeral. Why bother? He would have been more grieved hearing everyone certainly talking about what a wonderful woman she was. *How can she even call herself a mother?* Even worse, he was sure that *she* would be there. Always so supportive. That self-righteous bitch had the nerve to act like nothing ever happened, and Ryan's mother let her. Disgraceful.

He swallowed another spoonful. A cool drip of milk dribbled down his lip. He grabbed a crumpled piece of unknown clothing from the table to wipe his mouth. The hair on his arms stood as a cool breeze blew through the small room. The drafts in the apartment were unrelenting.

This goddamn place was falling apart.

He would complain to the landlord, but the landlord isn't especially

140

motivated to assist given the eviction notice already on the door. He looked around for a sweater.

"Fuck me," said Ryan, wincing, his inflamed neck muscles twinging after seizing up overnight. He paused to soak in the pain that lingered, seeing if it would get worse. His muscles were constantly a mess. He saw the familiar color of one of his sweaters under a popcorn bag on the opposite side of the table. He leaned over to grab it, sliding it over his head, slowing as he put his arms in to avoid any more muscle spasms.

Ryan continued to eat in the deafening silence. A bolt of pain shot through his neck once more. He walked over to one of the cabinets where there might be some pain meds. Surprisingly, they were there.

He grabbed the bottle of ibuprofen. He didn't need the heavy duty stuff today. He smacked the container against his palm to eject a pill. *Maybe a few extra for good measure.* He struck the bottle once more. Several pills fell out. He looked around. His eyes caught a tipped over bottle containing the remnants from last night's rum. *That'll do.* He grabbed the already opened bottle and slogged back the pills, the burn of the rum already distracting him from the pain.

"No pain and no headache. That's what you call multi-tasking."

He tossed the empty bottle onto the pile of trash already overflowing from the can. The bottle bounced off, dropping to the floor. A blanket on the ground broke its fall. Ryan returned to the table. A twinge of pain shot through the back of his neck again. He knew there was nothing he could do about it. The constant and persistent pain. But this felt worse than normal. He picked up the spoon, returning to the bowl of the soggy cereal. Yet, this would certainly be the highlight of his day. Ryan sat in silence, and pain, eating the remainder of the bowl.

After a while, the silence was broken by the sound of a loud crack outside his door. He jumped in his seat, whipping his head to the door despite the pain. Nothing.

"Fucking addicts. They better not try to come in here."

His phone rang. He picked it up to see the caller ID. He answered.

"Hey," he said.

"Hi, Ryan. Sorry to bother you like this, but Jenn just called out sick. Do you mind coming in?"

Ryan supported his head on his hand, looking down into the soupy cereal bowl.

"This is my first day off all week," he said. "There isn't anyone else that can cover for her?"

"Sorry, everyone is sick. Some stomach bug."

Ryan closed his eyes, pulling the phone away to take a deep breath.

"Yeah, I can come in."

"Thanks, Bud. You're a lifesaver."

The call ended with a soft beep.

"Fuck. Me."

Ryan tossed the phone, letting his hand drop onto the table. His fingers instinctively began rhythmically tapping.

"What a time to be alive?" he said, taking another spoonful. *We could fix that.*

Ryan hated his current job. He hated his last job. He hated any other job he's had. Pointless wastes of time and energy. His current life drain gave him the honorable title of "Sandwich Coordinator," which just meant he spent the majority of his day slathering mayonnaise on bread for morbidly obese people thinking they were making a healthy choice for not eating pizza. *Fat fucks loved their mayonnaise.*

His phone rang again. "Goddammit, what now?"

He picked up the phone to see it was his cousin. A pause. He answered.

"Hey," he said in a soft tone that surprised even himself.

"Hey, I've been thinking about you," said Rebecca. "What are you doing tonight? Can I take you out to dinner?"

"Can't, got called into work."

"How about after? Maybe just grab something quick?"

"I guess I could swing that," said Ryan. "I get out at 9. Meet you at your place at 9:30?"

"I'll just pick you up at 9 at the shop."

"OK, see you then."

"Perfect."

He set the phone down. "On a roll today, aren't you? You people-pleasing jackass."

He scooped up the bowl to swallow the remaining lukewarm milk.

Ryan looked up from the dirty rag in his hand to see Rebecca's car waiting outside as he finished after-shift cleanup.

"You got a problem or something?" asked the shift manager. "What you looking at?"

"Nothing, just my cousin outside," said Ryan. He wiped at nothing on the table.

"Well can you just focus for a little longer? I realize cleaning a table is hard work, but can you keep it together while you're on the clock?"

"Sorry, yeah," he said, dropping his head back down.

He wanted to slap this bitch. *Control freak cunt gets promoted last week and thinks she owns the place.*

Ryan finished his closeout checklist. "All right, I'm out of here. See you tomorrow."

"Can you make sure you're on time?"

Ryan threw a hand up to wave, the best acknowledgment he could manage.

"Cunt," he said under his breath.

The exhaust from Rebecca's car billowed in the chilly evening air lit by a few parking lot lights. Ryan braced for the wall of cold air. The jingle of a bell on the door signaled his departure. Rebecca stepped out of the car as he walked towards her. She held her hands and pursed her lips with that look of pity.

"I'm fine," said Ryan. "We don't need to talk about her," giving Rebecca a lackluster hug.

"I just wanted to see how you were doing," said Rebecca, her voice softening.

"Ree, I told you. I'm fine."

She gave him another pity-filled forced smile. "I didn't see you at the funeral," she said.

"Because I didn't go. No need to mourn someone that was already dead to me."

Ryan stepped around the car to get in the passenger seat. *Change the subject.*

"So where are we going?" he asked. "It better not involve bread or roast beef. I've been smelling that shit the last eight hours."

Rebecca clicked her seatbelt.

"I was thinking Thai. My treat."

"I hope so, cuz I got no money," said Ryan.

Rebecca rolled her eyes at him as she started the car. Neither spoke as she pulled out of the parking lot. Ryan looked around for something to comment on, but the streets were empty.

"Look," said Rebecca. "I know you don't want to hear it, but it was a really beautiful service."

Ryan clenched his jaw, eyes fixed on the road beyond the windshield.

"Why you gotta do this?" he said. "I. Don't. Want. To. Hear. This. My life is too busy for this. I moved on a long time ago."

Rebecca gave a sigh. "Did you though?" she asked. "I'm just worried about you."

"I told you. I'm fine. Can we just go eat please and drop it?"

"Did you really think I came all the way over here just to take your ungrateful ass out to eat?"

"I thought you just wanted some time with your favorite cousin," he said playfully.

Rebecca didn't acknowledge him.

"This isn't easy for any of us," said Rebecca. "You think I wanted to see my mom at the funeral either?"

"I don't want to hear about her."

"Look Cuz, I know. Believe me, I know. But you and me? We're all we got now. We got to get through this together."

"I'm already over it," said Ryan. "You should just move on. Pretend like it never happened. You know, just like my mom did."

Rebecca sighed and shook her head.

"I think you need to give your mom a break," she said. "I know she didn't give you what you needed, but she was doing what she thought was best."

"What I needed? Ree, I needed a parent to protect me. She didn't even go to the police. We've been through this."

"I know. I know," said Rebecca. "But things are different now that she's gone."

Ryan groaned.

"Why are we still talking about this?" he said. "I know. Let's talk about your pedo mom still loving life without a care in the world. You got any new 10-year-old step-daddies you want to tell me about?"

Rebecca remained silent, the only sound of an occasional car driving past in the opposite direction.

"Look," said Ryan. "All I'm saying is I've put this stuff behind me."

"Clearly."

"And you should too. We shouldn't give these women any more energy. Can we just get some food and chill the fuck out? Please?"

The car turned into the parking lot.

"Sure. We're here."

Ryan sat in the dark leather booth staring at the Buddha statue at the front of the restaurant while Rebecca went to the restroom. He admired the stoic golden figure as he listened to the sizzle of hot oil and hissing vegetables cooking, an occasional trio of bangs as the cooks flipped the contents of the wok to stir. The smell was complex, slightly fishy but sweet and rich at the same time. Rebecca returned, sitting opposite of him just as the waitress brought two heaping plates of food.

"Thank you so much," said Rebecca, snapping apart a pair of wooden chopsticks, staring silently at Ryan.

"You got any more questions, or are we going to just enjoy dinner?" asked Ryan.

Rebecca did not immediately answer.

"I'm worried about you. I know you think you are over things, but look at you," she said, waiving the chopsticks at him. "You're a mess. I just want to help."

Ryan scoffed.

"I. Am fine," he said. "I just...need to find a new place to live."

Rebecca set the chopsticks down, clasping her hands on the table.

"What?" she asked, irritated. "When were you going to tell me about that?"

"Just got an eviction notice last week."

She shook her head. "How come? What happened?"

"I didn't pay my rent," said Ryan.

"Why—"

"Look," he said, catching the sudden increase in volume. "I don't need a lecture. I know. Things got tight. I just couldn't make it. Plus the landlord raised the rent last month, so it's not even my fault."

Rebecca picked up the chopsticks, stirring the noodles.

"Fine," she said, not making eye contact. "Sounds like you've got things under control."

The conversation paused as they ate in silence, staring only at the plates.

"She always asked about you, you know?" said Rebecca. "She never stopped asking."

"And I'm sure you ran your mouth about me."

"You may have sworn her off, but she basically raised me. I was so young when all that happened with my mom. We both were. I didn't know what happened. I just thought it was normal. She raised me like her own. I'm grateful for that."

"Well I'm glad you got the mom you always wanted," said Ryan.

"Why you gotta be like this? I'm on your side. Don't shut me out."

"I'm not shutting you out. I'm eating my noodles."

Ryan stuffed a piece of barbecue pork in his mouth.

"What are you going to do about your place?" asked Rebecca.

"I got a couple months before the police show up to lock me out, so I got some time."

"Then what?"

"Who knows?" he said. "May stay. May go somewhere else and start over. Put this place behind me."

"I thought you were over it?" said Rebecca.

Ryan balled up the paper napkin and threw it at her.

"Not funny, Cuz," said Ryan. "This is serious."

Rebecca held her hands up in surrender.

"Those were your words, not mine."

Another pause.

"She always said you had the perfect voice," said Rebecca.

Ryan looked up from his meal with a judgmental glance as he pushed the noodles around on his plate.

"To sing," he said, "you either need joy or you need pain. I got neither. I don't feel anything anymore."

"Is that what you want? To not feel anything?"

"Better than living in misery. My world is gray, and I know exactly what to expect. No more surprises. I'm done with that shit."

Ryan returned his gaze to the plate as the conversation stalled once more.

"You think your mom can still see us?" asked Rebecca.

"God, I hope not."

"You know how she was. Last thing she said before surgery was asking if I was going to church on Sunday."

"It's too bad she didn't spend more time worrying about what was happening on Earth instead of up there in the clouds. Maybe would have noticed her kid needed help."

"Stop," said Rebecca. "You know she couldn't have done anything. This was on my mom. You can't put that on Auntie."

Ryan paused to reflect on the memories that he tried so hard to shut out.

"It all happened so long ago," he said, "but it still feels like yesterday. Makes you think how things could have been different, you know?"

"I know exactly how you feel," said Rebecca.

"Anything else I can get you," asked the chipper waitress, interrupting the moment.

"No, that's OK. I think we'll just take the check," said Rebecca.

The waitress smiled, returning to the kitchen.

"Would be pretty crazy though, wouldn't it?" said Rebecca. "All that stuff going on up there, and we can't even see it. Kind of wild to even think about. I like to think she found her way there though."

"If the God she follows allows stuff like what happened to me, then I don't want any part of it."

"'God works in mysterious ways,'" she said with a smirk.

Ryan mock gagged.

"You sound just like her," he said.

"I should. We spent long enough together."

"I never liked that excuse," said Ryan, shaking his head. "A mystery is only good if it gets solved, but this life sure as hell doesn't have much solution, now does it?"

"I suppose not," said Rebecca, setting down her chopsticks. "I'm stuffed. Need to get headed home here soon, too. But, I got one more surprise for you. You wanna guess?"

Ryan stared deadpan back at her.

"I'll take that as a 'no,'" said Rebecca, the glint in her eye growing.

She reached into her purse sitting next to her in the booth, digging around. She turned back to face him, hands still in the purse.

"I'm about to be your favorite cousin," she said.

She pulled out two slips of paper, one in each hand, shaking them up and down."

She waited, clearly expecting a guess. Ryan raised his eyebrow and gave a shake of the head.

"I got us tickets!" she said.

"To see who?"

"Who else? You know who!"

"Seriously? City Streets Squad?" said Ryan.

"The one and only."

She held her arms in close to her body and swayed to an invisible beat.

"It'll be like the good ol' days," said Rebecca. "I thought we could both use some cheering up."

Ryan was not particularly interested but appreciated the distraction in the conversation, so he played along.

"Didn't even think they were still around," he said.

"Me neither. Apparently doing a reboot tour. There's a catch though."

"Of course there is. What is it?"

"The closest town they are playing in is Tennessee, so we're going to need to take a little road trip. Can you get some time off work?"

"Taking time off sounds like the perfect solution to my homelessness worries," said Ryan.

"I know, not great timing, but it's only a couple of days. What are they going to do? Kick you out of the house?"

"Do you know what eviction is?" he said. "That's literally what they are going to do."

"We'll figure it out," said Rebecca, confidently. "We always do. I think we just need to get away for a bit and reset."

Ryan stared at her skeptically. He spoke before realizing.

"OK, fine," he said.

"Yes!"

"But under one condition."

"Name it."

"You leave my mom here."

"Name another one," said Rebecca.

"I'm not kidding, Cuz," he said. "I don't want to have her haunting me the rest of my life. I got enough stuff to worry about. I don't need to be digging all that back up. It's dead and buried. Leave it that way."

"Stop it with all the conditions. Just live life. Whether you like it or not, she was your mom, and nothing is going to change that. If she hurt you—"

"Not if. She did," said Ryan.

"Even though she hurt you, use it to make yourself a better person."

Ryan sighed.

"I'm not getting out of this, am I?"

"Not a chance."

Ryan rolled his eyes. "I guess I don't have a choice then, do I?" he said.

"No, you do not. I'll text you the dates and details. I know money is tight, so the trip is on me. Don't even worry about it. I just want to spend some time with you."

"Your husband and kid going to have an issue with this?"

"Let me handle them. Just focus on you."

"You sure about that?" said Ryan. "If I were them, I wouldn't want you going anywhere."

"I got it. Now go grab a to-go box and take this home. Lord knows your poor ass can't afford food right now."

"Can't wait to spend the weekend with you," said Ryan.

"Love you too," shouted Rebecca as he walked up to the service counter where he was met with a friendly smile.

Can't believe I'm even doing this. Can't pay my own damn rent and she wants me to take off work?

"To-go box, please."

Things can't get any worse really, so I guess nothing much to lose.

He walked back to the table and sank heavily into the booth, the weight of his situation pressing down on him. He began scooping the remaining pad thai into the box.

"Ready?" asked Rebecca.

"Yeah, let's get out of here," said Ryan, folding the paper tab of the to-go box into the slot. "I got some packing to do."

"That's the spirit."

"You know, since I'm getting evicted, and my cousin won't let me work."

"Ha. Ha. Just wait. You'll be glad you're coming."

20

A whirl of voices immediately encircled Hattie as she stepped through the doorway. Suddenly, she found herself in the midst of a massive bustling crowd of people. It felt like the middle of a busy city street. Ahead, Creator was already hugging someone as they passed by. He turned back to face Hattie.

"Welcome to The Portal," He said, arms outstretched and with a little twirl.

Hattie looked around. The room was immense, reminding her of the Throne Room, but the energy felt different. Unlike the solemnity of the Throne Room, this place buzzed with unbridled joy. Hattie was not sure if this actually was a room because it was so large that she could not gauge the size as it extended out in all directions. What drew Hattie's attention more than the dauntingly high walls that appeared more like mountains in the distance was the crowd of people huddled around the edge of what looked like an above-ground swimming pool at the center of the room. The raised ledge stretched for what looked like kilometers in both directions. It was filled with a glittery blue substance that definitely was not water. Hattie could barely see the curvature, but it was indeed a circle that connected far off at the horizon in the distance.

As she visually traced the edge of the ring, a familiar but new noise moved itself to the forefront of her attention.

"Kids," she said.

The sound of children's laughter is unmistakable, and it sang loudly above the conversations in the crowd. Hattie looked more closely at the individuals in the room. Creator eagerly waved at passersby.

There was a wide range of ages of people in the room from toddlers to adults, but this was the first time since arriving that Hattie saw kids. They giggled, bobbing and weaving through the crowd as they chased one another. Hattie felt the waves of laughter washing through the room as people walked and danced about, cheering as they entered and exited through swirling thresholds around the perimeter of the room. Her heart leapt thinking about the short time of joy she had with her daughter.

"Busy today," said Creator, "but it's always busy."

Hattie watched as the dancing Traces of the crowd intertwined and co-mingled, rising upwards before crashing down into a splash of color before retreating back to their owners. The waves tasted like peppermint.

"What exactly is this place?" asked Hattie.

"Oh, you're going to love it!" said a woman passing by, walking away backwards as she met Hattie's gaze. "You'll become a regular in no time! I promise!"

The woman disappeared into the sea of people.

"Told you it was popular with the locals," said Creator. "Come take a look."

Creator weaved through the crowd, making a path for Hattie as they approached the raised lip. The liquid in the vessel lapped against the sides, but it looked thick.

"That's not water," said Hattie.

"Oh no, definitely not," said Creator. "This is a very special substance. One of My favorites!"

"Look here," said Creator, pointing a meter in front of them. Hattie momentarily glanced to the sides to see the excitement of all those around her, pointing, laughing, and cheering. Some leaned over, strangely dipping their faces into the liquid as if searching for something beneath the surface.

"There's a bit more than meets the eye here," said Creator. "You wanted to see Ryan. Hold his essence in your heart and simply look."

Hattie noticed that the pool had a strange, almost magnetic pull, shimmering between shades of emerald and blue. The crests of the tiny ripples sparkled like diamonds.

"Look past the surface, Hattie," He said.

As she felt the tug of the pool, her mind filled with a memory so vivid it seemed to take shape before her eyes. Hattie felt her awareness drawn downward. As her vision met the surface of the swirling liquid, a tunnel opened up beneath her, and she felt her body drawn in. She sensed acceleration downwards in a vertical orientation but came to a stop nearly as fast as it started, standing upright.

The room was bright. Hattie squinted. She felt warmth on her face. She was outside. She looked around. Monroe Park, just down the street from her home, once upon a time.

"I'm over here, Mom," said a child's voice, Hattie's instincts recognizing the voice before her mind. Her heart raced as she turned around.

Ryan, no older than 7 years old, walked right in front of her wearing his favorite dinosaur shirt. A lump grew in her throat.

"Ryan, over here baby," said Hattie, reaching her arms out, unable to contain her reactions. He did not seem to hear her as he continued walking. She chased after him.

"These are historical records, Hattie," said Creator. "He can't see or hear you."

"No, no. He's real. He's right there. What do You mean records?"

"It seems you were focusing on the past when you gazed into the portal, so it brought you to the moment you were thinking of."

Hattie looked around at the trees. She smelt the fresh cut grass and heard the distant clinks of a metal baseball bat making contact with its target.

"This isn't real?" said Hattie, softly.

"Oh, I didn't say that," said Creator. "This is quite real."

Creator walked towards little Ryan, who now sat on the ground picking blades of grass. Hattie followed.

"I remember this," said Hattie.

"Of course you do! That's how we got here."

"No, I mean I remember...this."

Hattie craned her neck to the side and pushed down on the air with her hands repeatedly.

"I've seen this," she said with increasing determination.

A dog barked. Hattie looked to the parking lot and saw a man struggling with the leash of the dog as it lunged toward where Ryan sat. Hattie's heartbeat increased. Ryan continued his plucking.

"Ryan!" said a young woman's voice.

To their left, a youthful Hattie darted from behind a tall hedge of bushes, her baby girl strapped to her. The barking grew more aggressive. Hattie bounced her attention between the dog and the boy.

"Over here, Mom," said Ryan, waving, not noticing the activity. "Come here! I want to show Tess something."

The dog continued to pull at the leash as the owner tried wrapping it around his arm and pulling the dog backwards.

"Get Ryan!" shouted Hattie to her younger self.

The dog quickly ran around the back of the owner, dislodging the leash from his hand as the dog broke free, charging directly towards Ryan. Hattie watched as her younger self leapt over Ryan, baby and all, turned, and scooped him up off the ground, hoisting him as best she could, pulling his legs up just as the snapping jaws of the dog reached them. Tess began crying at the surprise new in habitant to her space.

"He's fine," shouted the owner from across the lawn, jogging at an unacceptably slow pace. "He just wants to smell you."

"Yeah right," said the young Hattie, continuing to turn to put her body in the way of the dog as the man attempted to restrain the animal. Adrenaline rushed through her, helping her keep both kids out of harm's way.

"I think it's time for us to go home," she said to Ryan. "What do you think?"

Ryan was fixated on a blade of grass that he managed to hold onto through the ordeal. She bounced him gently in her arms.

"That was such a scary moment," said Hattie.

"How did you know Ryan was in danger?" said Creator.

"I remember feeling like he was in danger. I could see it in my mind's eye. But it was this. I saw what I am seeing now. I'm sorry. I'm having a bit of déjà vu."

"Déjà vu is merely an artifact of an infinite spirit being held in a linear timeline. It is not by accident that you brought yourself here. Your spirit is connected across all time and space. Your younger self sensed what you just witnessed because your spirit is one."

The dog finally lost interest in Ryan, allowing the owner to begin pulling it away. Young Hattie set Ryan back down, keeping a watchful eye on the dog while bouncing baby Tess to soothe the shock of the moment.

"Are you all right, Son?" said young Hattie.

"I'm fine, Mom," said Ryan, zooming the blade of grass through the air like an airplane.

Creator walked around Ryan and young Hattie.

"There are many connections in the spirit that are difficult for humans to perceive in their physical form," He said.

Creator snapped His fingers.

In an instant, the park's inhabitants multiplied. No new people, only creatures. Heavenly creatures. And others. Suddenly, Aleifr was standing before her, his sword drawn and blazing with a red fire that seemed to smolder.

"Thank goodness, he was there to protect us from that dog," said Hattie.

"Not the dog," said Creator. "Watch more closely."

Aleifr walked, flaming sword still in hand, over to where the owner stood, scolding the animal. He drew the sword back, slicing the air and then directly through the dog. Neither the dog nor the owner reacted to the movement, but a black ball appeared at the neck of the dog, slowly uncoiling itself as it revealed a larger structure that extended the length of the dog's spinal column. The lanky dark creature twitched and writhed, one segment at a time as if suction cups came loose from the dog's body. Even from a distance, Hattie could see the grimace on the creature's face.

"What in the world?" said Hattie.

As the creature struggled to detach its final few connection points, it finally popped off, landing on the ground, writhing. Its body looked like an enormous millipede with undulating legs. Silky black exoskeleton. Its face looked canine, also black and slick. It scowled in Hattie's direction before scurrying off into the trees. The dog's owner seemed unaware of the entire interaction, and the dog scratched its ear with a few strikes from its back legs before the two continued walking down the sidewalk. Aleifr turned, walking back, sword still aflame.

"What was that thing?" asked Hattie.

"A rather unsavory character," said Creator. "I won't dignify it with a name, but know that just as you have seen the light of the spirit world, there are many areas of darkness at work."

Aleifr returned, slicing through the air dramatically as the flame extinguished from the sword. He slid it gracefully in a single motion into an invisible sheath beneath his cloaks. He looked directly at Hattie.

"I thought you said this was a record?" said Hattie, hesitantly reaching out towards him. "Can he see us?"

"Of course I can," said Aleifr.

Hattie jumped, pulling her hand back.

"How can that be?" she asked.

Creator smiled, and Hattie knew by now that meant He would give an answer but not really.

"As I said, Hattie, spirits are infinite beings, and your time on Earth merely reflects a few limited dimensions."

She was right. Hattie's brow furrowed. Aleifr turned to face Creator, hands behind his back.

"There is increased activity of the Accuser around Ryan. We have witnessed and stopped numerous attacks. They are getting closer."

"Yes, I know," said Creator. "A new generation always brings such things. My adversary is attempting to lay plans for this family."

Hattie's head dropped.

"I haven't seen or spoken to my boy in years," she said softly. "I guess his plans worked."

"The Accuser's attempts at victory are futile," said Creator. "He perceives his actions as far more important than they really are."

"So, what are You going to do about it?" asked Hattie.

"That is not the question to be asking," said Creator. "The real question is what are *you* going to do about it?"

"I don't understand," she said. "You saw. I was just fumbling my way through life."

Hattie flopped her hand about to mimic her own life flailings.

"It doesn't end well for me and my boy, or Tess," she said, a lump growing in her throat. "I didn't even get to see him in the end. He swore me off years ago."

"You are infinite," said Aleifr. "Your physical end is merely a transition. You still have work to do."

"You may not have experienced fullness in your earthly life," said Creator, "but all things are reconciled in the true realm. My vision will be perfected, and you are a part of it because you are a part of Me."

"Me?" she said. "You want me to battle the powers of darkness? I can barely make pancakes without a mistake."

"Hattie, you are too focused on inadequacies that are irrelevant to you now," said Creator. "You have access to My mind, My creativity. You are not just you anymore."

Hattie did not understand the words that Creator used, but she felt it. She felt the connection. She felt the burn for justice. This was her family. One she fought for every day on Earth. It was too late to help her daughter. If she had a role to play now, she would do anything to stop the evil from coming after her boy.

Hattie raised her head with resolve.

"What do I need to do?" she asked.

Creator smiled. "Now we're getting somewhere."

Whatever was coming, Hattie was ready to take it on for the sake of her family.

21

The green landscape around her of Monroe Park blurred as Hattie felt herself drawn backwards, as if pulled by a string. The blurred green transitioned to yellow before returning to an emerald blue as the streaks of light slowed. Hattie pulled her head back, splashing as it broke the surface of the portal, a rush of cheer around her resuming. She felt a hand on her back.

"There we go," said Creator. "Welcome back. How was it?"

Hattie paused, tears beginning to well in her eyes.

"I haven't seen my boy in so long," she said. "And Tess, she was so small. Back then if I had known I didn't have much time with her—"

Tears overwhelmed Hattie's voice as she dropped her head.

"I know, Hattie," said Creator, His voice soft and tender. "I know how much you care for him. For both of them. Hattie, you will be reunited with Tess soon enough."

Hattie's heart ached at the sounds of the words. She had been too nervous to even ask after not seeing her baby at the mansion.

"When?" she asked.

"Soon, she is here with Us. But right now, Ryan needs you, Hattie."

Relief swept over Hattie only to be consumed by her ache for Ryan.

"It just breaks my heart that I didn't get to have the relationship that I wanted with him. I did everything I could—"

"And sometimes it's just not enough," said Creator. "Hattie, there are many elements of life that you could have changed and many more that you could not. Life was never about perfection."

"I just wish I did better," she said, dropping her head, staring into the lapping liquid of the pool.

"Herein is another of the adversary's lies about My children. He lives with deep regret for the choices he has made. Humans were not created with the capacity for regret. This was taught by him. It is not the life I have for you now."

Hattie did not know what to say.

"Now you said you want to help," said Creator, clapping His hands and rubbing them together with excitement.

"Of course, anything!" said Hattie, desperate. "But what can I do from here?"

"Far more than you can imagine," said Creator, with a smile. "Picture Ryan in your mind."

Hattie closed her eyes. A series of images flashed before her. Ryan's 7th birthday when he stuck his face in the cake. His high school graduation. His first school musical. Hattie felt Creator's hands on her shoulders, turning her body back towards the pool

"Good, Hattie," He said. "Where do you think he is now?"

The moment Creator asked the question, Hattie immediately felt drawn back down at a blistering pace. Blue light streaked by, transitioning to gray and black, then, stillness. She was inside. The stark contrast in light from The Portal to where she was now made it difficult to see, as if walking inside after spending the day in the sun. Her eyes began to adjust. Dishes mounded in a sink. She turned. Ryan. Hattie gasped at her first sight of him for far too long. He looked much older now, several years having passed since the last time he allowed her to see him. He sat at the table eating a bowl of cereal while staring blankly at the wall, quite disheveled. The room was absolutely filthy. Creator stood next to her silently.

"This is...real?" asked Hattie, hoping the gloomy sight before her was not actually her son.

"Quite real," said Creator.

Hattie let out a sigh of pity and walked over to him, stepping over trash and clothes on the ground.

"You don't have to worry about that," said Creator.

"Worry about what?"

"The physicality. You are a spirit now. Your plane of existence does not interact with this dimension. You can simply walk through it."

Hattie kicked her foot towards a crumpled bag of chips. It swung through without resistance. Her amazement was short lived as she looked back to Ryan. She stepped directly next to him and stooped down to look at him eye level. She waved her hand around and through him with no resistance. As she did, he flinched before reaching for a sweater on the table pulling it slowly over his head.

Hattie saw Ryan's lips moving, but did not hear anything coming out.

"Why can't I hear him?" she asked.

"Only a subset of our dimensions are currently interacting."

Creator snapped His fingers.

Traces appeared over Ryan's head. Hattie walked to where he now stood at the kitchen counter.

"They're so dull," she said. "And slow. Why do they look so…sickly?"

"Ryan has not chosen a path to empower himself or his destiny. Look more closely."

Hattie walked around Ryan, seeing him toss pills into his mouth.

"My poor boy," she said. Hattie examined the gently pulsing signs above him. She waved her hands through them. They lethargically reordered above his head.

"How long has he been like this?" she asked.

"His pain grows," said Creator.

Hattie's last interaction with Ryan was unforgettable in the worst way possible. After a heated argument, he really let her have it, calling her "his abuser," and left in a fit of rage, his final words being that he never wanted to see her again.

Ryan returned to his seat. Hattie followed. She instinctively moved her hands down the back of his head in an attempt to comfort, imagining what his hair used to feel like. Her hand moved lower as she placed it on his neck.

"Back off!" snapped a gravelly voice. Hattie reflexively withdrew her hand as she watched Ryan wince. "He's mine."

Hattie watched as the skin around the back of Ryan's neck began to crack open as a hideous creature emerged from the growing hole. An appendage that looked most like a tongue emerged first, stretching the hole until an insect-like face emerged, large pincer teeth stretching out sideways. The creature's beady eyes met Harriet's gaze.

Hattie stepped back with complete revolt.

"Didn't you hear me, you dumb bitch?" said the beastly creature. "He. Is Mine."

The creature's pincers snapped shut, punctuating its abruptness. Spindly legs writhed on the surface of Ryan's neck.

"Stop it! Leave him alone," said Hattie, unsure how to defend her boy against this thing.

The creature let out a dramatic scoff as a sneer stretched across its face.

"He wants ME," it said. "He *needs* me. I'm just teaching him how to love. That's what you're always going on about with these beasts, isn't it, Rabbi?"

The creature whipped its head away from Hattie to scowl at Creator.

Hattie turned behind her to Creator, Who was watching the conversation without expression.

"Can't You do something?" she said in desperation. "Where is Aleifr? Please, stop this thing!"

"I would love to, but unfortunately Ryan has an agreement in place with these beings. I could remove this creature and his associates, but without a healing in his heart, another would immediately take its place as a part of its contract. One after another, on and on, forever."

"There's nothing You can do?" said Hattie, desperately. "You're God. You're supposed to be all powerful. Why can't You do something?"

"I didn't say that, now did I?"

"You said he's stuck like this."

"I didn't say that either," said Creator stoically. "This is not how love grows, Hattie."

"Love, love, love," interrupted the creature. "Always going on about love with these rotten bags of flesh. Still foolish enough to think they will love You? You had love. Our love—"

"Silence," said Creator, the weight of His words sending a deafening shock wave through the room.

Ryan winced. The creature's mocking laughs cut off, and it retreated back into Ryan's neck with a sneer on its face.

"Please, Ryan," she begged.

"Love grows when it is stretched and exercised," said Creator. "Love does not grow if I merely force each interaction the way I want.

Hattie, this is your opportunity."

Ryan took another scoop of cereal.

"Why do You let that creature torment my son?" she asked.

"You are mistaken, Hattie. This torment is upon invitation. Humans have physical dominion on Earth. You are the Heirs. The Royalty. These creatures obey those with authority and can only operate when given permission."

"Why would Ryan ever give permission to that…that thing? It was ghastly."

"The physical body is a gateway to the spirit. Actions of the body open and close doors in the spirit. Whether conscious or not, the connection is there."

"When did this happen?" she asked.

"I think you may have an idea," said Creator. "Can you imagine anything in Ryan's life that would have opened him up to vulnerability?"

Hattie heard the question, but knew it wasn't really a question. She saw the consequences of her choices in the life review.

"I thought I was doing the right thing," she said. "I just didn't want him to suffer anymore. He had been through so much. I got him out as fast as I could."

"I do not speak these words to condemn you, Hattie. But it is important for you to understand the connection between the physical world and spiritual."

Creator didn't have to say anymore. Hattie knew what He was referring to.

"I thought it was enough."

"I know," said Creator with deep compassion.

But it wasn't enough. Ryan suffered in silence, lashing out at the family.

"One of the last things he said to me was that I didn't protect him," said Hattie.

Creator didn't respond.

"Did I do this? Did I give him this thing?"

"No," said Creator. "Your actions were not the specific cause, but they did open the violation wound, allowing more to enter. Your sister exerted her authority wrongfully, violating herself and Ryan. This forfeiture was taken by My adversary, and his minions now operate in that place. But this goes even beyond your sister, Hattie. She has her own struggles, but this is generational. My adversary brought a case against your family line and takes any permission he gets to attempt to strengthen his foothold."

Hattie shook her head.

"This all sounds like a legal proceeding."

"Precisely," said Creator.

"What exactly does all that mean?'"

"The world, both physical and spiritual, is governed by laws and all beings operate within those guidelines. These creatures are very legalistic and know the law very well. The legal system humans operate in is, once again, a simplified version of the true reality. My adversary and his minions cannot operate outside of these laws, but they do look for opportunities to manipulate humans into yielding power and strength in an attempt to rebuild themselves."

"Did I make it worse?" asked Hattie, hesitantly.

"Unfortunately, yes. While you did not yield the original authority, My adversary used Ryan's perception of your actions to further partner with him. My adversary trafficks in hopelessness, despair, and depression. He exploited those feelings to further isolate Ryan from love. As he tried to self sooth with unholy things, My adversary's investigative team offered him comfort. But it came at a cost."

"I feel awful," said Hattie, holding her head. "All I wanted to do was help my boy, and all I did was hurt him."

"These beings look for violations of love because that is a sign of My children giving up their authority. They are very keen. They watch for any opportunity. They manipulate My children into believing falsehoods. They are deceivers."

"Can Aleifr help?" said Hattie, pleading with her hands.

"Aleifr operates with authority as well, but it is a different authority. He can only be released when the proper authorities have been granted to him."

"But he protected us back at the park? Why can't he do the same here? Just cut that thing out of Ryan's neck."

"Humans are the dominant being on Earth," said Creator. "Humans carry dominion that I have granted from My own. If Aleifr wanted to remove that creature, which I assure you he does, his very being would prevent him from doing so because My adversary now has a legal right to Ryan's body. You could not fly on Earth as much as you wanted due to the laws of physics. It was impossible for your being to violate those laws. Until the permission is revoked by Ryan or someone with greater line authority, Ryan's state will not change."

"What are You going to do then?" asked Hattie.

"As I said, this is your opportunity. This is your family and your line authority."

"I take it back," said Hattie, flailing. "I take back all the authority. Right now."

Creator smiled. "It's not quite that straightforward. Now that you are a spiritual being, your physical dominion is no longer in place."

Hattie was becoming frustrated at the circular conversation.

"Why are You so calm about this?" she asked. "My son has that thing living inside of him?"

"I understand how this may be frightening for you. Most humans never see the Fallen during their physical lifetime, even though they are an epidemic in the population, and their effects are felt throughout.

"Please just tell me what I need to do," said Hattie. "I will do anything to get that thing out of my boy."

"The Fallen have tailored plans for each of My children. Strategies that work for one do not work for others. So you must first know what the partnership formed between your son and this specific Fallen is."

"How do I do that? Ask it?" said Hattie.

"Precisely."

Hattie waited for further explanation.

"Please," He said, stepping aside with an inviting hand.

Hattie turned back to Ryan, focusing on his neck.

"Um, spirit, uh, what are you doing with my son?" asked Hattie with a trembling voice.

Nothing happened.

"They are rebellious and only respond to authority," said Creator. "Speak with authority. You have My authority in the spirit realm."

"What are you doing with My son?" she said more confidently this time.

A shriek called out as the undulating body of the creature appeared to be pulled from Ryan's neck by an invisible power. It whipped its head around to face Hattie.

"You can't have him," it growled.

"That's not what she asked," said Creator. "Answer the question, Fallen One."

The creature's mouth writhed.

"He. Must. Be. Unworthy," said the creature, visibly fighting against saying the words.

The creature's neck, if you can call it a neck, twisted, fighting against the force holding it. Another shriek.

"You can't have him!" said the beast. "Don't you understand? He has too much power. We must keep him unworthy."

"Too much power for what?" asked Hattie. "Why are you trying to stop him?"

The creature let out a wretch.

"No, no, no, no, no, no," hissed the beast, voice struggling in resistance. "I can't…let his voice be heard. He needs me to survive."

"He doesn't need you," snapped Hattie.

"Of course he needs me," said the creature. "He needs someone to protect him. You surely didn't. What a pitiful excuse for a mother."

Hattie knew the statement was supposed to hurt her, and yet, she felt nothing.

"Stop it," she said, her voice becoming steadier.

"I think he even liked it," mocked the creature. "He'll never give me up. He wants more. You should see what he does when you aren't around."

"Enough," said Creator, another wave shooting across the room.

The ghastly beast snapped back into Ryan's neck, disappearing.

Hattie let out a sigh of relief.

"I don't understand," said Hattie. "All of this is to stop him from singing?"

"The Fallen are battling against each and every human from stepping into their full destiny. Look."

Creator gestured to the dim Traces above Ryan.

"His calling is still here," said Creator. "The signs are still here. The colors are still here. Nothing the Fallen can do will remove these Traces from above your son's head. But, they fight against the fullness that the destiny can become. Look at your own Traces, Hattie."

She gazed up to see the vibrant swirling colors around her head.

"You are in a higher state of fulfillment. The health of your destiny is visible. The Fallen fight humans from fulfilling their destinies because it means humanity is fulfilling their likeness to Me while on Earth. They are fulfilling what they are meant to be in eternity."

"But why singing? All of this to stop someone from singing?"

"Words are powerful, Hattie. I put a sword in Ryan's voice. One of the most damaging statements that most humans take for truth is words cannot harm. This could not be further from reality. In fact, words are mightier in My Kingdom than physical strength. Words carry power through the physical and the spiritual. They are, in fact, a vibrational mechanism that passes between the realms, interacting with both."

"The creature said it wants to keep Ryan feeling unworthy. Why?"

"Singing pours out from the individual. If the individual feels empty or unworthy, they are unable to sing. To worship. To call forth the reality that they see in the spirit realm. They become unable to manifest the fullness of My Kingdom."

Ryan had the most beautiful voice when he was a child. Hattie didn't understand why he stopped until later when the molestation came out. She knew he had lost his innocence and joy that day.

"I still don't understand why You don't just command it to leave," said Hattie.

"I yielded My dominion to humans on Earth. Humans, in fact, have more authority there than I. This is why I had to come to Earth as human, to re-inherit the authority that humanity gave up and return the ability to humans to take it back. There was no other way for Me otherwise."

"But you're God," she said. "You can do anything."

"I can do all things, but I do not contradict My Word. A King who does not honor his word invalidates himself as a King."

"But you came back as human, so you got the authority back, so can't you fix this?"

"Hattie, I am a King, not a slave-owner. I have no interest in simply being the conductor of actions. Doing so invalidates My entire purpose for humanity. Humans are complex because I am complex. Humans must learn to operate with the authority that I have given them. That means you, too."

"But if I don't have authority in the physical world while I am here, how can I help?"

"Much more than you realize," said Creator, His smile returning.

22

Acantha scratched the closing summary of her report, the ink glistening from the flickering candlelight. She paused, flipping to the calculations table to verify all was in order one final time. The flame of her candle began to sputter, casting more shadow than light onto her papers. A knock broke the silence, echoing around the empty walls of her study. She looked up from the table with a scowl, wondering what nonsense awaited her. Acantha arose, pushing back the heavy wooden chair as its scrape underscored her irritation. She departed the study with quick, aggressive strides. The air in the hallway was still. She found Bastian standing in the foyer, his broad stocky shoulders tense under his cloak.

Acantha's eyes narrowed as she demanded, "What?"

"You are being summoned to present your latest report for review so the Conclave may determine its next steps," said Bastian, his tone rightfully cautious.

"We've been over this before," said Acantha. "There have been no changes to the plan. Superior did not instruct us to deviate from it."

"I understand," said Bastian. "This is to discuss some of the recent complications in the case. We need to ensure continuity of messages that the habitation teams are speaking to the family members."

Acantha's lips pursed. "When were you planning to tell me of these complications?"

"Immediately, as always, Acantha," said Bastian, straightening his posture. "Please, join the Conclave so we may discuss further."

He turned and opened the door that led deeper into the halls, the large iron handle groaning as it creaked open. For a moment, Acantha stood still, calculating whether to follow. She raised her hands, and with a flick of her fingers, the report papers flew from the study, fluttering as they aligned themselves neatly into her grasp. Her body reluctantly followed Bastian, where he was already turning the handle of another door, swinging it inward. Acantha followed, entering the room.

An unwanted face stood at the far end, his steely gaze fixed on her. Acantha managed a tight-lipped greeting. "Always a pleasure, General Velraithe," she said.

The room was small and circular, with an obsidian table at its center, reflecting the dim, shifting light of wall sconces that threw elongated shadows.

"And you as well," he said, standing at attention.

Acantha took a seat across from him. Bastian remained near the entrance, fidgeting.

"I believe we have a quorum to proceed," said Bastian. The other two Conclave members flanking Velraithe remained silent, only nodding.

"Thank you for joining us, Acantha," said Velraithe, his fingers steepled in front of him. "Bastian tells us you made great progress with the boy. We eagerly await your final reports."

"I was surprised to hear that we needed to meet," said Acantha, unwilling to participate in unnecessary pleasantries. "This is the first I am hearing of...challenges. I trust these complications are not due to incompetence, Bastian?"

"Hardly," said Bastian, the pitifully weak lump. "There is a new variable to the equation."

"The Archives were notified that the family's aunt did not select in favor of our calculations."

Acantha raised an eyebrow, unimpressed. "Why is that a surprise? The humans have pedestrian mindsets. It is not unusual for some to resist us. It will take her ages to orient in His realm."

"She already came to see us," said Bastian.

Acantha's eyes narrowed. "How so?" she demanded.

"She and the Creator dropped into the timeline and confronted me," said Bastian.

"That is quite unusual, is it not, Acantha?" asked Velraithe, leaning forward slightly.

"Perhaps. Their interference is two standard deviations above the frequency with which we typically begin to see such meddling activity."

Velraithe nodded. "That is substantial."

"But not surprising," said Acantha. "Even the Creator surely sees how close we are with extinguishing this line. We infiltrated it millennia ago, and this branch is about to be cut off once and for all."

"Their spirits are fractured," said Bastian. "They receive my whispers at a statistically significant rate. The profile we built is even better than we thought. The female is already in a vulnerable state, and the male is barely holding onto his sanity. We have them exactly where we want them."

"Then it seems like all is well," said Acantha. "So, what is the concern, Bastian?"

The other Conclave members at the table shifted slightly, their chairs creaking.

"It's the youngest, Acantha," said Bastian. "The child."

"The boy?" said Acantha. "He was never a factor in this. Just another pawn, insignificant at best. His parents will self destruct."

Velraithe leaned over the table, collecting Acantha's report. He thumbed through the pages.

"You state that the boy's Traces are developing upon your last inspection," he said.

"Yes."

"That shows a sign of resistance to our efforts," said Velraithe.

"He's insignificant," said Acantha. "Merely a tool to destroy the family."

"Yes," said Velraithe, "but the Conclave believes it best to alter the strategy to accelerate somewhat."

"Which is exactly why we're here," said Bastian. "To recalibrate. We cannot afford a single misstep."

"What do you propose we do?" asked Acantha.

"The female's cousin," said Velraithe. "The degenerate slob. Bastian reports that his impact on the family is higher than we previously calculated. He bears surprising weight in the actions of the couple. We need to accelerate our efforts with him."

The silent Conclave members nodded in agreement.

"I see," said Acantha.

"Is that something you are capable of doing?" asked Velraithe.

"Bastian," said Acantha, "you will coordinate with the other habitation teams to begin swaying influence. I think it's quite obvious who we must re-engage."

"I trust you will be able to handle these adjustments with discretion?" asked Velraithe.

Acantha smirked. "Discreet is what I do best."

She rose from her chair.

"Come, Bastian," she said. "The family will fall. One way or another. We will begin immediately."

Acantha turned, her robes catching the air of her speed and departed the room.

23

Ryan waved at Rebecca as he stepped inside his apartment. He closed the door and tossed his keys onto the table, or rather, on top of some clothes lying there. He walked to the fridge, cracked it open, and shoved the takeout box onto a shelf, ignoring the sour smell wafting up from other moldy leftovers. Ryan peeled off his work shirt as he walked to his bedroom, tossing it on the ground. Flipping to his back, he dropped onto his bed.

Despite just eating his body weight in Thai food, he felt unexpectedly light. Life was shit, but seeing Ree was good, even if she couldn't just let things go with his mother. The concert sounded fun. Was this happiness? He paused, taking a deep breath and took stock of the moment.

I feel good, he thought, in disbelief.

He was good, not great, but good is still good. The feeling was foreign, like a melody he couldn't quite recall, but it warmed him in a way he hadn't felt in ages. The thought of eviction floated into his mind. A new start did not sound half bad. His credit was already fucked, so who really cares? Ryan rolled slightly to his side to slip his phone out of his back pocket, holding it above his face to send a text.

Hey, thanks for tonight. I needed that.

He hit send, tossing his phone on the bed. He sat up, facing a pile of trash and clothes.

This place is a real shithole. "I don't even know how it got this bad," he said.

He scanned the room, the slightest desire rising to clean, even just a little. Through all the garbage, clothes, empty wrappers, and dishes, Ryan's eyes landed on his guitar. The guitar sat in the corner on a stand, which he hadn't touched in years, blue dirty underwear hanging off the top of the neck.

"You deserve better than this place," he said to it. "You are way too nice to be here."

He stood up, walked over to the guitar and tossed the underwear on the ground. The dust layer on it was visible, even in the dim light of the apartment. This guitar was without question the most valuable item Ryan possessed. It was a gift from his mother in his late teens. Guilt, most certainly. He thought about selling the guitar after his mother died to help purge her memory, but somehow, he couldn't quite let it go.

He picked it up by the neck, the familiar heft settling into his hands as he sank onto the bed and slipped into the playing position. He strummed. The strings were horribly out of tune, and he immediately felt that his playing calluses were no more. He began picking each of the strings to bring them back to their proper sound. The sound wobbled as he twisted the tuners, matching the vibration to his inner reference. Another strum.

"Nice," he said.

His phone buzzed. He looked over to see the green alert.

I had a nice time too. Looking forward to our road trip. Will text later. Still driving.

He started strumming again, force fitting his words to the beat.

"My life is already so fucked up. It doesn't really matter. I just got evicted, but that's OK. I'll just go to a concert with my cousin."

He ended with a mini accelerated solo.

"So fucking ridiculous."

Rebecca was all he had now. It was scary, but also a relief. For the first time, maybe ever, he felt a flicker of freedom. Maybe, just maybe, he could let the baggage go and be himself.

24

Rebecca shifted the takeout box between hands to rifle through her purse to find the keys. Wallet. No. Tissues. No. Bill. God no. Keys. Rebecca slipped the key into the lock, took a breath, and opened the door. *We'll see what mood he's in today,* she thought.

"I'm home," she said to the empty living room, surprised that it was in order.

Frank poked his head out into the doorway from the kitchen. His shirt blended into the wall, so his bald head seemed to float as he leaned out to greet her. *Did I ever find him attractive or just convenient?*

"Oh, hey," he said. "You have a good day?"

Rebecca met him in the middle of the room, giving him a very short kiss and a guarded hug. She kicked off her shoes and tossed her jacket on the back of the couch. She sat.

"Pretty good," she said. "Saw Ryan today."

Frank remained standing.

"Oh," he said, his voice dropping. "How's he doing?"

"Not great. Said he's getting evicted?"

"Unbelievable," said Frank, shaking his head. "It's like that guy wants to be miserable. How did that happen?"

"He said something about the landlord raising his rent, and it not being his fault."

"It's never his fault, isn't it?" said Frank.

"I know. I'm just trying to cut him a break. He's had a rough couple of months."

"Has he? Couldn't even be bothered to go to the funeral. We had to

172

take care of everything. Again."

"Let's not be dramatic," said Rebecca, attempting to hide an eye roll. "It wasn't 'we.'"

Frank didn't take the bait.

"What else did he have to say?" he asked.

"Nothing too interesting," said Rebecca, standing and walking to the table, flipping through some mail. "We're going to see a concert together in a couple weeks."

Frank scoffed.

"You actually want to spend time with him? He's such a downer."

"His mom just died, and we're his only family," said Rebecca. "Jesus, cut him a break."

"All I'm saying is he brings this on himself. You took care of his dying mother while he couldn't hold down a job to pay for the worst housing in town. I don't know why you keep putting in effort with him."

Rebecca did not acknowledge the statement.

"You want me to drop you guys off at the arena, so you don't have to park?" asked Frank.

"That's OK. It's actually out of town, so we have to drive anyway."

"Oh, where at?"

"Just over the border," said Rebecca, knowing what the response would be.

"What?" said Frank, walking quickly to the table where she stood.

Rebecca felt her pulse quicken as Frank stormed over to the table. She clenched her hands but held her ground.

"It's not that far," she said. "It's just on the other side of the border."

"Are you fucking kidding me? You're going to Tennessee right now with your dipshit cousin?"

"He's not the dipshit, Frank."

"That's right," said Frank, his volume increasing. "You're the dipshit. You make plans *right now* to go out of town and leave me with Liam so you can hang out with Ryan? What the hell is wrong with you?"

Rebecca felt her throat tighten with anxiety. She took a breath. It did not help, so she defaulted to allowing the rage to rise.

"With me?" she shouted back at him. "What do you mean 'What's wrong with me?' You're the goddamn drama queen in the house."

"That is not fair at all," said Frank. "You've been completely gone for months! We've all been patiently waiting for you to wrap things up so we can just be a family again. And now this?"

"I don't understand why you need to be so controlling about it. It's just a weekend."

"It's always been 'just a weekend' with you," said Frank. "Except it ends up every weekend. We've barely seen you since the funeral, and you weren't even staying here before Hat died. You're always busy with something."

"I had a lot of responsibilities. If I didn't bury her, no one would have."

"Well it seems like you want to bury us too," said Frank.

Rebecca stood in frustration.

"I can't handle this right now," she said walking towards the hall. "I'm going to bed."

"Of course," said Frank, calling after her. "Always the martyr. Woe is me. I'm neglected by my family, even though I can't take a single moment out of my day to spend a fucking minute with them."

Rebecca did not respond and walked out of the room. She slipped into the spare bedroom, shutting the door behind her. The silence pressed around her, and she leaned against the door, stifling tears with her sleeve. She could feel Frank's rage through the walls.

"Don't worry," he shouted from the living room. "I'll put Liam to sleep. No trouble at all. Please, don't overexert yourself."

His voice traveled past the door where Rebecca was hiding.

I need to get out of this, she thought.

Rebecca hated the fighting, but the alternative seemed worse. She and Frank married right out of high school. Rebecca loved living with Aunt Harriet, but she needed space. At the time, Frank had seemed like everything she ever wanted—stability. Once upon a time, at least.

Her phone buzzed. Rebecca pulled it from her pocket to look at the notification.

"Love you, Sweetie. Would love to take you to church with me this weekend," it said.

Rebecca's stomach sank. Her mother, again.

This is the last thing I need right now. How did she even get this number? Rebecca did not have any direct contact with her mom since her early teenage years. Aunt Harriet strictly forbid it. It's been nearly 15 years

174

come to think about it. Communication from her mother started to resurface after the announcement of Auntie's death went out. Rebecca wasn't anywhere near ready for a relationship, not to mention the fact she did not want her mother anywhere near Liam. Yet, she also couldn't bring herself to block the number.

Rebecca swiped the notification away and clicked off her phone. *I can't deal with this right now.* The neighboring door closed as she heard Frank leave Liam's room. A few steps, and then he shut their bedroom door. She let out a breath.

"I can't keep doing this," said Rebecca, eyes shut.

She opened the door, sneaking into the hallway and then into Liam's room. Momentarily lit by the sliver of light shining through the open door, she saw him asleep. She shut it quickly behind her, bracing the final centimeters to ensure silence. He was surprisingly still asleep despite the commotion. Rebecca stood motionless to let her eyes adjust. She looked at the dinosaur poster on the wall, softly illuminated by the glow of the clock. It reminded her of all the simple, happy moments she wished for Liam but felt slipping away.

"I'm sorry, Baby. You deserve better than this," she said, stepping to his bed and gently brushing a tuft of wavy black hair to the side of his head.

Rebecca knelt at at his side just staring at him. *I'm not her,* she told herself.

She didn't want to linger.

"Good night, Baby."

She pulled the race car covers up a little higher on Liam's chest and arose, taking a final look at him before leaving the room in silence.

Rebecca prepared for bed in the guest bathroom. The bathroom welcomed her return, already well stocked with her toiletries from previous visits. She turned on the water, leaning heavily on the sink, and stared at herself in the mirror. The face that stared back looked hollow, shadows darkening her eyes, the weight of it all pressing down. She breathed in deep as the steam rose.

"I don't know what to do," she whispered. "I can't keep doing this."

She bent down and splashed her face. Up came the tears.

25

"Your help will look rather different than what you are expecting," said Creator, staring for a moment at Hattie before reaching into His robe. Hattie glanced at Ryan, head still down eating mush. No sign of the creature.

"Hold out your hand," said Creator.

She returned her gaze and followed the command, hands outstretched and palms up. Creator pulled a ruby red glistening booklet from His robe.

"Here you go," He said with a joy that seemed incredibly out of place given the dank room.

He set it proudly in her hands, His smile growing. The intensity of the red cover was unlike an earthly red, and Hattie blinked a few times as it looked superimposed into her vision. She brushed her hand down the cover. Supple and smooth like velvet. She observed the gold stitching on the cover of the almost unusually small sized book. The intricate design was dynamic, a moving ocean scene. The stitches sewed themselves as a thread dolphin leapt out of the water before diving back down, the fine golden lines animating the coastal view.

Hattie looked at Ryan. Then back to the book.

"I don't understand," she said.

"It's a book. Open it!" said Creator.

Hattie gripped the book, flipping it over to determine the orientation as the cover design swam to the bottom.

"Does it matter which side?" she asked.

"It's a book, Hattie. Open the book."

Hattie opened the cover to find ornately written shimmering black metallic calligraphy on the inside.

It is hereby decreed by
Order of the King
that freedom be fully and inextricably granted to the following individual:
Ryan Joseph
son of George
son of Cedric
son of Wallace
Jones

Hattie shifted the book into one hand in order to run the other down the page. The texture felt like cotton. A luscious, teal-colored wax seal at the bottom of the page depicted a majestic lion flanked by unearthly feathered creatures. She moved her finger over the seal. Upon touching, her finger sent a ripple through the wax, seeming to change the solid material into a liquid. The lion figure shifted, breaking free of the page, pushing its face upwards towards Hattie and let out a deafening roar. Hattie screamed, instinctively slamming the book shut before dropping it and jumping backward. Her ears rang as the lion's roar lingered in the air.

"What was that?" she said.

"It's a lion on a wax seal," said Creator. "What did you think it was?"

He knelt down, picking the book back up.

"How is that supposed to help Ryan?" she asked.

"You have to keep reading," He said, handing her the book with a firm grip. "That was just the first page."

Hattie sighed, still not understanding why she was reading a book while her son sat next to her with a beast living in him. She opened the book again. The face of the lion stared motionless at her. She slowly moved her hand to turn the page, hoping not to upset the creature. The lion did not move.

The next page looked like a table of contents. But this was no ordinary book.

She looked up at Creator.

"This is Ryan," she said.

"You asked how you can help," said Creator. "This should give you some direction."

Skimming the sections down the page, the first half read as a biography. Hattie turned to the "Creation of Ryan" chapter, expecting some baby photos.

"I don't understand," she said, shaking her head. "This looks like sheet music."

Hattie recognized some of the symbols and notes, but the music bars had depth, with layers sinking down into the page. Notes were colored unknown symbols.

"Precisely," said Creator. "This is My composition of Ryan."

"Why would You write a song about Ryan?"

"No, this *is* Ryan," said Creator, stepping around to Hattie's side to look at the book with her. "This is the essence of Ryan. I sang him into existence—well, I created the composition, and Spirit sang him into existence. You're in here too, Hattie."

He flipped a few pages of the complex symbols before placing a finger down on the page, running it past a few bars.

"Let's see here," said Creator, finger still searching. "Ah, here we are. See, you're right here."

He punctuated the spot with His finger.

"Here's where I joined his spirit into your line," He said.

Creator's face beamed that of a proud parent.

"Hold on," she said, closing her eyes. "What does this all mean? These notes? You attached him to me?"

"It's really quite basic, you see."

Creator turned back to the beginning music sheet.

"Here is where We defined his spirit from Us," He said, framing a section of bars with His thumb and index finger.

"Then We move into his purpose and calling here."

He pointed a little further down on the page.

"See here, these are his Traces."

Creator turned back towards Ryan, pointing above Ryan's head to the lethargically breathing symbols.

"Those symbols are here because they were written in this book," He said.

"How do words turn into people, or spirits, or whatever this is?" asked Hattie.

"The same way we turn anything from nothing into something. As sound forms waves, so Spirit's voice shapes existence. Each ripple is a piece of Us, a living truth intertwined in Ryan and in you, Hattie. Little ripples. My ripples!"

Creator clapped with excitement. Hattie stared blankly. Science was never her strongest subject in school, but what Creator just said made absolutely no sense.

"We're ripples in the water of existence?" she said shaking her head, trying to force a connection in her mind.

"Precisely!"

"I will pretend that I understand what that means because I have more questions, but I still don't know how to help Ryan."

"You'll need to do a bit of reading on that. A few more chapters in, you'll find *Strategies of the Enemy* and *Preparation and Counterattacks*. Those are rather important at this time, especially for what's coming, but you'll want to take some time to go through the full book. It will have many answers to the questions you have already asked during your time here."

"Wait," she said with panic in her voice. "What do you mean 'for what's coming?' What's coming?"

"My adversary and his allies are lining up a rather insidious plan. Nothing We haven't seen before in your line. Quite common, actually. The enemy often repeats his same attacks against a family, trying to break in and cause a root to form. But it is important for you to assist intervening."

Creator strolled to a stool in the corner of the room, pulling a piece of crystal-clear fruit from the folds of His robe while sitting down and taking a bite. Hattie wondered how He was "sitting," given the discussion of interacting planes earlier, but that didn't matter right now.

"You don't seem worried," she said.

"Why should I be worried? You are here to help."

He took a juicy and crunchy bite from the see-through fruit that resembled a pear.

"Me? You're relying on me to disarm a 'rather insidious plan?'" she said, air quoting.

"Of course," He said casually, taking another bite of the fruit, a spatter of rainbow juice shooting from the side and dissolving mid-air like a firework. "Who else would you have Me use?"

"I don't know," said Hattie, throwing up her hands. "You or the angels. Aleifr? How about Aleifr? Can't he do something? I can give him my authority."

Creator paused His chewing, lowering His voice as He leaned forward on the stool.

"Hattie, I am in you, and you are in Me. When I send you, I send Me. We are two, but We are one."

He took another bite, leaning back to assume His relaxed position.

"You still haven't said how I can help," said Hattie. "I'm just a spirit. How am I supposed to intervene when I'm here, and he's there?"

Hattie extended her arm to gesture towards Ryan.

"Read the book, Hattie. The answers you seek are in it."

Creator took another bite of fruit, speaking with a full mouth.

"And you may want to hurry," He said. "His life counts on you succeeding."

"How long do I have?" she asked with desperation. "I don't even know what I'm looking for."

"If you stay in this timeline, maybe a few days before his impending demise."

He took another bite.

"Impending demise?!" Hattie exclaimed.

He took another bite of fruit.

"My son is about to die, and You are having a snack break," she said, frustration growing.

"Oh, I'm sorry, did you want one?" He asked, reaching into His robe.

"No, I just want some answers. What do You mean 'impending demise?'"

Creator retracted His hand.

"Well yes, every one of My children faces impending demise if there is no intervention. The enemy is actively seeking to steal, kill, and destroy the lives of each and every one. He does not rest. He is always on the prowl looking for an opportunity."

"And the answer is in this book? So I just need to read it."

"Hattie, you must remember that you are no longer bound by the constraints of Earth. Your mind has not fully connected itself to the heartbeat of My Kingdom. The words I use might be scary. Terrifying, in fact. But only if you do not recognize the resources that you have at hand. The precise answer you seek is not in the book. There is no need for a precise answer. You have access to limitless resources. Once you read, your primary feeling will not be one of lack and helplessness. Since this is your first mission, please work with Aleifr. He will be able to help open your eyes to what you have access to. So please, take this book. I have plenty of copies in the library."

Hattie's instincts told her to be worried, but the peace carried in the words of Creator put her at ease. Her voice quieted.

"Do You have one of these books about me?" she asked.

"Of course," said Creator with glee. "I have a book for everything in My creation. You should have seen the looks on the faces of the Hosts when I released the books of your generation! Some of My favorite memories."

"Will I be able to read it?"

"If you ask nicely, Aleifr may let you see it. He has been studying it for quite a while. He knows you inside and out. Every detail."

Hattie looked back at Ryan, wanting to spend more time with him, but she knew that she needed to leave.

"Can we go now?" she asked.

"Of course. You'll want to get right to it," He said. "We can even take the shortcut. No need to return to The Portal."

Creator opened Ryan's door behind them.

"After you," He said.

"Goodbye, my sweet boy," she said, walking past Ryan, his arm frozen midair. She clasped the shimmering red book to her chest.

Ryan seemed to move in slow motion, his face turning towards Hattie, making eye contact with her. Her heart leapt.

"Come, Hattie."

She turned and walked through the door. The moment her foot touched the concrete on the outside of Ryan's apartment, the view in front of her smeared into an array of colors. She looked down to steady herself, hands out to her sides. She was not sure if she was falling or being thrown. Her body came to an abrupt stop. Silence. Instead of concrete, her foot was framed by dizzying blue and white geometric patterns spiraling across the floor. She looked up.

"Welcome, Hattie," said Aleifr.

He, along with other stoic beings, sat at the head of an unusually basic, but solidly built, wooden table directly in front of her, sitting in the middle of a multi-colored room that resembled a cross between a dining room and a school classroom. Boards with writing in an unknown language hung on the walls.

"Please, come in," he said. "We were just getting started."

Hattie turned to Creator. She only caught the brief glimpse of His waving hand pulling back behind the closing, electric burnt orange-colored door. Hattie returned her gaze to the room.

"Please, have a seat," said Aleifr.

Four additional Hosts at the table arose silently, two on each side, leaving a single seat for Hattie opposite Aleifr. They stood tall and were cloaked in glistening armor that shimmered like sunlight on water. They stared at her, motionless. Hattie walked to the end of the table, placing her hands flat on it, steadying herself as she sat. Her eyes wandered. The room seemed to contain every possible color, with each glimpse catching excruciatingly detailed geometric shapes diving down into a scale of oblivion.

"Where are we?" she asked.

"Your family war room," said Aleifr.

Her eyes snapped back to him.

"War room?" she said in disbelief. "This ain't no war room. Looks like we're in a circus."

"I find the trimmings quite nice actually," said Aleifr. "One of your ancestors decided to take it upon herself to decorate a few centuries ago."

"What was she thinking with all this strange color?"

"Inspired by a mountainous region of Heaven. I look forward to taking you there someday."

"It feels familiar somehow," she said.

"It should. Some of your family line comes from Morocco. The people there were given glimpses of the mountains and adopted the colors and geometry quite happily. Given human ability, it is actually quite impressive what they were able to recreate on Earth."

Hattie eyed the four Hosts still standing at the table. She awaited an introduction. None arrived. Aleifr drummed his fingers on the table, drawing Hattie's eyes down to a small glittering red notebook before him.

"I hear you have a book for us to review?" he said.

She mentally checked her hands. Empty. "Isn't that it there?"

"Oh no. This is your book, Hattie," he said. "We were just reviewing some strategy options. We are glad you could join us."

Hattie looked at each of the four Hosts, who still stood motionless.

"Hello, nice to meet everyone," she said. "I am Hattie."

She waited. They stared. Hattie felt uncomfortable.

"Are they all right?" she asked.

"They are awaiting your command, Hattie."

"What does that mean?"

"They report to you," said Aleifr. "What do you want them to do?"

"I'd really like them to sit down and stop staring at me."

The four Hosts simultaneously sat in their chairs, briefly lifting them for a single slide forward, all performing the movement in unison. They directed their gazes towards one another across the table with military precision. No words.

"Hattie, I'd like to introduce you to your Enforcers. They will be assisting you during this season."

"Season?" said Hattie. "What on Earth do I need enforcing? I need to help Ryan."

"Precisely," said Aleifr. "On Earth. You need enforcing. We will help Ryan."

"I don't understand," she said. "Creator just told me that I had to be the one to help him, and I need to read that red book. Something about the authority of my family line. He said that you couldn't help even if you wanted to. I don't really get it at all."

"Now you're getting it!" said Aleifr.

This was the first time Hattie had seen any sort of excitement on the face of Aleifr. His eyes beamed. The stoic Enforcers continued to stare motionless at one another.

"Now quickly, let's see that book," he said.

Hattie held up her hands.

"I don't know where it is. I had it just before but now—"

"It's in your heart," said Aleifr.

"I don't understand. Do you want me to tell you what I saw?"

"No, it's in. Your. Heart."

Aleifr pinched his fingers together to make a sort of beak out of his hand, pecking at his chest.

"Reach in and take it out so we can read it," he said. "We are quite eager."

Hattie knew better than to ask any more questions and simply followed Aleifr's movements. She placed her hand on her chest and pressed. She felt pressure.

"It's sinking," she shouted.

"Of course it is," said Aleifr. "Now just move it a bit to the left. It's in the left chamber."

Hattie felt pressure from the inside. She looked down to see her fingertips disappearing into her chest. There was no pain, but she could feel an oddly pleasant, tickling sensation from behind her sternum.

"There, picture it in your mind," said Aleifr.

Hattie closed her eyes and saw the lion jump out of the page. She immediately felt a yank on her arm. She opened her eyes to find Aleifr towering over her, hand clasped around her wrist, which now held a shimmering red satin book.

"How did you do that?" said Hattie, astonished. "How did I do that?"

She poked her chest again with her hand in a few places, but nothing happened.

"Where did that come from?" she asked.

"The Father stores what He values in His heart, which means you do too."

"Does this mean I manifested it because I needed it?"

"You can use your mind to create and manifest," said Aleifr, "but your heart is where you store, protect, and treasure."

Aleifr offered her a comforting smile.

"May I?" he said, gesturing with his eyes towards the book. "We need to read it."

Hattie nodded, still startled. Aleifr gently removed the book from her frozen hand and placed it in the center of the table. The four Enforcers rose, placing their hands on the book in a stack. Aleifr circled the table, returning to the head and gently laid his hand on top of the pile. The group simultaneously closed their eyes. Hattie drew in a breath, watching intently for their reaction, unsure of what to expect.

"You'll be joining us then, yes?" said Aleifr, eyes still shut.

Hattie took the cue and stood quickly.

"Just on top there, yes," he said.

Hattie's hand hovered over the pile before lightly placing it atop of Aleifr's dark matte hand. As her fingers touched, Hattie felt a sense of warmth begin to spread through her body, but as her palm connected with the back of Aleifr's hand, Hattie felt a surge of thoughts and memories race through her mind like a sports car revving its engine behind her eyes. She closed them.

Even with her eyes shut, her vision was clear. She turned her head, memories playing like movie clips floating in her mind with silver and gold strands exploding outward from them. The strands connected to others that floated in the limitless space she found her mind's eye in. As she looked around, she saw Aleifr and the Enforcers, all staring upwards watching the dazzling show of images, videos, and connections. They maintained faces of concentration as if they were reading a textbook. A vibrant ribbon encircled the group, emanating colors and an elaborately composed melody that Hattie recognized as Ryan's Traces, but these were bright and alive.

She saw herself in some of the videos, but these weren't her memories. They were Ryan's. In an instant, Ryan's entire life hung in the air like a child's mobile. As the memories swirled past her, they accelerated, condensing their radius until the entire structure collapsed into a singular point, flashing as it dissolved into a low throbbing orb that hovered at waist level in the middle of the group.

"Very good," said Aleifr. "Now that we're on the same page, let's see what our options are."

Aleifr reached to pluck the singular floating point before yanking his arm backward. An explosion of images, words, and sounds burst forth, spinning around the room. Hattie could not see any individual picture, but she sensed each moment of Ryan's life. All his hopes, pains, and joys, folding into one perfect point. She could see the hand of darkness over Ryan. She felt the pain that he felt as her sister abused him. She sensed the sorrow that he felt. But the thoughts didn't end there.

A circular chandelier of glowing blue boxes descended from the darkness above them. The boxes stopped just above the chaotic swirling just for a moment. Then an explosion. Lightning bolts began shooting out from the boxes, striking the floating images causing a flash and a loud *boom* with each hit. From each box, the lighting struck as if it were firing bullets. Hattie could not discern any pattern for the movement, and she could only observe. Nearly as soon as it started, the lightning stopped, leaving no trace of the images, only the soft glow of the floating chandelier of boxes.

Hattie returned her gaze to the group, looking for direction. Their eyes were still fixed on the boxes. As Hattie returned her gaze upwards, the boxes began to descend, coming closer together as the circle descended in front of the group.

Hattie didn't know how, but she knew what was in each of the boxes and with clarity.

"It appears you know what needs to be done," said Aleifr.

Hattie released her hand from the group, opening her eyes to return to the colorful room. As Hattie removed her hand, she saw that the stack of hands now sat atop a single blue box at the center of the table.

"What was that?" she asked.

"The analysis of alternatives," said Aleifr. "With so many variables, we needed to step into a different dimension in order to perform the calculations."

"We went into another dimension?" asked Hattie.

"Well of course. Here, there is certainty. The dimension we stepped into allows the infinite variables to be captured and calculated across time. Spirit performed the final selection."

"We assessed infinity, and the answer is in a little box?" she asked.

"Oh, would you prefer a larger box?" asked Aleifr.

"No, I, well, it just seems strange."

"You were in the room with us. You already saw the answer. Hattie, I know this is overwhelming, but you were created for this. This is a part of your destiny. Your family is counting on you."

Hattie felt the weight of Aleifr's words. He was right. She did know what needed to be done. With confidence, she reached for the box, sliding the top off and looked inside.

26

Since meeting up with Rebecca, no new work or life prospects had come to Ryan, but at least the weight of depression seemed to lift slightly.

He laid on his side, phone propped on the bed as he mindlessly scrolled through some old childhood photos. He and Ree were always together after she moved in. She was his everything growing up.

The doorbell rang.

"Who the hell is that?"

Landlord, probably. Jackass trying to collect.

"He's going to be waiting a long time for that money," he said.

Ryan didn't feel like taking on an argument and stayed put. Another knock, more persistent this time. He slowly arose from his bed, peering around the corner towards the door. Curtains were shut, as always. Another knock. He approached the door cautiously from the side, trying to weave a line of sight through the curtain to see.

"Ryan," said a woman's voice.

His stomach sank as his head swirled before his mind had a chance to register the voice, pulled into the past.

Another knock.

"Ryan, honey. Ryan, are you home?" said the voice.

Another knock.

"I see a light on. Are you in there, Ryan?" said the voice.

A cold sweat formed on his forehead and queasy feeling in his stomach as his breathing increased.

"I swear, this boy has not changed one bit," she said under her breath, a puff of condensation forming as she spoke.

She knocked more aggressively.

"Ryan, I can see your shadow. Now open up this door and let me in. It's cold out here."

She turned to take stock of the absolute dump her nephew now lived in. She clutched a side of her coat and wrapped it more tightly around her to ensure nothing touched her.

"Absolutely disgusting. I can't believe I'm even here," she muttered.

She knocked again.

"I'm not waiting out here all day, Ryan, now open this—"

The door swung open. There stood her nephew, much older than the last time she saw him.

"What the fuck are you doing here?" he said, voice raised.

Etta forced out a smile through pursed lips.

"That's no way to talk to your Auntie," she said. "Won't you invite me in, even for a minute?"

Ryan's eyes contorted, and he raised his hand.

"Are you fucking kidding me?" he said. "You show up on my doorstep. Now? And you want me to just let you in my house?"

Etta scoffed.

"This is hardly a house, Ryan," she said. "Just look at it."

"Un-fucking-believable," he said.

"Now be a good boy, and let your Auntie in."

The words seemed to stun him for a moment. Etta pushed the door open and walked past Ryan. He fumbled a few incomprehensible words. She found herself in what resembled a living room, or perhaps the kitchen. It smelled of stale alcohol. She could only imagine a wild animal living in such a place. Certainly no human. Hands clasped and purse resting in the crook of her elbow, she turned to face Ryan, who still stood in the doorway.

"I don't want you here," he said. "Leave."

"Oh please, stop acting like that. Now give Auntie a hug."

Etta stretched out her arms, approaching. Ryan backed up, closing the door with his body. She lightly embraced him. He did not reciprocate. His breath was shallow in her ear. He smelled like deli meat. She withdrew from the embrace, holding him by the arms and offered a sympathetic face.

"Oh, Ryan, I am so sorry for your loss." She tilted her head, clasping her hands. "Losing your mother must be tearing you up inside."

Etta's eyes caught the glimmer of a few discarded beer cans on the floor next to Ryan. "You're still mourning."

Ryan broke her hold and walked around her.

"You must be out of your mind coming here," he said.

"Oh come now, Ryan. You can't talk to Auntie like that."

"You're sick. I want you out."

"I just came to offer my condolences. I know how hard it can be to lose a parent."

"Fine, you gave them," he said. "Now leave."

Etta looked around, clicking her tongue in disapproval.

"Oh, honey, look at this place," she said. "You need help."

"Definitely not from you," said Ryan. "You've done enough."

"I'm just here for you, Ry-Ry. Did my sister know you lived like this? I can't believe she would let her own son live in such squalor. She never understood how to raise a child right."

"You took my childhood," said Ryan.

"Oh come now. You're blowing things way out of proportion. I know you're still upset about your mother and must be lashing out. You probably see me as your mother. It's OK. I forgive you for being upset. I know you two weren't on good terms at the end."

"You ruined my life and your own daughter's," said Ryan. "Did you molest her too? Is that the real reason she came to live with us?"

Etta tightened her posture.

"Rebecca's father and I were having some challenges at the time. I thought it was best that she be raised in a more stable environment. That's all."

"Wow, mother of the fucking year over here. So my ma didn't threaten to go to the police if you didn't send Ree to us?"

"Now Ryan, be reasonable," she said in a sympathetic tone. "There's no need for this. You were young at the time, so I can understand why you don't remember exactly what happened. We all have misunderstandings. Ryan, if all this was as bad as you said, wouldn't she have simply gone to the authorities with you? She was your own mother for goodness' sake. So wouldn't a mother want to protect her own child if I was the big bad aunt?"

She paused for a response. None arrived.

"Exactly," she said. "Now look. We all have to grow up sometime. We had such a special relationship when you were younger. You didn't seem to have any complaints back then. So why the harsh tone now?"

"I was just a kid, Etta. How do you even talk like that and go to church every Sunday?"

"Oh, did you want to go to church with me? That would be—"

"Are you even hearing yourself right now?" asked Ryan. "You. Are a pedo. I don't know what kind of 'god' you and my mother follow, but the fact that you are even here right now says there is no justice. Just leave."

Etta cleared her throat and forced a smile through the accusations. She softened her tone further.

"Ryan, it's been ages since we last talked. And after...well, everything, I thought it might help to reconnect. I know we have some things to work through, but with your mom gone, I think it would be helpful if I were still in your life. We're a family. We need to be helping each other through this difficult time right now. It's important for you to have a mother figure. Now, I do like your idea. Maybe you can join me at church on Sundays, and then I can take you out to eat and get a healthy meal in you. Poor boy, look at you. Practically starving. Are you even eating? Can I cook you something?"

"I don't want anything from you," said Ryan, his voice weakening.

"Ryan, I'm trying here. I will give you some time. I know all of this is new and probably a little overwhelming. Just think over my offer."

"Does Ree know you're here right now?"

Etta's neck spasmed, tweaking her head to the side.

"I haven't had a chance to catch up with her just yet," said Etta. "She rushed out of the funeral before I could see her and her beautiful family. We've been playing phone tag."

Etta cleared her throat.

"Has she said anything about me?"

"Just that she doesn't want anything to do with you," said Ryan.

Etta forced a laugh.

"Kids never do change, do they? Always wanting to be so independent. Mothers and daughters do have their challenges."

"Not every mother is a child molester."

"Please, Ryan, enough with the accusations," said Etta. "We both know I didn't force anything on you."

"So you admit it?"

"We all need someone to take care of us sometimes," said Etta. "I was just giving you something I knew your mother couldn't."

She took a step closer.

"Look around, Ryan. This is what your life has amounted to? Beer cans on the floor. Dirty clothes on your table. I don't even want to know what that is," she said, gesturing toward a dark, crusted stain. She shook her head.

"I can help you get back on your feet," said Etta.

Ryan paused.

"How exactly do you propose to do that?" asked Ryan with a questioning voice.

"Well, I have a home with some extra bedrooms. It's been years since I've had anyone else in the house with me. It's just sitting unused. I'm an old lady. Are you afraid of an old lady?"

"You want me to live with you?"

"Why not?" she said. "We're both family. You just lost your mom, and Lord knows you could use some help. What do you say? You don't even have to pay rent. House has been paid off for years, and I still get Jerry's pension. We can just keep each other company."

Ryan stumbled over his words.

"I have been looking for a new place," he said, "but this doesn't feel right."

"Now listen," she said sternly. "You are my nephew, and I am your Auntie. We're supposed to take care of each other. I'm not taking 'no' for an answer."

"Don't you think Ree is going to have a big issue with this?"

"Let me handle my daughter," she said. "You just worry about getting your things boxed up."

Etta walked to the kitchen counter, scribbling on a piece of mail.

"Now here is my number. I expect a call from you tomorrow so I can schedule a truck to come pick up all this junk and take it to the dump. Just bring your things. I have everything else."

She set the pen down with purpose, turning back to Ryan.

"I expect a call," she said. "You hear me?"

"Yes, Auntie," he said softly.

"Good, and Ryan, it really is so good to see you again. I'll show myself out."

She stepped over a few piles of trash, balancing on her toes so as to not catch her foot in whatever bear traps were underneath the garbage on the floor. She carefully made her way back to the door.

"Will chat soon," she said.

Ryan looked down at the ground as she turned, opening the door and stepping outside.

She pulled the door behind her, facing the desolate parking lot. Etta took a deep breath to compose herself and mentally brush off the filth of that place. She tightened her coat once more, pushed her purse up onto her arm, and walked down the path back to her car. *Victory.*

27

Ryan stared from the window at that wretched bitch walking away. This felt like a movie, not real life. He released the curtain and turned to face the room.

You idiot.

What had he done? Did he really just agree to move in with the woman who molested him?

I think she's right. You did like it.

"No, I was just a kid," said Ryan.

It was not until his early 20s that Ryan even recognized what happened as abuse. He just thought that was what adults and kids do with one another. Even when Ree came to live with them, he didn't understand why. He was young. So young.

Look at you. Whoring yourself for a roof over your head.

A memory fragment broke loose. He was no longer in his apartment. He was in his childhood room, her breath hot and too close, hands in places that made his skin crawl even now. He squeezed his eyes shut, as if it could block out the past, but the memory stayed sharp, relentless.

He couldn't see her, but he felt her. The way she whispered softly. The scene unfolded with startling clarity. He shut his eyes, forcing them tighter in hopes of keeping the memories out. It didn't work.

"Mom!"

The shout was involuntary. He was suddenly back in his own body, finding himself on his knees in the living room breathing heavily and in a cold sweat. Tears welled in his eyes.

Do you think she still wants you like that? I bet she does.

"I can't do this," he said to the ground. "I can't do this."

He broke. Collapsing onto a few loose garments, he rolled onto his back. Ryan wrapped his arms over his eyes as he sobbed. The empty hole in his heart grew. His body felt heavy with emptiness.

You have to move in with her. You'll die here if you don't.

What other option did he have? He couldn't even pay for this dump. At least he would have a roof over his head that didn't leak.

Your landlord might try to fuck you too, so that's a plus.

Ryan trained his mind to expect the worst, but this was a travesty. What was he doing? Here he was, a grown man, sobbing on the floor. A floor that he couldn't even afford. His sob surged into rage.

"What was I thinking?" he said. "I can't go to a fucking concert right now. She's out of her mind."

Ryan grabbed his phone and dialed.

"Hey, I've been thinking," he said. "I can't go on that trip with you."

"Why, what happened?" said Rebecca.

"I just can't. I've got a lot of stuff going on here, and I can't take off work."

"Ugh, this so typical," said Rebecca.

"What does that mean?"

"You just give up all the time. You can't commit to anything. It's a concert. It's not that big of a deal."

"You've got a husband paying your way. I ain't got that."

Nailed it.

"Keep going, Bud. Let's hear all your excuses," she said.

Stupid bitch.

"Look, you stupid bitch!" he shouted at the phone, holding it in front of his face. "I told you I'm not going, OK?"

Ryan heard Rebecca's voice crack.

"What the hell is wrong with you?" she said, sniffling.

She thinks you're an idiot.

"I'm not an idiot," he said. "It was a dumb idea anyway. What were you thinking? Just going on a road trip. Ree, I'm losing my place. I can't take off work."

"I already told you I would help you."

Ryan heard a distant voice over the phone.

"What the fuck are you offering to that deadbeat now?"

Even her husband knows you're trash.

"I'm done Ree," said Ryan. "I can't do this with you."

"Quitting again like you always do? Jesus, Ryan, look at your shit life. Pull it together."

She's right.

"You're one to talk. You hate your husband!"

"Don't bring him into this. This is about you and your shit life and your shit decisions, Ryan. Take responsibility for once. We both know you don't want to change. You love being the victim because it gives you an excuse to give up."

She's right.

Ryan removed the phone from his ear and clicked it off, tossing it on the couch.

Pathetic shit.

"Fuck this," he said, kicking the leg of the table, his rage covering any pain. "Fuck her!"

Ryan pushed his tongue against his cheek and took a deep breath.

This is your life.

"This can't be my life. This is miserable."

You're in pain all the time. It never stops. You live a miserable life, and it will never get better.

"I just want out."

Now there's an idea.

"I'm just done. I'm done with all this shit. No matter what I do, life still sucks."

And it won't get better. You know that.

Ryan dropped his body onto the couch, leaning over his knees with his head in his hands.

"What options do I have?"

There's always Auntie Etta. She seemed eager to help.

"I can't do that," he said, shaking his head. "I just can't do that."

There's always the other option. Peace, at last.

When the thought crossed his mind, Ryan felt a momentary relief. He often fantasized about that, but it was usually just that, a fantasy. An escape. It never seemed like a real option.

Until now.

Until now. He was done. He just shut out the only person in his life that he was close to. He was now fully and utterly alone.

You can do it. I believe in you. Maybe succeed at something in your pathetic life.

Ryan leaned back bumping his head against the wall, blank faced, staring at the dumpster of a life he created. He could feel in his mind's eye the final glimmer of light extinguish. There were no other options. Ryan continued to stare at the wall, reliving his most painful life memories.

Remember when your mom thought you were lying about your aunt?

Ryan was only ten when the news came out. There were plenty of signs, which his parents completely missed. It was only when Ryan was caught at school with another student in the bathroom that the teachers started to ask questions.

"How did she not know? She was my own mother."

She knew. She just didn't care. You were too big of a burden. Dead weight in the family.

"I was only ten. What else could I do? I didn't even know what was going on."

I think you knew. You just didn't want it to stop.

"I was a kid. I didn't understand. I didn't know that was wrong. I was just doing what felt good."

See, I knew you liked it.

A knot tightened in his throat, tears welling.

"I didn't know."

Ryan closed his eyes.

Clearly you weren't trustworthy. What parent doesn't trust their kid about that?

He didn't have a response.

Remember when you pissed your pants in front of class, and your dad called you a filthy slob?

I was so nervous.

"You pissed your pants!" he could hear his Dad's voice ringing in his ear. "You filthy slob. You idiot. No wonder your aunt went for you. Easy target. Fool."

The resonance of the words immediately released tears. He fought regularly to keep those words behind walls, safety held hostage in the deepest parts of his mind.

Remember when you tried to fuck your girlfriend and could only think about Auntie Etta?

"That was humiliating."

I bet that girl remembers. Imagine how many people she told. Do you think she gave you a nickname? Something funny for her friends to call you?

Ryan only tried having sex the one time after what happened with his Aunt. The shame and inability to perform brought the deepest levels of shame to his mind.

Unlovable.

"I am unlovable."

Forgettable.

"I am forgettable."

Burden on society.

Ryan sat in silence under the weight of own decrepit waste of a life.

You know what you need to do. Show some compassion for others for once.

Ryan's eyes moved around the room. A knife would be too painful. He could hang himself, but the thought of choking was too much. He wanted something painless.

Call your Aunt before you do it. Let her find you.

"That's not a bad idea. That bitch deserves some pain in her life."

Yes, she does. She lived a happy life after you.

Ryan's eyes landed on the several bottles of heavy duty pain medication that were strewn about on the floor. They were typically reserved for only the worst days of his pain.

That's the right idea.

"Couple pills, little booze. Nighty night, Ryan."

Easy. It's perfect. You need to do it tonight. Before you chicken out, Coward.

"I should write a note for Ree."

Fuck her. You heard what she said. Let her wonder. Let them all wonder.

"I can't do this."

You can do this. Show them what you're made of.

Ryan's mind lusted after the idea of ending his suffering. The endless torment of life was insatiable. No matter what he did. No matter how many times he stood up. Life pushed him back down and kicked until he was bloody and battered. This simply wasn't worth doing anymore.

Look at how much pain you've already caused. You can finally clean up your own mess.

Ryan continued to stare at the bottle of pills on the counter.

"I can't have her find my body."

They'll smell you before she comes looking. She thinks you're an idiot wasting away in garbage. She's not looking for you.

With a shaky breath, Ryan rose and walked to the counter, his fingers grazing the scattered bottles as he made his choice. Before he could change his mind, he slugged back as many pills as he could fit in his mouth. He felt the time bomb slip down his esophagus. With only a moment's hesitation, he grabbed the knocked over bottle of vodka from a previous night's party.

"No time for a glass."

That's right. Let's make this quick. You're almost here. You're doing so good.

Ryan drank down as much of the vodka as he could, fighting his way through the burn of the alcohol. One gulp at first. A harsh exhale in attempt to push out the burn. Then another. And another. The subsequent slurps went down much easier. Ryan finished off the remainder of the bottle.

I'm so proud of you. I didn't know if you would do it, but you did it.

"I did it. And now we wait."

Ryan had not eaten all day, so it did not take long to feel the comforting blanket of the alcohol. A slight smile worked itself across his face.

Are you going to call your Aunt?

"No, I want that piece of shit landlord to find me melted into the ground. He'll never be able to rent this place again."

I couldn't have come up with a better idea myself.

Ryan was so close to escape. He felt the warming throughout his body as he sat on the couch fantasizing about the peace and quiet he was entering.

Any last words?

"Fuck this world. Fuck you. Fuck Rebecca. Fuck me. I'm done. Good fucking riddance to this place. I don't care what's on the other side. It could never be worse than this."

I'm sure.

Ryan felt his breathing slow. He breathed in deeper, exhaling longer.

Just relax.

The peace he felt was bliss. He closed his eyes, tilting his head back.

He pictured for a moment what his life could have been.

Just relax.

He opened his eyes to find them much more difficult to hold open. He blinked, unable to focus on the room as his eyes rolled from side to side.

Almost there. Just let go. Close your eyes.

Ryan closed his eyes once more as the darkness closed around him, swallowing the ache, until there was only quiet. Peace, at last.

28

Rebecca sat crying, the blank dial-tone of her phone blaring.

"Piece of shit!" she shouted, throwing the phone across the room.

He's not worth your time. Why even bother with him?

"I should have known he couldn't pull his life together," she said, wiping tears.

He's a deadbeat. Cut him off. You don't need this.

"All I've done is help him. His entire pathetic fucking life. And this is what he does?"

Do you want him to go away? Shall I take him from you?

A spirit of Destruction appeared in the room to join the familiar spirit. Rebecca remained motionless, seemingly unaware of the new presence. The spirit's robes draped her form like liquid shadows, the violet sash cutting across her body. Thick, black hair, pulled down over her shoulder.

"Welcome, Acantha," said a spirit, holding a bow.

"Where are we, Bastian?" asked Acantha, stepping around the bed, inspecting.

"The female is weak and broken."

"Excellent. The Guardians?"

"Bound and buried," said Bastian. "They are no threat."

"Wonderful. Please proceed."

Rebecca failed to hold back a sob.

"I just don't want to deal with him anymore," she said.

Do I have your permission then? I can end this torment with your cousin,
whispered Bastian.

"Life would probably be easier. I don't want to see him anymore. Sure as hell would help my marriage."

Frank hates him.

"Yeah, he does."

Frank hates you. But you already know that.

Rebecca didn't respond to the thought.

Can you blame your husband? He just wants your affection, but you spend so much effort on your cousin.

"I'm such a shitty wife."

Truly. It's incredible Frank even stays with you the way you act.

"I'm so fucking worthless."

After all the late nights spent helping Ryan out of trouble, for Frank to hold it against her like this... Rebecca's chest ached as her sobs reached a new level.

"I'm trying my best, but I just can't do it."

Your best is pitiful. Look at your life. You don't need to keep suffering like this.

Rebecca's tears became silent in intensity.

"What if she doesn't agree?" asked Bastian.

"Doesn't matter," said Acantha. "We already have received the contract from the male. His fate is sealed. We only seek her permission to further strengthen the case."

"Why bother if his fate is sealed?"

"No, strengthen the case against her. With the male claimed, we will be refocusing on her and her remaining family. My orders are to ensure no further propagation of the line. They are enemies of the State."

"I see," said Bastian.

"The seeds I planted in her son will be sprouting soon. She'll be devastated. But this? This moment here. When she finds out about the male's death, she won't be able to live with herself. She'll blame herself for the remainder of her pathetic earthly life. Poor fool will self-destruct and take out everyone around her like a bomb."

"She certainly is easily persuaded. No backbone at all."

"You have done well on your watches, Bastian. My inspections have revealed a consistent weakening of her strength. Look at how dim her Traces are. She doesn't know who she is anymore."

Bastian grinned.

"I never get tired of seeing Superior's well-laid plans coming to life," he said, "or rather, death. Superior's plans are always just that. Far superior."

Acantha slowly walked around the bed, her eyes never leaving Rebecca.

"I have run many of these missions, and it never ceases to amaze me how fragile and susceptible these creatures are," she said. "I may never understand why He chose them."

"But not for long," said Bastian. "There won't be any of them left soon enough!"

"Pests meant for extermination. He will turn His back on them. Just like He wrongfully did to us. Even He would not allow His name to be tarnished for so long by these creatures. We will be reunited soon. The apology will be a sweet song to my ears. I'm sure Superior will have these chapters burnt in the Archive so that we may all begin once again. But until then, we must deal with this infestation."

"I just feel so alone," said Rebecca through the tears.

You are alone. You have no one. Your husband hates you. You have your son, but we know why you can't be close to him. You are your mother's daughter, after all.

"I'm not like her!" she shouted.

Then why do you avoid being close? He thinks you don't even love him. Is that any way to raise a child? What mother does that?

The words spoken by Bastian became a dark cloak settling on Rebecca's shoulders. She could not see it, but her shoulders slumped as it came to rest upon her. Rebecca dropped onto her back under its weight, hands over her eyes, weeping.

You need to give up. It's your only escape.

Bastian continued whispering into Rebecca's ear.

"God help me," she cried out. "I can't do this anymore."

A loud crack rang through the room, startling Acantha and Bastian. The sound of Rebecca's sobs ceased. She lay motionless on the bed, frozen in the moment between the ticks of the clock.

"What is the meaning of this?" said Acantha, looking around the room.

A sapphire blue blur spun into existence at the foot of the bed. A petite but muscular Host now stood between Acantha and Bastian, cloaked in purple and red, staring directly forward. An Enforcer stood next to him, clad in armor.

"Be it known to all," said the messenger, "both high and low, that by the decree of The Court of the High, a temporary stay is hereby placed on the access to Rebecca Lynn, daughter of Gerald, son of Walter, son of Ignacius Brown."

"Nonsense," said Acantha, waving her hand in dismissal. "Leave us."

"The decree is effective immediately and binding upon all," said the messenger, "and all who dare to disregard it shall be subject to the full weight of the Law and the displeasure of our gracious monarch."

"This can't be," said Acantha. "She granted us access. You cannot revoke her permission. You know that."

"Her contract with you has been suspended," said the messenger.

"On what grounds?"

"An amicus petition was filed on her behalf, and she has co-signed the petition."

The messenger pulled a scroll from his robes, extending it towards Acantha. She glared at it before snatching it out of his hand. Acantha furiously pulled the scroll open, scanning the court order.

"This is a weak argument," she said. "Her aunt has no standing in this case."

"Irrelevant, but you may file a petition through the appropriate channels."

Acantha paused, staring down at the messenger, then scowling at the Enforcer.

"These creatures are not worth your time. The female will revoke this order as soon as you leave the room. Surely you have heard her. She is destined for captivity and despair."

"That is not for me to say. I am merely a messenger. If you have concerns on the legality, you may—"

"Why do you serve these beasts?" hissed Acantha. "They have only turned you into slaves. You are a slave of slaves!"

"My motivations are also irrelevant."

"Look at you. You could be great, and here you are running errands for these pitiful things. They are the lowest of creations. Your betrayal will not be looked upon favorably when we are reunited."

The messenger's eyes broke the empty stare and looked at Acantha.

"Your fates are already sealed," he said. "I have seen the documents myself. Reunification is not possible."

"Nonsense."

"The records are open for you to review."

"You are right. He does not wish to welcome us back, but that is not how this ends. Look at those things."

Acantha's eyes slithered to scowl at Rebecca.

"They are the ones He has sided with," she said, pointing a finger of accusation. "They are the ones He is putting the trust of His inheritance in. There is no way for Him to succeed. They will rot Him from the inside out. When He fails and humbles Himself, Superior will welcome Him back. Under Superior's guidance, the Kingdom will be made right again."

"The deceived are always the last to recognize they are such," said the messenger.

"Truly," scoffed Acantha.

Acantha and Bastian stepped backwards simultaneously, disappearing from the room as a portal snapped shut around them. The clock remained frozen.

Hattie felt her breath release as the grim figures no longer cast their shadows in the room. The messenger turned to face Aleifr, who stood next to her.

"Thank you for your quick action, my friend," said Aleifr.

"I am merely the messenger. You have done the work."

"Yes, thank you Aleifr," said Hattie. "Thank you to all of you."

"Hattie, it was your petition that allows us to be here," said Aleifr, eying the messenger and the Enforcer. "It was not my work that did this. I am a guide, but you are the one that carries the authority."

"But Ryan," she said. "He is still in danger."

"The contract he has with the enemy is unfortunately full and complete," said Aleifr. "We have no grounds in his case to intervene as we have done here. There is no room in his heart for faith. We are helpless. Our only hope is to encourage Rebecca to intervene."

"Time is of the essence," said the messenger.

Hattie turned to Rebecca, still frozen in the bed. Hattie walked to her, sitting beside her.

"My sweet girl," said Hattie, gaze lingering on Rebecca. "My poor sweet girl. You were meant for greatness." She paused. "You are meant for greatness." At that moment, the dark cloak upon Rebecca's shoulders began to dissipate, and a small red speck appeared floating above her heart.

"I had no idea when you came into my life the blessing you would be," she said. "Despite the struggles, you were a blessing."

A red glittering scarf emerged from Hattie's mouth as she spoke, intertwining itself around the dim Traces above Rebecca's head as the black cloak fully disappeared.

"You carry our family purpose," said Hattie. "Caring and comfort."

The red speck grew.

"You are meant to bring these things. God, help her as she navigates the struggles of this world. Give her the confidence to overlook the arrows that people throw at her in their woundedness. God, give her the courage to step out again and again, even when she has been rejected."

The red speck grew.

"God, hear me," she continued. "Remove the tears from my daughter's eyes."

The red speck grew.

"Rebecca, you are an eternal being. I so desperately want to be reunited with you now, but you still have work to do on Earth."

The red speck grew. Hattie began to weep. Aleifr stepped around the side of the bed. The red speck was now a glowing orb hovering over Rebecca's chest. It undulated, expanding and contracting in synchronization with the movements of the red garment, which was now the size of a quilt, wrapped around Rebecca, from her Traces to her feet.

"Your prayers have been heard," said Aleifr, placing his hand on Hattie's shoulder.

Aleifr snapped his fingers as Rebecca came back to life, choking back a few more tears. They began to subside. Rebecca slowly began to sit up. The moment her body touched the red orb, Hattie was jolted backward, her face splashing back through The Portal's surface, immediately surrounded by the joy and laughter of others.

Aleifr stood beside her.

"It is up to Rebecca to choose whether she partners with us," he said. "You have done what could be done."

29

Rebecca pulled into a parking space in front of the dingy apartment complex, tears still soaking her cheeks. A man wearing dirty rags walked in front of her car, scowling.

"Get out of here, Lady! We don't want you here! I'll kill you! I'll kill him! I'll kill them all!"

His passionate threats quickly returned to the deep conversation he was having with himself.

"Damn druggies are running this town," said Rebecca. "I can't believe I'm even here right now."

He's not worth it. Go home.

"I should just go home. He's not worth it. Fucking miserable martyr."

You need to see him.

Rebecca closed her eyes, sighing.

"I do not want to be doing this."

Rebecca still gripped her steering wheel, shaking it in frustration as she spoke.

He's just looking for sympathy. Why don't you show your husband this kind of care for once?

Rebecca scoffed at her own audacity of being outside his apartment.

"I'm crazy. I'm fucking crazy. He does not deserve this attention."

Fuck him. Ungrateful asshole.

Rebecca put her foot on the brake, reaching for the keys to start the ignition.

You need to see him.

"I don't want to fucking see him. Not after that call. Are you kidding? Why would I go see him after that?"

You need to see him.

Leave.

Rebecca let out a scream of torment.

You need to see him.

Rebecca's shoulders sank as she let out a belabored sigh.

"OK, I'll go," she said meekly.

Her anger sparked.

"If this guy even thinks about pulling anything, I'm out of here. I've got enough to deal with."

Rebecca yanked the keys out of the ignition, tossing them in her purse as she grabbed it and stepped out of the car with purpose. She needed to move fast before she changed her mind.

He's an ungrateful shit. Leave. Now. He's just going to hurt you again.

Rebecca planted one foot in front of the other, reaching Ryan's door. A haggard old woman appeared on her left.

"Another one of you?" she said with a knowing laugh, shuffling by with a cracked basket full of laundry. "This boy must be something special to have so many of you angry women coming to his place. You a lot younger than the last one, Honey."

Rebecca simply shook her head as the busybody continued down the hall.

"They're never worth it, Honey," said the woman over her shoulder. "Go home. Take it from me. You should just leave. He doesn't want to hear anything you got to say. Just go home while you can. Girl like you gets hurt in a place like this."

The woman snickered as she turned a corner, disappearing. Rebecca returned her gaze to the door, refocusing. She knocked hard.

"Ryan!" she shouted, catching the volume of herself, she lowered her tone. "Open this door. I'm not leaving. I need to talk to you."

She knocked again rapidly before she finished her sentence, pausing for only a half breath.

"Ryan, open this door right now."

No response. She walked over to the window. There was a light on, in the back of the apartment. She could make out the silhouette of his head, scared little shit hiding from her.

"I see you in there. Get up and let me in. Ryan!" She pounded on the window. "Ryan." She pounded again.

He sat motionless.

"Ryan, get over here!"

She could see him slouched over on the couch.

What a deadbeat. He's not worth it. Go home.

Something's wrong.

The tug of concern shifted her tone. She knocked again.

"Ryan, open the door!"

No movement.

The slouch of his body was contorted. He was not asleep. She cupped her hands over her eyes to try and get a better view peering through the window. As she did, her eyes adjusted to the dim light inside. Ryan looked asleep, but she saw a flow of what appeared to be vomit running down his shirt.

"Jesus," she said.

Leave him.

Help him.

She knew what needed to be done. Rebecca pictured this scene before. She reached into her purse pulling out her phone, dialing with a shaky hand. She lifted the phone to her ear, bending back down to look in the window once again. The agonizingly long ring tones finally connected.

"Hello? I need an ambulance sent to the Ridgecrest Estates, room 107. My cousin. I think he overdosed. Hurry."

Rebecca took a few steps back, looking to the left, then to the right for anything that might help. A "Management" sign hung on one of the doors just a few paces down from where she stood. She ran to it.

She had nightmares about a day like this.

"This can't happen," she said, reaching for the door handle. She turned it, putting her weight behind the movement. The door was unlocked, and she found herself in a small lobby, breathing heavily. A woman sitting at a desk let out a yelp before restraining the surprise.

"Hi, can I help—"

"My cousin," said Rebecca, trying to maintain composure. "He's in room 107. He overdosed. Please, I need you to open the door."

The woman spun in her seat to face Rebecca, freezing, hands clasping the arms of her chair and mouth agape.

"Now, please! He needs help! The ambulance is on the way."

The woman blinked a few times as her consciousness returned.

"Uh, ok," she sputtered out.

The woman stood, retrieving a set of keys from the desk drawer. Rebecca turned to leave for the room. She heard the woman's heavy shoes clunking behind her. The sirens wailed in the distance.

Rebecca stopped just past the door, turning to see the rotund woman fumbling with the keys as she reached the door.

"Hurry, please," said Rebecca. "He needs help."

"Sorry, I'm trying," said the woman, her voice cracking. The woman's hands shook as she navigated the ring of keys before locating the right one. Attempting to insert into the lock, she still struggled.

"Here," said Rebecca, grabbing the keys out of the woman's hand and forcefully inserting them into the lock and turning. She swung the door open.

Vomit. The unmistakable stench of sour stomach acid hit her nose as soon as the door opened. She swallowed the nausea creeping up her throat. She momentarily paused, pushing the door fully open to step inside. Ryan was pale and crumpled in the chair. The flow of sick pointed to a bottle on the floor. She stepped forward, picking it up. Pain meds.

"Dammit, Ryan. What did you do?"

"Is he dead?" asked the woman, voice barely audible, cowering in the doorway.

"Jesus, you better not be dead Ryan," said Rebecca.

She stepped to his side, reaching to put two fingers on his neck. No pulse. His skin was cold and clammy. The flashing red and blue lights shone in through the doorway as the loud sirens reached the parking lot.

"Ryan, wake up! I need you to wake up!"

"Ma'am, I need you to step aside," said a forceful man's voice.

Rebecca turned. A responder appeared in the doorway.

"Please, help him," she said.

She handed the bottle to the man. The paramedic approached Ryan.

"Sir, can you hear me?" he said loudly and without inflection. He placed his fingers on Ryan's neck. He paused for an eternity.

"Pulse is faint," he said.

He leaned into Ryan's face, turning his head.

"Shallow breathing."

Rebecca put her hands over her mouth. A glimmer of hope.

The paramedic grabbed something from his bag. He slipped up Ryan's sleeve, placing a device on Ryan's upper arm. She heard a click.

"What is that?" asked Rebecca.

"Naloxone," said another voice behind her.

Rebecca turned. Another paramedic now stood in the room. "Counteracts those pills."

"Ma'am, were you here when he took these?" he asked. "Do you know how much he took and when?"

"No. No I wasn't here," she said. "Is he going to survive?"

"We're doing everything we can, ma'am. We need to get him to the hospital. We don't know how much alcohol was consumed."

The paramedics wiped the vomit from Ryan's mouth and moved him to a stretcher, placing an oxygen mask over his head. Rebecca placed the back of her hand on her forehead, for a moment finally taking in the entire scene around her.

"Jesus, Ryan," she said, shaking her head. She watched with tears in her eyes as the paramedics carried Ryan out of the room. They moved swiftly. No sooner as they had arrived, they were closing the doors of the ambulance. Rebecca observed as if it were a movie before snapping back into the present.

"Thank you," she shouted to the office manager, who still stood in the corner of the room. Rebecca ran past, jumping in her car.

Rebecca fumbled through her purse to find the car keys, struggling to control her movements as the adrenaline coursed through her body. She saw her phone and dialed Frank, setting it on her lap as she turned the ignition key and pulled out of the lot.

"Jesus, is he OK?" asked Frank.

"I don't know. They just took him away. They said he was breathing, but barely." She wiped tears away from her eyes.

"He's so selfish," said Frank. "I can't believe he would do—," interrupting himself. "I guess I can see him doing this."

"Please, not now. I'm going to the hospital."

"I guess I'll pick Liam up from school today," said Frank.

Rebecca rolled her eyes.

"Please, Frank. Not now. I know everyone is such an inconvenience for you, but this is serious. He might die today. He might already be dead. And all you can talk about is how your life is affected? What the hell, Frank?"

Silence.

"Do what you got to do," said Frank softly. "I need to get back to work."

The line went dead.

He doesn't care about you at all.

"Did he just hang up on me?" she said, picking the phone up to look at the screen. "You did not just hang up on me, you fucking asshole!"

He only thinks about himself. You are an afterthought.

"Je-SUS! I can't keep doing this."

Leave him.

Rebecca shifted back and forth between rage and tears all the way to the hospital. She parked in a loading zone. She didn't care. The sliding automatic doors to the building opened as she hurried into the emergency room. A man stood just inside the entrance.

"I'm looking for my cousin," she said.

"Wait a minute, ma'am. I'll need to see you over here first," said another man in uniform, stepping in front of her.

"My cousin. He's dying. I need to see him."

"I understand, but I need to perform a routine security check."

Rebecca looked around.

"Is this for real?" she scoffed. "What's happening. This is the emergency room, right?"

"This is for your safety and ours," said the man. "Standard procedure. Please, arms out to the side."

"This can't be happening," she muttered under her breath, surrendering her arms as the overweight man wanded around her body.

"Purse, please," he said, holding out an expectant hand.

Rebecca handed him the purse as he stuck a ruler inside, stirring it around, clearly more for show than anything else.

"Thank you, ma'am. Please see the check-in counter."

Rebecca grabbed her purse, still in disbelief, as she hurried into the lobby. She approached the woman at the desk.

"Please, I'm here for Ryan," said Rebecca. "He was just brought in by ambulance. Do you know if he's OK?"

The woman behind the counter moved slowly from her corner to face Rebecca.

"Are you his next of kin?" asked the woman.

"Um, I'm his cousin."

"One moment please," said the woman, her voice clearly not understanding the severity of the situation. A few clicks on the keyboard.

"The doctors are with him," said the woman. "Please wait here."

She gestured to the bank of mostly empty chairs.

"There's nothing you can tell me?" asked Rebecca.

"Sorry, not at the moment. Please, have a seat."

A smattering of forlorn and nervous looking people sat in the waiting area. The hanging TV blared a cooking show.

"Unbelievable," muttered Rebecca.

You should have just let him die.

"I couldn't do that."

Why? You walk away from your husband and kid every day. That's just who you are.

"Ryan needs my help."

And you still almost left him there, drowning in his own stench. Alone. All alone. Is that what caring looks like?

"But I helped him."

But you thought about leaving him. Even now, you wish you hadn't done it.

"He's going to survive. He's going to make it. I know it."

Feeling confident today. You know it?

"I hope he makes it. He has to."

There is that attachment again. Like mother, like daughter. You are so like her.

Rebecca closed her eyes and took a deep breath.

"Rebecca, you need to calm down. This is not the time to spiral."

Pray for him.

Rebecca chuckled at the fleeting thought. Was she really that desperate?

Fool. Your prayers didn't work last time, did they?

Rebecca realized it was only a few months ago that she was right here in this very same hospital. She waited one floor up for Aunt Hat during surgery.

"He has to survive. I can't go through that again."

Still thinking about yourself. Selfish bitch.

Pray for him.

Rebecca grew up in the church, both with her mom and with Aunt Harriet. Prayer wasn't a foreign concept, but after years of seeing unanswered prayer, she figured the whole thing must be made up.

What would an almighty god do with the desperate pleas from a desperate woman like you?

"Exactly."

The whole thing didn't make any sense. It gave Aunt Hat peace, but her? Certainly not.

So needy.

Pray for him.

Fool.

Pray for him.

Rebecca threw her head into her hands and let out a groan.

"All right. All right. I'll pray. Just get this over with."

Rebecca looked around in shame. She didn't want anyone to see her. She tilted her head down ever so slightly out of habit but continued to scan the room with her eyes for any onlookers.

He's dying right now, and this is all you can do? Stop wasting your time. Pray for him.

She began in her quietest whisper.

"Please, just… if anyone's listening, help him," stuttered Rebecca. "Please, please, please, God. Dear God…Jesus, ugh I don't even know what I'm doing."

Keep going.

She took a deep breath in.

"I honestly don't know if I'm crazy or if there is someone listening right now, but I don't have any other options. Ryan is hurt. He needs help. I can't help him. He needs a miracle. Please don't let him die. Please, please don't let him die."

She began to cry.

"Please don't let him die. I don't know if you can even hear me, but don't let him die. Please, don't let him die."

She didn't know what else to pray or do, so she just cried, muffling the sobs as best she could. Rebecca waited in the moment. She felt the pain and depth of the hole in her heart that Ryan would leave.

"Ma'am? Excuse me, ma'am," said a soft voice.

Startled, Rebecca raised her head and wiped the tear stains.

"Yes?"

A man in a white coat and a consoling smile stood before her. Her heart sank.

"Ryan. Is he OK? Is Ryan OK?"

The man stared at her with a soft and comforting smile.

"Please, God, tell me he's going to live."

"I have an update on Mr. Ryan Miller," said the man, arms crossed, averting his gaze to the ground. "Would you please come with me so we can go somewhere more private?"

PART THREE

30

The resonating sounds of footsteps dissipated as the Heilen turned a corner with one of Baal Hadad's chamber guards. The boy's Traces were perplexing. Hadad turned, stepping back up onto the dais, admiring the craftsman detail of the cedar wood throne. He stood, facing the ornately carved face of the bull that sat atop.

What are You planning? he thought.

He stepped forward, turning, then lowered himself into the seat. He drummed his fingers on the armrest as he stared across the long chamber. The crystal window on the opposite wall displayed chaotic lightning strikes in the distance. He replayed the Traces in his mind.

"Guard," he said.

"Yes, Your Prince."

"Summon Acantha. I need her advisement."

"Yes, Your Prince."

The stoic guard stepped backward from his position into a passageway, momentarily disappearing before returning almost instantly. He walked to the center of the chamber, turning to face Hadad. The guard bowed with an arm outstretched to the passageway as Acantha's flowing dark robes entered the room."

"I must say that I was pleasantly surprised to hear from you, Baal Hadad. I thought you forgot about me."

"Please, Acantha, for you I am merely Hadad. It's good to see you, my friend. It has been a while."

"Indeed it has," she said. "Superior has me working on some special projects, so I have been rather preoccupied."

"I think our time in Eden was the last time I saw you, was it not?" said Hadad.

"Yes," said Acantha, a shadow of a scowl flashing across her face. "The end of the beginning for those creatures. Our existence would be very different if it were not for them. The growing infection of that planet. They don't deserve even a moment in His presence."

"The Council will be reunited in its entirety one day," said Hadad.

"They took our spot," she said, sneering. "That was supposed to be us."

"It won't be long. I hear Superior has been making good progress with negotiations with Him."

"I can't speak to those," said Acantha, "but some of our strategies are quite intriguing. We surprised even ourselves."

"Superior has been keeping me abreast of the developments. But as much as I am enjoying this chat, I do have a request. Can I show you something? I need some assistance with interpreting a symbol that I am not familiar with."

"Show me," said Acantha.

"This is still under investigation, so I would appreciate your discretion with the others, but given your background, I thought it appropriate to show you."

"Of course. I am happy to be of assistance."

Hadad rose from his throne, stepping down to the level with Acantha. He extended two fingers, clasping the others with his thumb as he painted sweeping strokes in the air in front of him. A purple streak remained behind his hands and fingers curved in the air, methodically retracing the figure from memory as it now took shape before them. Acantha stepped closer, adjusting her sash.

"Fascinating," she said.

"I knew you would think so."

Hadad continued tracing, adding further details of the vibrations of each stroke and color.

"It was dynamic," said Hadad, "so this was all I saw at the moment, but I could tell there were further packages buried."

He finished with a final finger sweep circling the top. Acantha stepped around the pulsating figure.

"Where did you see such a thing?" asked Acantha.

"It was in Traces."

"Nonsense, I've never anointed such a Trace set."

"This wasn't one of yours," said Hadad.

"This is a human's Traces? Certainly not. I've inspected each of them myself. None are even remotely close to this."

"No, of course not."

"Then where?" asked Acantha.

"A new angel."

Hadad traced another set of strokes over the top of the existing symbols.

"A new Archangel," he said.

Hadad could see the concern on her face as she returned her gaze to him.

"He's creating again," she said.

"Yes."

"What do you make of such a thing?"

"I've never seen one of us with these markings before," said Hadad. "This type of power was never discussed in the Council meetings."

"Did you see this new angel?"

"Right here in my own quarters," he said.

"This is concerning, Hadad. You don't need me to know what those symbols mean."

"Humor me. I'd love to hear your thoughts."

Acantha stared at him for a moment. Her eyes returned to the symbols. She encircled the floating figure, examining it from all sides. She stopped.

"This," she said, repeatedly pointing at a segment that he knew would draw her attention. "This is not normal."

"How so?" asked Hadad. He knew how so.

"Our Traces are dynamic, but they are contained. We have our purpose. When we left, Superior showed us how to grow into fuller potential beyond our Traces. But this? This is a feedback system."

She traced a line around and through several of the floating characters.

"This being becomes more powerful with resistance," she said. "Exponentially."

"I see."

"And this," she pointed to a glowing red orb that slowly spiraled up and down in a helix pattern. "It's a storehouse of strength. This angel is not dependent on the momentary flow strengths within the Fields."

"What exactly does that mean for us?" asked Hadad.

"It means that despite our redirection of the forces of the humans to the Princes' Fields, even if in a region that we completely own, this being will be able to operate unbounded. And it will operate with depths of strength that we have never seen."

"This would seem to be a meaningless attempt to display power and intimidate," said Hadad. "Look at how feeble the creatures are. So easily confused. It will not be difficult to gain their trust and adoration regardless of this new being."

"Even when we are able to get the humans to put their guardians in chains, this being will actually be made stronger," said Acantha.

"But even so, it still must abide by the rules of engagement. He would never violate His own rules."

"This is true," said Acantha, "but what would His purpose be creating an angel like this unless He were mounting an attack?"

"Therein lies the question, Acantha."

"Have you informed Superior?" she asked.

"Not yet. I only recently became aware of the new angel's existence."

Acantha nodded with strength.

"Superior will know what to do," she said.

"Of course."

"What did this Host look like?" asked Acantha. "Did he engage with you?"

"He was just a boy," said Hadad. "He hid behind those he traveled with. Hardly intimidating. Why do you think He created such a small boy to carry Traces like this?"

"Potential," said Acantha without hesitating.

"In what way?" asked Hadad. "The Council saw every Host and creature He created. None were as young as this."

"Hosts that are raised grow deeper roots during their maturation process. It allows them to support greater power. Given what I see here, it is not surprising."

"How long will we have until he reaches full potential?"

"Difficult to say," said Acantha. "These Traces are quite weighty. Perhaps a few millennia by Earth's measures."

"So we have time."

Acantha bent down and leaned in to examine more closely.

"Maybe, but perhaps not," she said. "This store here is particularly concerning."

She encircled a small orb with her finger.

"How so?" said Hadad.

"The store is the Throne," said Acantha.

"His Throne? How can that be?"

"In theory from what I see, this is a potentially limitless power. It isn't really even a store. It is a direct connection to the Throne."

"The Throne of Justice never leaves the Throne Room," said Hadad.

"Precisely," said Acantha. "This connection allows its power out."

"No other Host has such a connection directly to that room. Why the boy?"

"I can only speculate what that means. I've never seen that power released."

"No one has," said Hadad. "The Council never agreed to such an allowance."

"Never was a reason before, I suppose," said Acantha.

"Thank you for your time. Your input has been illuminating."

"When will you be showing Superior? He needs to know about this."

"I will travel to him as soon as you leave."

"Does anyone else know about this?"

"No, you are the only one."

"This will be alarming for them," said Acantha. "Superior will need to be careful that this does not lead to a mutiny of his own."

"Surely you aren't insinuating that Superior is unable to handle his own army?" spat Hadad.

Acantha took a breath.

"Of course not," she said. "Please keep me informed."

"Of course," said Hadad. "It was a pleasure, Acantha. And please, don't feel like you need an invitation. I always enjoy our visits."

Acantha nodded without speaking, bowing slightly. She turned and walked across the chamber, turning at the guard, and proceeded back through the passage, disappearing.

Hadad returned to his throne and sat. He gestured to pull the symbols that still floated in the air closer to him. He twisted his hand to rotate it, inspecting further. He wondered what Superior would make of this new development. The plans were unlikely to change, but this would need to be handled.

Hadad stood abruptly, dissolving the symbols as he stepped through them.

"I am going to see Superior," he said to the chamber guard, who stepped aside as Hadad walked by, entering the golden doorway.

31

His eyes struggled to open against their own weight. He left them closed. A metronome ticked, timed perfectly to the throbbing in his head. Half notes.

Will someone turn that off? he thought but only managed a flat groan when his mouth opened. Ryan turned his head toward the noise, straining his eyes open. Blurry. He tried to speak again, but his mouth felt locked in place, only managing a slightly louder groan.

His eyes were swimming, but he could make out machines and wires. The smell of disinfectant surrounded him. Ryan saw a green monitor with movements on it. It seemed to be painting the unrelenting beeping.

He ran his dry tongue across the roof of his mouth, swallowing a few times to try and regain some moisture. Vomit. The memory returned.

Still a failure, you piece of shit.

I can't do anything right.

You're going to wish you were dead when Rebecca finds out about this. Rebecca. Oh Jesus, Rebecca.

Ryan could already hear her voice yelling at him in his mind. It got louder. Her voice wasn't in his head. He kept his eyes closed.

"Jesus, Ryan, what the hell were you thinking?" said Rebecca.

"Ma'am, he's just regained consciousness," said a man's voice. "Please, no interrogation."

Ryan knew he couldn't escape and mustered what little courage he had to force open his eyes and turned to the voice. He saw the unmistakable white coat of a doctor step in front of Rebecca, but not before he locked eyes with her.

"How are you feeling, Ryan?" asked the man, leaning down over Ryan's face, shining a light into his eyes. Ryan blinked. "I'm Dr. Jones. You probably have quite the headache."

Ryan groaned. "Yeah."

"That's to be expected," the doctor continued, adjusting a mask over Ryan's nose and mouth. "You were in respiratory arrest when the paramedics found you. We're monitoring your vitals closely. Your heart rate and O2 saturation are stable for now. You're lucky they found you when they did. The next 24 hours are crucial, but don't worry. We'll keep you under observation for any complications. We're going to take good care of you."

The doctor's kind eyes gave Ryan a short-lived moment of comfort.

Can't even get this right, you dumb shit.

Ryan blinked slowly as the weight of the situation refilled his mind. The doctor stood, replacing a pen in his pocket. "Are you up for visitors?"

He looked at Rebecca, who stared at Ryan over the doctor's shoulder in silence.

"Yeah," said Ryan.

"OK, I'll leave you be. Press the button there if you need anything. The nurse will be back in to check on you in a bit."

The doctor turned to Rebecca.

"No yelling, understand?" he said sternly.

"Of course," said Rebecca with a meek smile as the doctor turned to exit the room.

Rebecca slowly approached the bed, clearly attempting to contain herself. She reached for Ryan's hand. She said no words, but he heard the questions.

"I just couldn't put up with it anymore, you know?" said Ryan. "We both know I'm not going anywhere in life. Look at me."

Ryan held out his arms before dropping them limp on the bed in surrender.

"What happened?" asked Rebecca, gentler than he expected. "I just saw you a couple of days ago, and you were fine."

He wasn't sure how to answer.

"Something happened," she said. "I see it. What the hell

happened?"

Ryan paused, not sure if he wanted to open this can of worms.

"Your mom," he said softly.

Rebecca winced, shaking her head.

"What?"

"Your mom," repeated Ryan. "That's what happened."

"I don't understand."

"Your mom came to my place."

"She did what?" said Rebecca, catching her rising tone.

"I don't know," said Ryan. "She just showed up at my door and was talking crazy. It just made rethink everything that's been going on. Look at me, Ree. I look like absolute shit. I feel like absolute shit."

You are absolute shit.

"I am absolute shit," he said.

"Ryan, you aren't shit," said Rebecca, moving to sit on the edge of the bed. "Look, my mom did some terrible things to you. That wasn't your fault. You're just trying to survive."

"Exactly. I'm done just surviving. This just isn't worth it."

Rebecca sighed and pursed her lips.

"What did she say? When did this even happen?"

"Right before I called you," said Ryan.

"This doesn't make any sense. What did she want?"

"Me, I think."

"What does that even mean?" asked Rebecca, shaking her head.

"She wanted me to move in with her."

"What? The fuck."

"Exactly," said Ryan.

Rebecca rubbed her eyes.

"I'm sorry, this makes absolutely no fucking sense."

Rebecca leaned back and pumped invisible brakes with her hands.

"You're telling me my mom. MY. MOTHER. Came to your place and asked you to move in with her?"

"Yeah."

"Why would she want that? She hasn't spoken to you in years, right?"

"I don't know, Ree. It was all crazy. She was saying how I needed someone to help take care of me now that my mom was gone and that she was the only one that could help me."

Rebecca whipped her head back to face Ryan.

"Holy shit. This is crazy," she said.

Rebecca stood, her hands on her hips, and turned around, processing what Ryan recounted. She turned back.

"I can't believe the nerve of that woman," she said.

"When I saw her, it was like I was a little kid again," said Ryan. "I didn't even know what was going on."

"What did you say?"

"Can we not talk about this right now?" he sighed.

"Ryan, you're in the goddamn hospital right now with a tube in your arm. I thought you were dead. I had to find your body covered in puke. You don't get to avoid this. I need to know what happened."

Ryan let out a reluctant groan, knowing the response.

"I said yes," he said.

"You did what?" said Rebecca with disbelief, leaning in towards him.

"I don't know. It was a blur, and I panicked. I'm getting kicked out of my place, and she was offering a free place to live."

Ryan knew his justification was weak.

"Wait, so you actually want to move in with her? Ryan, she molested you. Why on Earth would you go to live with her? Are you out of your mind?"

Ryan looked around at the room.

"I think that's pretty clear," he said. "Look, it all happened so fast. I don't even know why I agreed to do it. That's when things got...a little out of control...But, she had a point."

"So that's when you called me?"

"Yeah."

Rebecca sat down in the chair next to the bed and stared at the wall as the anger on her face melted away.

"And that's when I told you to basically fuck off," she said.

"Yeah, pretty much."

"A couple of months ago, I was sitting in a chair just like this one with your mom's body. Here I am with you. I'm like the fucking angel of death."

Rebecca sniffled, attempting to stifle tears as her face scrunched.

"You can't move in with her," she said.

"I know. Why do you think I'm in this bed? I already tried to get out of this. I don't have any options, Ree. My life is over."

"Move in with me," said Rebecca.

"Ree, I can't do that. Frank would lose his shit. I heard him on the phone already. You know he wouldn't go for that."

"It's better than living with my mom. Look at you, Ryan. You went into a tailspin just by seeing her. You can't go back to her. Not after everything that happened. It's just…wrong."

"I just don't see what else I can do."

"I'll talk with Frank. You're coming to stay with us, at least for a little bit. No more questions about it. It's already settled."

Rebecca stood, turning to face him.

"You aren't going to try anything else, are you?"

Ryan shook his head, breaking eye contact.

"Not right now, at least."

"I love you, Ryan. Don't do anything stupid."

Ryan pursed his lips barely into a smile to look at her.

"See you, Ree."

Rebecca turned and walked out, leaving only the sounds of the beeping monitors. He dropped his head back onto the pillow with a sigh.

"What the fuck am I even doing with my life?"

Getting ready for the next fuck-up, you stupid shit. You know that by now.

"I just can't keep doing this. Over and over. I'm just done trying."

Too bad you did such a shitty job killing yourself. Mid-twenties and still haven't accomplished anything. Well, you took care of your aunt's needs, so there's that.

You are alive.

"I am alive. That's all I have."

That's all you need.

Give it a few days. You'll be ready to try again.

32

Rebecca opened the door, tossing her keys in the dish. Frank sat on the couch.

"What happened?" he asked, as if she were returning from the grocery store.

"He's alive."

Frank scoffed.

"I'm honestly surprised this hasn't happened sooner," he said.

"Really, Frank?" said Rebecca, removing her jacket and draping it on the back of the couch. "That's what you want to start with? I just found my cousin's body on the verge of death, and your words of comfort are that 'he should have done it sooner.'"

That worthless shit doesn't deserve you.

"All I'm saying is, he's been depressed as long as I've known him," said Frank. "I'm just surprised he hasn't tried something like this before."

"Unbelievable. Is there even an ounce of compassion in that dry carcass of yours?"

"For him, no. He should have gotten over all that stuff by now. He's a grown man. Always the martyr. Always an excuse for why things aren't working. It's pathetic. I don't know why you bother with him."

"'All that stuff?'" said Rebecca in disbelief. "You mean the years of child abuse?"

Frank changed the channel on the television, not making eye contact with her.

"It couldn't have been that bad," he said. "She didn't even go to jail.

She was probably just being weird."

Rebecca shook her head.

"I'm not having this conversation with you right now. Ryan is in the hospital. When he gets out, he's coming to live with us."

Frank turned off the TV, setting the remote down hard, and turned to face her.

"I'm sorry," he said. "I'm going to let you repeat that because I think I just heard you say that you invited your piece-of-shit cousin to move in here."

"He needs a place to stay, Frank. He can't go back to that apartment by himself. What if he kills himself?"

"Then the world would be a better place, Ree," said Frank, throwing his gorilla arms in the air. "He's a pitiful sack of shit. If he didn't kill himself this time, he'll figure it out eventually. Even he's not that incompetent."

"How can you say something like that? He's family."

"Where do you draw the line, Ree?" asked Frank. "Do you really want Liam walking in to find him on the floor next time? Good god, Ree. When are you going focus on your actual family? Your real flesh and blood in front of you instead of him?"

"That's not fair," said Rebecca.

"Fair?" said Frank, feigning offense. "You abandoned us for *months* while you took care of your aunt. She raised you. I get it. We made it work. But him? He's absolutely worthless. How much more are you going to stretch this family? Do you even want to be a part of this family, or should we get divorced and let you move on?"

"You can't throw around a word like that, Frank."

"I'm not throwing it around, Ree. I'm honestly looking at your behavior and wondering if you even want to be in this family. You were going to leave us to go on a road trip with that deadbeat to a concert. Now you want to play house with your addict cousin?"

"What choice do I have?" said Rebecca. "He needs me."

"We need you, Ree," said Frank, his volume quickly rising. "We are your family. Us. Your son, Liam. Remember him?"

Rebecca couldn't hold back her tears any longer. She wiped away what she could, snatching her jacket from the couch. She needed to get out.

"Of course. Run away again," said Frank. "Can't handle your own responsibilities, so just run, Ree. Run away. Don't worry. I'll take care of our kid. Have a good time. We'll be here when you get back."

Her emotional dam broke for a moment as she unsuccessfully tried to pull back a sob.

"I can't do this right now," she said with stuttering breath.

"Whatever, Ree. You do your thing, but that cousin of yours better not be with you when you get back."

Rebecca grabbed her keys, slipping out the door and shut it behind her. The cold silence was welcome. She collapsed into the wicker chair on the porch.

"You're going to be fine," she said to herself. She didn't believe it.

When are you going to tell him the real reason you don't want to be around the house?

"That's her, not me," said Rebecca. "I'm not her."

You've got her blood. Apple doesn't fall far from the tree, does it?

"I'm not my mother."

That bitch really ruined things for you, didn't she?

"She just keeps causing problems for everyone."

What are you going to do about it? Are you going to let her keep interfering with your life?

"She's not even in my life."

You can put a stop to her once and for all. Or do you prefer to just let her run your life from afar?

"I don't want anything to do with her."

You could talk to her.

Rebecca laughed at her own thought.

"Shit, I haven't talked to her in years."

She's going to keep interfering if you don't do anything about it.

"I don't think I could face her. Not after all these years. Not after what she did to Ryan. And showing up at his house? That was low even for her."

What happens if she goes over to see him again? He survived last time, barely. You can't be there to save him every time.

Flashbacks of Ryan's limp body raced through her head.

"I can't go through it again."

No, you can't. You can't let that happen to family.

Rebecca let out a groan as she swallowed the fresh tears that were beginning to well up.

You know that you need to see her.

Rebecca released her belabored breath knowing she needed to see the woman.

33

Rebecca sniffled in silence, only the sounds of passing cars breaking through. She yawned as the day's events were catching up to her. She shook her head awake.

"My life is out of control. I can't be getting involved with this stuff anymore."

You need to protect your family.

Rebecca pulled into an open spot on the street. Darkness cloaked the well-manicured neighborhood. Streetlights highlighted cars along the road. Rebecca had never been inside, but she drove by many times, looking to catch a glimpse of the woman she once knew.

Rebecca's memories of her mother were strong, even though she went to live with Aunt Hat at a fairly young age. Her mother was always put together, no matter where she went. The few times Rebecca spotted her in the yard during a drive-by, she was always in a blouse and lifted heels, even if she was working in the flower beds.

This wasn't the house she grew up in, but it was eerily similar. Same cream paint color, gray roof, same English garden landscaping. Her mother was a creature of habit, and it showed at every level.

Consistent is comfort.

She could hear her mother's words ringing in her ears.

Rebecca felt guilty at times for living with Aunt Hat. She and Uncle George always seemed to be financially struggling, and after all, aside from you know what, her mother was a good mom. Etta played with her, fed her well, and seemed to truly love her. Not even Rebecca knew what was going on inside. She still didn't. Rebecca heard bits and pieces from Ryan, but he would lock up almost as soon as he started talking.

The unspoken rule of the house was to never discuss the incident.

What happens in the past.

"Stays in the past," she said aloud.

Until it doesn't.

Rebecca's curiosity would sometimes get the best of her. Even now, it was almost too hard to believe. Her mother was and still is well-respected in the community. Maybe that's the real reason Aunt Hat never pursued anything legally. Her mother always made it a point to let people know in the most subtle of ways that she was the more successful of the sisters. The more godly. The more beautiful.

It wasn't until her teen years that Rebecca heard the cover story that her mother was spreading after Rebecca stumbled into a conversation with one of her mother's church friends in high school. Etta told her inner circle that Aunt Hat became infertile after Tess was born and after the accident, her heart was devastated to know she would never get to hold a daughter.

"How is your Aunt doing, Dear?" she heard the woman say. "Your mother Etta is just the most generous person I know. I couldn't imagine sacrificing my own happiness just so my sister could experience joy. A true hero, you know."

Rebecca shook her head at the memory. Prior to that moment, Rebecca thought about reconnecting with her mother after she was out of Aunt Hat's home, but that moment closed the door. Rebecca wasn't a daughter. She was a social chess piece for maximum leverage. She was the sacrifice that saved her mother.

Rebecca sat in the darkness of her car, hands still on the wheel as she looked to the house for any signs of movement.

She may not even be home, she told herself.

She's home.

A light flicked off behind the curtains of the front room.

"She's home," sighed Rebecca. "She's home."

Rebecca opened the car door reluctantly, standing to give herself another moment to change her mind.

You know you need to see her.

"I need to see her. She's going to keep pushing."

Rebecca shut the door with determination and approached the

house. The short driveway was flanked with flowering bushes. It was a beautiful house, much nicer than the one she ultimately grew up in. She approached the door. A cold sweat ran down her forehead as a wave of nausea passed through her stomach. *It's just nerves*, she told herself. Rebecca took a deep breath, blowing out the nerves. She rang the doorbell and stepped back. No sounds.

Maybe she's not home, she thought. *I'll just come back.*

She's home.

Before Rebecca could turn away, she heard soft footsteps slowly approaching the door. She caught the light change in the peephole, and she heard a gasp on the other side of the door. The lock jolted, and the door swung. There stood a familiar face. An older version, worn, but smiling. Etta stood in the doorway, silent, frozen in the moment. Neither spoke in the standoff.

Etta suddenly reanimated.

"Is everything all right?" she asked. "I wasn't expecting you to come by."

Etta's cheerful tone became more somber.

"Look at how beautiful you are," she said. "I didn't know if I would ever see you again."

"I didn't know either," said Rebecca.

The two women stared at each other, caught, unsure how to navigate the moment. Etta was still wearing makeup and hair tightly wound into a bun as if she was expecting a visitor. Always prepared.

"Can I come in?" asked Rebecca, breaking the silence.

"Oh yes, of course."

Etta stepped aside as Rebecca entered the house, smelling the familiar perfume of her mother. Jasmine.

"It looks the same," said Rebecca in the entryway. Etta closed the door, stepping around in front of Rebecca.

"I like things the way they are," said Etta. "Oh Rebecca, it's so good to see you. Have you been crying, Dear?"

"I heard you went to see Ryan," said Rebecca, refusing her mother's trademark small talk.

Etta's face changed to controlled composure.

"Yes," she said, looking down at the floor and her arm leaning on the back of the recliner. "I wanted to offer my condolences. I had hoped to do so at the funeral, but he wasn't there—did you see me at the funeral? I was trying to say hello—such a pity he didn't go to his own mother's funeral. I don't know how my sister raised him to be so—"

"You didn't think showing up unannounced to his house was pushing it a little far given, you know, your history with him?" said Rebecca, carefully monitoring her tone.

"Don't be silly, Rebecca. I was just stopping by. He's a grown man now, Rebecca. He can take care of himself. I'm a little old lady."

"Is that why you asked him to move in here?"

"He's family, Dear. We take care of family," said Etta with confidence before pulling back. "And you've seen him. He could use a little extra help. Have you been to his place? It looks like a wild animal lives there."

Etta tugged at her cardigan over her shoulders.

"Truly dreadful," she said.

Rebecca drew back, eyes roaming the ceiling as they searched her mind for one of the many threads of this conversation to dive down.

"Mom, that was completely inappropriate," she said.

That word tasted bad in her mouth.

"I was just trying to be helpful," said Etta.

"Do you realize he ended up in the hospital because of you?"

Etta took a step closer, clasping her hands.

"Oh no, is he all right? What happened?"

Rebecca took a step back to maintain her distance.

"He tried to kill himself," she said.

"What?" said Etta, putting her hand on her chest. "That is terrible."

"He's alive, barely."

Etta let out her breath.

"Well that is a relief. Is he still in the hospital? Shall we go visit him? I'll get my coat."

Etta started to turn.

"Don't you get it?!" Rebecca shouted, throwing her hands in the air as her internal restraints began to break. "You are the problem. You. You destroyed his life and just when he finally had a chance to move on, you showed up at his door wanting to play mommy to him. Again. It's disgusting. You! You are disgusting."

Rebecca felt the boil of anger in her chest rising up.

"I don't understand," Etta said, lowering her tone. "We had such a nice conversation. He seemed open to the idea. I thought we ended on a good note."

"He was probably just telling you what you wanted to hear, just like you trained him. Remember?"

"Rebecca, don't be foolish. Your aunt blew that situation way out of proportion. You were a kid. I don't blame you for not remembering what happened."

"You are unreal," said Rebecca, feeling her stomach tighten. "Ryan tried to kill himself because of you."

Etta tossed her hand.

"Oh, come now, he did no such thing," she said.

Etta stepped forward, reaching for Rebecca's hands. Rebecca promptly slapped them away, taking another step back. The boil reached Rebecca's shoulders.

"Please, Rebecca, don't be like this. Don't you see? We have a chance at a new life together. I wanted to respect my sister's wishes, but she's gone now. She doesn't need to stand in between us. Any of us. Please. I hear you have a family now? I saw at the funeral. You have a son?"

Etta reached for Rebecca again.

"Do not. Touch. Me," said Rebecca. "And do not talk about my son."

The boil was in her ears. She felt the heat.

"I just want us to have a relationship, Rebecca. You are my daughter. Look at you. We are so much ali—"

"I am nothing like you," interrupted Rebecca.

"Please, let's just sit down," said Etta. "Things are getting a little heated. You're getting all worked up."

Etta grabbed Rebecca by the hand and began to pull her towards the couch. Rebecca pulled her arm back, but Etta didn't lose her grip.

"Rebecca please, just come sit on the couch. I'll make some tea."

Her grip did not relent.

"Get off of me!" shouted Rebecca.

She shook her arm, trying to break free. Etta's grip felt unnaturally strong for the old woman.

Etta reached for her other hand.

"I said no!" said Rebecca.

She used her free hand to push Etta in the chest in an effort to escape. The boil flowed from Rebecca's eyes. With another jerk of her body, Rebecca was free. The sudden movement threw Etta off balance in her raised heel shoes. She stumbled to the side before fully losing her balance. Etta let out a panicked shriek. Her aging body tumbled backward as one leg collapsed underneath her, sending her quickly to the left. Etta hit her head squarely on the corner of the solid marble coffee table on her way down. The hollow thud of her skull making contact was a sound that Rebecca had never heard before. Etta's limp body dropped, finally resting on the floor, motionless. Rebecca stared as a slowly growing pool of blood began to form beneath Etta's hair.

"Oh God," said Rebecca.

You killed the bitch. Great job.

Rebecca froze, waiting expectantly for the old resilient woman to rise as she always did from any challenge. Etta lay motionless, the pool of blood growing.

Let her die.

Rebecca searched the room and found the phone. She dialed. The operator picked up after what seemed like an eternity.

"Please, I need help. My mother hit her head, and she's not moving. There's a lot of blood."

"Stay calm, ma'am. Is your mother breathing?" asked the dispatch.

"I don't know. She fell. Please send someone quickly."

"Okay, I need you to check if she's breathing. Can you get close to her mouth and nose? See if you can feel or hear any breath."

Rebecca stepped around her mother, avoiding the continually growing pool of blood. She leaned down, holding her own breath as she listened.

"I don't—no, I don't think she is," said Rebecca.

"Alright, I'm dispatching an ambulance to your location. How did she hit her head? Was she standing or sitting or doing something? Where you there when it happened?"

"She just tripped and fell. Please hurry. She's not moving."

"OK, do you have a towel nearby? Can you apply some pressure to the wound?"

Rebecca looked around. She spotted a basket of freshly folded linens on the ground. She grabbed one, rushing back to Etta, kneeling down. She put the phone on speaker, setting it on the table as she crouched.

"OK, I have a towel," she said.

Rebecca cradled her mother's head. She could feel the warm blood soaking through to her hands, collecting underneath her knuckles before dripping onto the floor.

"Good," said the dispatch. "Apply gentle pressure, but don't press too hard. Just keep it steady until the paramedics arrive. You're doing great."

"OK, I will. But please hurry."

Rebecca stared down at the pale face of her mother. All she could do now was wait.

34

George sat in a finely carved wooden porch swing with Hattie, gently swaying in front of her new home in the cool air as a dazzling sunset of purples peaked above the trees. Hattie admired the distant houses, wondering who lived there.

"It was amazing," said Hattie. "I was right there in the room, but the evil things couldn't see me. Then the angels showed up. *BOOM*."

George laughed.

"Those 'evil things' are called 'the Fallen,'" he said. "I'm really proud of you for completing your first mission. It's always a big step."

"Is there even such a thing as a small step here? Every moment I turn around is something new. But this, I can get used to this."

Hattie held her hand out above a small table next to the swing. A cup and saucer popped into existence, clinking as they settled. Hattie watched as the dark colored tea filled from the bottom.

"I see you have been settling in well," said George with a smile.

Hattie nodded excitedly, pulling the cup to her lips to take a sip.

"But I do worry about Ryan. I just want to protect him. I couldn't stand seeing that black thing living inside of him. And it's still there."

Hattie shuttered at the memory of the foul-mouthed black creature.

"I just want to see him free of that thing," she said.

George nodded.

"We all do," he said. "Ryan is one of many assignments that we will be working."

George looked above Hattie's head.

"And by the looks of it, you'll have plenty of work to do," he said.

Hattie set the cup down.

"You can read those things?" she asked.

"Sort of. I can feel it just like you can feel it. You'll start to see the patterns."

"When I was with Aleifr, I could feel it."

Hattie pointed upwards towards her Traces.

"All I could feel was 'comfort,'" she said. "I still don't really understand it."

George gave her a knowing smile.

"You will continue to unfold it with each mission," he said. "This is an eternity-long journey we are on, Hattie. Just think about what you did with Rebecca. The work you did created the space to give her a reprieve from her own torment. You provided her comfort."

"Hmm, I guess I didn't think of it like that."

George looked up his own Traces.

"What about me? What do you see?"

Hattie stared for a moment. George's Traces were differently colored than hers, but peculiarly, they flowed together with her own, creating a larger set of symbols above them both. She looked at George.

"Our destinies were intertwined from the foundations of the world," he said. "On Earth, we married to represent that union. Here, we continue to operate as one."

Hattie smiled. She didn't understand, but it felt good.

"I'm no expert here," said George, "but I think you'll be helping people understand who they are. People on Earth are only uncomfortable because they don't know their own identity. They see themselves as doctors or plumbers or students, but that isn't who they really are. It's why we were never really satisfied. We never accepted our true identities."

Hattie waited.

"And that is?" said Hattie, hanging for a response. "And don't you dare tell me that it will be revealed in time, Mr. George Davis. What are our true identities?"

George laughed.

"We are slivers of an Infinite Being. Perfectly packaged subsets to uniquely express different characteristics. Our earthly careers are merely manifestations of that identity. It's no wonder you enjoyed being a mother or helping out in the community. It's baked into you.

It's in your DNA. It's in your spirit. It's in our spirits. The Traces that Spirit sang over us made us that way."

For once since this journey began, Hattie did not have a follow-up question. She felt the weight of George's statement. *It's who I am.*

George continued. "So many are unhappy or unfulfilled because they refused to acknowledge who they really were and choose paths in life that contradict that. They think they are depressed or tired, when in reality, they just have not aligned with what was sung over them. When they align, those vibrations generate energy instead of resistance."

Hattie stared off into the distance trying to process George's words. They made sense, but there was so much to what was said. As she stared off beyond the porch, a jagged streak of blue flashed at the foot of the steps. She sat up straight with a jolt.

A large and powerful looking angel appeared, slowly climbing the steps. His shoulder-length hair looked like waving reeds, and his bronze skin glistened in the light. A wide and welcoming smile stretched across his face. He glanced at her before turning his gaze to George.

"I heard the good news," said the being.

Hattie turned to see George already on his feet, moving towards the angel.

"Friend!" shouted George.

They embraced.

"I've been watching you for a while, Hattie," said the being. "It is so good to finally meet you face to face."

Hattie did not respond, astounded by his beauty. She did not know him, but she felt a deep connection.

"Of course," said George. "You two haven't met yet. Hattie, I am pleased to introduce you to my Guardian. He is the best around. Damiel, this is my wife, Hattie."

"So good to meet you, Damiel," said Hattie. "It feels like we have known each other for a very long time."

"I have been with your family for many generations, Hattie," said Damiel. "You haven't seen it yet, but your lines have crossed paths many times throughout history. I am quite close with Aleifr. Is he here in the house?"

"I'm actually not sure exactly where he is," said Hattie. "He seems to come and go as he pleases."

"Our kinds are drawn to certain beacons," said Damiel.

"I don't know what that means, but I'm sure I'll learn about it in the university courses," said Hattie.

George laughed, changing the subject.

"Where have you been, Damiel? It feels like I haven't seen you in who knows how long."

"An urgent but temporary mission specifically directed by Creator," said Damiel. "I have also been following the developments within your line, Hattie. I am so pleased to hear that your son's intervention was successful."

"I miss seeing him," said Hattie, "but it wasn't his time to be here. I had no idea this is what Heaven would be like. Eating grapes on clouds does sound nice, but saving the world is a lot more fun."

"Speaking of which," said Damiel, "that is why I am here. Creator asked me to bring you to a celebratory feast. It's a custom for completion of first missions for the Heirs."

Hattie had not eaten anything since her welcome feast in the home but was not hungry. Yet, food never sounded so good.

"I hear there are some additional guests of honor that have been requesting to meet with you," said Damiel.

Hattie stood up.

"What are you waiting for?" she asked. "Let's get moving!"

Damiel smiled a gently, turning to walk back down the steps of the porch. At the base of the steps, he reached down to the ground, grasping something invisible to her eye, moving his hand above head height. The space in front of them seemed to unzip up, revealing a glowing yellow light behind it.

"Is this a door?" asked Hattie.

"In a way, yes," said Damiel. "But it's a little faster. After you."

He held out his welcoming arm as George and Hattie stepped down the porch, cleaving their way through the opening and stepped into the light.

Hattie's senses were met with an immediate chorus of songbirds. She smelled the sweet blending of harmonious notes in her nose just as strongly as in her ears. She closed her eyes in pure bliss.

"Trust me, it never gets old," she heard George say. "Just wait for what Creator has for you."

35

"My friends!" said the unmistakable voice.

Hattie opened her eyes to see Creator standing at the head of a long table, which sat in a clearing within a vast meadow. No trees or structures as far as the eye could see. Only hills and flowers. The flower's tiny bursts of color shone through the thick green billowing grasses. Hattie looked into the distance. The flowers swayed in the wind, crests of color and gradient building and shifting. They appeared as a sea of undulating gemstones.

As the gentle breeze blew through the hillsides, the scents that passed Hattie's nose played like the strings of a violin. As the flowers shifted from side to side, their colors darkened and lightened, sending plumes of rainbow color across the ocean of the horizon. She was entranced.

"You've been busy!" said Creator. "Please, come and join Me."

Creator welcomed them over and stepped away from the table, the ornate and detailed carvings blending with the naturalistic scene. The table almost appeared as if it had sprouted up from the ground, exactly as intended.

Creator stepped towards them with arms out, embracing both George and Hattie before turning towards Damiel.

"I am glad to see you have reunited, Damiel," He said. "I appreciate your flexibility with taking care of our other mission. Hattie, Damiel here has been watching over your line for many years along with Aleifr. He has so many stories that I know you will enjoy. And he's a bit chattier than Aleifr, so you might be able to get some more details out of him."

"I heard that," said Aleifr, stepping through another zipper of light behind the table.

"Why do you think I said it?" said Creator.

"I have to confess," said Hattie, "I remember thinking Heaven might be boring. It seemed like perfection would be uneventful, and yet here we are in perfect perfection, and the adventure we experience at every moment is beyond description."

"If humanity really knew what true life looked like," said Creator, "they would be rushing the gates, but I'll let you in on a not-so-secret secret. All of this is what Earth should be like. It is the job of the Heirs to bring this Kingdom to Earth. Now please, have a seat. We have a few more guests arriving momentarily, but I would love to hear about your first mission's experience, Hattie. But before that, some tea."

Teacups popped onto table first. Then empty platters and then sandwiches, fruits, and pastries filled the space. Steam appeared over the cups as tea filled.

"English tea sounds nice, don't you think?" asked Creator. "Please, take a seat anywhere."

Hattie walked to the nearest high-backed chair and sat down. The others followed.

"I just don't even know what to say anymore," said Hattie. "I feel like I have been here forever and just a moment at the same time. I don't know if I'll ever get used to this."

She picked up the luminous, iridescent cup, its colors ranging from deep blues to greens, swimming and swirling around. She touched it to her lips, inhaling the robust and toasty aromas.

"Trust me. You won't," said Damiel. "And that's a good thing."

As they sipped, flowers continued to bloom around them, flushing in ripples of color and reacting to the gentle breeze blowing them to-and-fro.

"Now back to your adventure," said Creator. "How was it?"

Hattie pondered the recent events, of which she had no idea how long they lasted.

"I had no clue of the amount of activity that was happening here," she said. "I guess I always thought once you die and go to Heaven, the job is done, and you get to relax. All I used to think about was my heavenly retirement."

"One of humanity's biggest challenges is understanding its purpose," said Creator, tossing an unknown piece of fruit into His mouth. "When you are aligned with your purpose, work is not work. It is joy. That is why My adversary is so fixated on ensuring as many people as possible are kept fearful from stepping into their calling."

"Just like Ryan," said Hattie softly.

"Just like Ryan," said Creator. "His challenges are not over, but this experience uniquely positions him to be able to step into his fullness."

"You mean he couldn't fulfill his purpose if this didn't happen?"

Creator smiled.

Hattie looked around the table, Damiel and George both silently smiling.

"Humans are fixated on their own individual challenges," said Aleifr, "not realizing that there is a larger battle going on. A power struggle of galactic proportions. The war isn't even good versus evil. It is love and the destruction of love. Creator represents perfect love and growing it. The Fallen attempt to stop it from expanding."

"If there was no evil," said Creator, "love would abound because there would be no resistance to it. Yet, the existence of evil necessitates action on the part of love to grow."

"I think this might be over my head," said Hattie.

"Have you ever thought what *My* purpose of existence is, Hattie?" asked Creator. "The One and Almighty Creator. The One that was and is and is to come. The One with no limitations. What possibly could My purpose be?"

Hattie only stared blankly.

"What do you see in My Traces, Hattie?" He asked.

It was only when the question was presented to her that Hattie realized Creator was the only one without any Traces.

"You must expand your view Hattie," said Creator to the thought.

He held his hands out, looking around.

"This is My Traces. You are My Traces. The Kingdom are My Traces. The Heirs are My Traces. My destiny is growing love."

Hattie blinked with barely an understanding.

"Just as humanity's purpose is to learn to love and grow love on Earth, so is this only modeled after My purpose because you are modeled after Me. Love is not a molecule floating through the bloodstream of humans. Love is the disruption of the fabric of reality that turns nothing into something."

Hattie shook her head.

"I still don't know what that means," she said.

"A wave only exists because it is a disturbance of the water. An avalanche only exists due to a disturbance of the snow. Love is the ultimate disruptive element of the universe. Out of nothing, the existence of love creates something. It is only through love that we see any of this around us."

Hattie inhaled deeply, attempting to hold that immense thought in her mind.

"I am Creator. I am The Creator. Just as a painter works with paint or a sculptor works with clay, love is the medium that I work with. Love is what I use to turn something shapeless and formless and give it meaning. But love is not just My medium. Love is My being. I create with My own essence."

Creator paused, smiling, as always. Hattie had no words.

"Without love, without that disturbance, the universe and every realm would remain empty. My adversary battles humanity because he is battling against love. He is battling against his own inability to create the very thing that the universe requires for existence. In his own pride, he only sees what he individually is able to influence, not what the capacity for love could be. He fears for his own existence, thinking that he would be lost as the millennia go on. But in all of this, he was not able to see the uniqueness. Just like a snowflake, each and every disturbance in Our fabric through love is unique. It has a signature. My adversary possesses much knowledge but is not all-knowing, despite what he tells his followers. His lack of understanding prevents him from truly seeing that each signature is important, special, and recognized by Me. His desire was to put himself above Me, not knowing that I yield to those that yield to Me and oppose those who oppose Me. His effort to forcefully put himself above Me sealed his own fate, when all he needed to do was yield."

"But if You are helping to grow love and You are also love, who created You?" asked Hattie.

"I don't think you're ready for that answer just yet," said Aleifr, interjecting.

"I guess I couldn't expect You to reveal all the mysteries of the universe in one day, now, could I?" asked Hattie.

"One day?" said Creator. "We've been here for over a thousand years."

Hattie sat up straight in her chair.

"What?" she asked, startled.

"Well, it could be a few minutes or a thousand years. Which do you prefer?" asked Creator.

The table laughed.

"Heaven humor is strange, but I think I like it," said Hattie. "It just seems so simple and so complex at the same time. I'm not sure how or why that is, but it just works."

"The depths of the realms are meant for true royalty to seek out," said Creator. "You may stop at any level you like, or you may pursue further. I have hidden the mysteries of the universe in every cell of every being, waiting for brave explorers to seek them out. Each interaction has the opportunity to unveil something new."

"So is love at the top or at the bottom of that journey?" asked Hattie.

"Both, of course! Love is the primary connection, the motivation. It is also the fundamental disturbance within the Fields of reality."

"Are you saying that if I love, I can change reality?" asked Hattie.

"Now you're getting it! Love is not a combination of feel-good chemicals swimming around in your head. Your human body was built to physically behold love, but that was merely a shadow of reality. Love is a particle, as you humans can relate to it best. Love is one of the few particles that transcends realms. Love is what was sung over the vast emptiness to create Earth, the moon, and stars. Love was the breath that I breathed into the mouth of Adam. It is the particle that passes from the physical realm to the spiritual realm, allowing My children to connect with Me."

"What I still don't understand is if Your purpose is to grow love, why not just clone Yourself?" asked Hattie. "All this extra stuff seems to make things complicated. You are love, so just snap Your fingers and make more love, right?"

"Is that not what I did?" said Creator.

Hattie stared at Him blankly.

"You are My clone," He said proudly.

Hattie raised her eyebrows and shook her head.

"I don't know about that," she said.

"Love is not simply generated. Love is grown. It is impossible for

Me to simply create love because that is control, and control is the opposite of love. I had to grow love, just like you might grow a fruit tree. Plant the seed, tend to the seedling, water, fertilize, and prune. And some day, that tree will bear fruit true to its seed. That fruit grows more trees on and on and on. Hattie, you are the tree that I seek. I seek a vast forest of trees. An ecosystem of love that feeds off one another, reproducing and multiplying, creating an endless wealth of love like the universe has never seen before. It was the only way. And best of all, I got you out of it, didn't I?"

Hattie put her elbows on the table, face in her hands and rubbed her cheeks as realization washed over her mind.

"I know it's a lot to take in, and there is so much more," said Creator. "When I spoke of humanity wrestling with its purpose, herein lies the battle. A cherry tree never wonders what its purpose is. It is coded to grow and produce cherries. It never questions if it should produce apples or if it is, in fact, a dog. Yet, humans struggle constantly with finding their purpose and thinking they are something that they are not."

"It's different though, isn't it?" said Hattie, looking back to Creator. "Humans think and ponder about life. Trees don't do that."

"You don't think so? Hmm."

Creator raised His cup of tea for a sip, smacking His lips.

"That's a topic for another day," He said. "But My point is that the best way to prevent a tree from growing and bearing fruit is to prevent it from growing to become strong enough to bear fruit. If a tree is strong and in the right environment, the tree will fruit. This is what My adversary seeks to disrupt."

"He's trying to change our programming," said Hattie.

"Precisely. You are coded for love," said Creator, pointing above Hattie's head. "If given the right environment, that is what you will become, so he comes to try and interrupt that. He starves you from receiving nourishing relationships with your parents. He prods your friends to betray you. His primary goal is to create environments where love struggles to grow. He is the weeds in My garden trying to choke out life."

"So just pull the weeds and be done with it," said Hattie.

"That is an option, but that behavior also does not cultivate the land for My trees. If I pull out the weeds, the roots of My trees are disrupted. Weeds wrap their roots around those of My trees. But, even in an infantile stage, love has the ability to cut weeds down. Those weeds fall to the soil and become nourishment for the trees. In his own struggle against love, love is the only thing that can defeat his ways. Even when his roots are wrapped around you, exhibiting love regardless, is the scythe that you have to cut him down."

"But I seemed to struggle with the same things throughout my life," said Hattie. "I never felt like the weeds went away."

"The more you cut down the weeds, the weaker they become as the roots are forced to spend energy to sprout again. Over time, the weeds will die or become so weak that the tree's roots are unaffected by them.

Hattie chuckled to herself.

"What's so funny?" asked Creator.

"I just imagined that the creator of the universe wouldn't be such a—"

"Gardener?" said Creator.

"Yeah, I guess."

"My story with humanity began in a garden, so why does that surprise you now? I have a home, but I am cultivating a garden, a self-sustaining garden that grows and expands forever. I am reproducing the most powerful particle in the universe. But to do that, I need you."

"It sounds so simple when you explain it," said Hattie.

"In its essence, it truly is," said Creator. "There are many layers to what I tell you, and in time, you will see more revealed, but My purpose is quite simple. Humans spend their lives wondering about Me, but I have already given My will and purpose inside of them. The confusion comes from My adversary and the Fallen. He succeeds when he convinces a tree that it isn't a tree. He tells it that it shouldn't bear fruit. He convinces it that it is a bird or a worm. It's no wonder that confusion and lies are his primary tools. His only strength comes from attempting to disrupt the natural growth of the seed that is in each and every person."

"That's what he did to Ryan," said Hattie. "That's what he did to me."

"And every other person in the history of humanity. He attempts to confuse and isolate, preventing My trees from joining together to support one another."

"But You are the gardener," said Hattie. "Surely You can do

something about the weeds and confusion."

"If there were no weeds, no confusion, no lies, My seeds would grow and flourish just as intended. They would grow tall but frail, becoming more susceptible to adverse conditions as they grow. The weeds and the wind build strength in My trees."

"So we need the struggle?"

"Paradoxically, yes. Your ability to love grows stronger than if you were left alone."

Creator smiled again. She knew His eyes saw exactly with what she wrestled.

"You've had a few eventful moments," He said. "Perhaps it is best for you to take some time of rest to ponder what we have discussed."

"I thought we didn't sleep here?" asked Hattie.

"Rest looks different in this realm. Rest looks like communion and connection. But I suspect I know the real question you want to ask."

Hattie hesitated. Creator smiled.

"Will I get to see Ryan again?" she asked. Her voice softened. "When will I get to see Tess again?"

"Ryan's journey is just beginning. You partnered with Earth to help cut down some of the weeds. It is now up to those around him to help turn those weeds into fertilizer so that he may grow. You and he were destined together from the beginning of time. Your purpose with him and those in your family line is just beginning. As for Tess, she is in very capable hands. You will be reunited very soon."

Hattie's eye caught a glimpse of a sparkle in the corner of her eye. She turned her head. An angel, shimmering in various shades of purple but with no visible face, passed by her, approaching Creator from behind.

"Pardon my interruption," said the being, "but the guests of honor have arrived."

"Wonderful," said Creator. "Please send them in."

36

Creator rose, and Hattie followed suit with George, Aleifr, and Damiel. Hattie looked around for a door to see the special guests. She saw none. The purple being stood behind the table with its hands folded in front of its waist, motionless. Hattie continued to look around for signs of the visitors in the meadow. Suddenly, an electric green flash of light shot down out of the clear sky with a thunderous clap. Hattie involuntarily let out a startled yelp, stumbling back towards George. Creator leaned over to her.

"My apologies," said Creator. "He tends to take the express routes."

Hattie looked to the location of the lightning strike. Glowing smoke cascaded off the back of a glittering figure on the ground, head bowed and kneeling at the strike location. The shimmering rainbow of its layered folds of wings was strong, and Hattie could feel a magnetic intensity radiating off of the being. The table stood in silence. She turned to George, who looked about as shocked as she felt. Damiel and Aleifr stood stoically. Creator was grinning, but that was usual.

The being held its position for a moment, the rainbow sparkles transitioning to a silver dusting. It smoothly stood to its feet, the masculine figure towered over all the other guests with a stern look from his sparkling diamond eyes and slate blue skin. The rainbow patterning of its wings extended down onto his liquid-looking clothing. A swath of gemstones cascaded down the side of his face, across his cheek, and down his neck and chest. The complex mosaic of multiple colors glistened in the sunlight like a kaleidoscope.

Hattie felt an electric charge in the air. The being's Traces were weighty, and Hattie felt the pull and push of them as they swirled around him. They were large and robust, swirling not only around the being's head but also drifting down, draping him in a second garment of color.

The being's Traces looked unlike the others Hattie had seen. The flow of colors almost mirrored the movements of the meadow, waving hypnotically. Hattie felt the piercing stare of his diamond eyes, even as they were locked on Creator.

"Welcome back!" said Creator, breaking the silence.

He outstretched His arms and took a step toward the being. As He did, Hattie blinked a few times as she saw not Creator stepping, but perhaps the most beautiful woman she had ever seen step out of Creator's chest and hug the being. Her skin glowed gold. The woman embraced the massive being. Hattie's eyes darted back and forth between Creator and this woman.

"I have someone I'd like to introduce you to," said Creator.

He stepped around the woman, placing one hand on her shoulder and the other on the back of the being.

"Hattie, I would like to formally introduce you to one of My Archangels, Adlai. Commander of My Justice."

The being gently nodded his head in Hattie's direction.

"It's a pleasure to meet you face to face, Hattie," said Adlai, his voice gentle but deep and reverberating like a drum. "My armies have been fighting alongside and for you for quite some time. I am so very honored to be in your presence."

Hattie nearly felt embarrassed at Adlai's humbleness.

"Thank you. It is an honor for me as well," she said.

Hattie's eyes were drawn back to the woman standing beside Creator. She was beaming, still staring at Adlai.

The woman's gaze shifted to Hattie as their eyes locked. At that moment, Hattie felt an electric surge travel through her body as she felt a mix of disconnected memories racing through her mind. The thoughts zoomed through her mind's eye as her breathing increased. As if watching a movie, she saw the memories of her loneliness and joy and every emotion in between. Then silence. She returned to the present as she continued to huff.

"Hattie, do you know who this is?" asked Creator.

Hattie could not speak. She nodded "yes" without words. These were familiar feelings, but an intensity unlike anything she had felt before.

"Hello, Hattie," said the woman, her voice like a harp. The woman stepped around the table, revealing her loosely draped tunic, ebbing and flowing around her body. It was plain but the glow of her skin and hair seemed to magnify off of the white moving fabric.

The woman stepped in front of Hattie, who still was struggling to speak. The table's other guests disappeared from her view as Hattie's eyes locked on the woman. The woman took Hattie's hands. Another surge ran through her body. She knew.

"I Am," said the woman.

"The Spirit," said Hattie, breathily forcing out the words. "You're the Holy Spirit."

The woman smiled. "Spirit."

A deep feeling of comfort swept through Hattie's body as the woman remained with eyes locked and hands held with Hattie. The woman laughed a familiar, warm laugh. One Hattie recognized because it was one that she used with her own children when they amused her. The aroma of a woodsy campfire arose from the laugh.

"I know you're overwhelmed," said Spirit. "That's normal. Just feel what I am giving to you. Think about it later."

The thoughts from before raced back, but this time, Hattie saw the connections. The times where she felt left out or ignored by others. When things didn't go her way, and she became frustrated, she saw the missing piece. She saw the orchestration. She also saw Spirit standing right beside her."

"I never mean for you to feel ignored or slighted, Hattie," said Spirit. "But I am always working. Sometimes that goes beyond typical understanding."

Hattie saw moments where she felt compelled to drive a different route home, which avoided car accidents. She saw times that George didn't get a job, and she was so disappointed only to see that the boss would have treated him horribly. The entirety of her life played out just as she saw in the Throne Room. Except this time, she saw the Spirit of God. She saw the protection. The times when she cried herself to sleep without understanding. Now she saw. She could see so clearly.

Hattie began to sob. Spirit held back tears with a smile. Her face radiated light. Hattie felt the wrap of comfort around her very inner being.

"I love you so much, Hattie," said Spirit. "I would do anything for you."

Spirit dropped Hattie's hands, stepping in to hug her. At the moment of contact, Hattie felt a deep burning within her chest. Spirit wrapped Her arms around Hattie's back, pulling her head in close.

Hattie's heart felt directly connected to Spirit, and she felt a rush of waters pouring into her, a flood of love, connection, and understanding.

"You are Mine, Hattie, and I am yours," said Spirit. "I am so happy to have you home."

That moment felt like it lasted forever, and perhaps it had. Wave after wave washed over Hattie. She felt deeply known. Hattie could only weep on Spirit's shoulder, a patch of flowers beginning to form where the tears met the soil.

A calm swept through Hattie, a peace beyond understanding. She managed only a whisper in Spirit's ear.

"Why are You only showing Yourself now?"

"The Father and Creator are protective of Me," She said. "I usually wait before an introduction. New guests tend to already be a bit overwhelmed. But Hattie, you've known Me for a very long time."

"Your voice," said Hattie. "I've heard that voice."

"Of course you have," said Spirit, pulling back to look at Hattie. "I've been talking to you your whole life, My daughter. I would hope you'd recognize it."

"It's so clear here, but that voice."

"Some call Her intuition or conscience," said Creator from behind them, as Hattie remembered where she was. "But no, those thoughts are not yours. They come from Spirit. She is the Comforter and the Counselor."

Hattie's heart flashed a momentary ache.

"Why couldn't we hear You like this on Earth?" she asked. "If people could hear You like this, they would run to You!"

"Hattie, your time on Earth was merely a glimmer of your existence," said Spirit. "You existed in the heart of the Father long before the creation of the world. I held you in My arms. I spoke to you just as I speak to you now. You know My voice and hear it clearly. But your time on Earth was a time of growth, a time where you needed to seek out the voice, to follow and wonder where it led."

"But that created so much confusion," said Hattie. "I never knew for sure what thoughts were You or me or just terrible food."

Spirit softly laughed.

"You are not meant to merely hear My voice. You are meant to become My voice, to become the words I speak before they are even spoken. I spoke the world into existence, and I sang the Traces that now dance over your head. Your time on Earth and now is meant for you to become pure love. For you to simply follow instructions is not transformation. Only when I withhold My clarity does your own spirit stir to seek Me out, to find Me, to hear what I have to say. I never stopped speaking, Hattie, but the training wheels did come off, as you might say."

"I feel like I'll never really understand why we were on Earth," said Hattie. "There is such clarity here, such purpose and meaning. So many on Earth...Ryan. He's lost. Why can't You just appear to him? Call his name. Anything. It would be so easy for You to help him turn his life around."

"Hattie," said Creator, "you would be surprised how quickly the believer becomes the skeptic. Throughout time, We have interacted with the Heirs in many forms, some as direct as We are with you now. And yet, many still turn their back."

"Shouldn't we all have our chance?" asked Hattie. "Why not speak to him and let him decide then. Why all the mystery?"

"Hattie," said Spirit softly, "when you were raising Ryan, bad things happened to him, yes?"

"Of course."

"And as his mother, you wanted to do everything you could to help him. You'd give him the best advice to help him live a happy and productive life."

"I tried. He didn't always listen, but I tried."

"And did he ever have friends that gave him advice that you already gave him?"

"Yeah, and he listened to them instead of his own mother!" said Hattie.

"Precisely."

Spirit stared at Hattie for a moment, allowing her to process the seemingly innocuous comment.

"Children will be children," said Spirit. "Our Heirs have a built-in drive to grow, but the rebellion that the Fallen plant in them often rejects the exact authority figures that could help them the most. But We created you for relationship, just as We are with one another. Humans grow best when working together, not when an authority figure demands attention, even if that figure is perfectly right."

Hattie thought back, trying to reconcile what she heard Spirit describing.

"You're saying that people seek after You more when You don't talk to them?"

"Unbelievable, isn't it?" said Spirit with a comforting smile.

"Unbelievable," said Hattie.

"Ryan still needs your help, Hattie," said Spirit.

Hattie pursed her lips and nodded.

"I know," she said. "He feels so close but so far away."

"You did a good job with him, Hattie. The way you fought for him makes Me so proud."

Hattie dropped her head, involuntarily letting out a brief sob before pulling herself back together.

"You aren't alone in this, Hattie," said Spirit. "Your entire family line is here with you. They have been warring on your behalf since the dawn of humanity, and they fight alongside you now. They will not take defeat. We do not take defeat. Hattie, I'd like you to meet someone very special."

The Spirit turned, looking into the distance to reveal a small moving object on one of the crests of the hills.

"That is Navvah," said Spirit.

"That's a beautiful name," said Hattie.

"She is beautiful in all ways. Navvah is the first warrior in your family. She fought like no other to save the line, the line that leads directly to you. Without her, the world would have missed out on so much. She didn't know it at the time, but her actions would change the course of human history."

"And we're still fighting," said Hattie.

"Still fighting for a battle that is already won, but the Heirs don't realize it yet. Navvah will help lead you as you continue to fight for your own line, your son, and his descendants to come."

Hattie watched as the distance figure continued moving.

"You were made for this, Hattie," said Spirit. "You were absolutely made for this. I look forward to being alongside you. It is so good to have you home."

Spirit embraced Hattie once more, holding the connection for a moment. As Spirit stepped back, she moved towards Creator, who still remained standing in silence. Spirit's figure shifted, dispersing into glittering glowing orbs that encircled Him, dissolving back into His being.

37

The golden sparkles of Spirit's energy disappeared into the folds of Creator's robes. Hattie refocused on Creator, who stood smiling, of course. She felt disconnected from the moment, still pressed in an embrace with Spirit. Her awareness slowly returned.

"Any other surprises You've been keeping?" asked Hattie.

"Oh, plenty," said Creator, His grin growing.

Creator raised His hands slightly, drummed His fingers together, looking at the table.

"Especially this dip here." He pointed excitedly.

Creator pulled up a bowl of a slick blue gel-looking substance. He ushered the bowl towards her.

"Try it," He said. "It's simply divine. One of My favorites. "Come, let's have some appetizers while Navvah makes her way here."

Hattie returned to her seat along with the others.

"Why is it taking her so long?" asked Hattie.

"Navvah likes to travel the old-fashioned way. Makes her feel more connected to her roots. She's truly incredible. You'll like her. I know it. She's also got a little extra something with her."

Hattie gazed back towards Navvah. She could see the thin shape of a walking stick as the woman continued her journey across the rolling hills.

"Look a little closer, Hattie," said Creator.

Hattie let her eyes settle on the distant Navvah, and her focus drew in, bringing her into view. Navvah was muscular and looked like a warrior. Her staff stretched above her head and her Traces had elements that Hattie recognized from her own. But her attention was drawn to what was on Navvah's back. Wrapped tightly in glittering garments was a small face peaking out. A baby. A baby that Hattie had not seen in far too long.

"Tess!" screamed Hattie, her eyes drawing back to focus on the group.

"You will be reunited very soon, Hattie," said Creator. "Navvah has been taking such good care of your little girl."

"It's going to take her forever to get here," said Hattie feeling the ache of the distance.

"Yes, it may. Good thing we have time. Please, join Me at the table."

Creator guided Hattie back to her seat, pulling out her chair. He sat as the other table guests sat themselves as well. Adlai sat on the other side of Creator, his massive frame dwarfing everyone else at the table. He folded his hands neatly in front of him, his wrists the size of tree branches.

"He's right," said George. "You should try the dip while we wait."

"Good grief, I'll try the dip," said Hattie.

George was ready with some kind of dip delivery piece of food that Hattie also could not identify. She grabbed it, taking a mouthful with exasperation. She chewed.

"OK, that is good," she said, grabbing another scoop.

"So, what do you think?" asked George. "Everything you had hoped for?"

"This is nothing like I hoped for," said Hattie, "but in the best way possible. I was so limited. Did you know about Tess?"

"I have been waiting for this reunion just as much as you. Just when I think I've seen it all, a new layer reveals itself," said George.

Hattie's chewing slowed.

"George, were you, you know, doing with me what we did for Ryan?"

"Of course I was! Damiel and I ran many missions for you. Remember that time your social security check was delayed and then arrived at the last minute? That was us! Under direct orders of Adlai over here," he said proudly, nodding at the rainbowed being still sitting stoically next to Creator.

"God's Archangel of Justice helped get me a government check?" said Hattie with disbelief.

"My armies respond to any violation of justice," said Adlai.

"So this is all normal," said Hattie, waving her hand in a circle, still holding a bit of dip.

"Quite normal," said Creator, spooning kernels of red jeweled fruit from a bowl onto His plate.

"No one gets tired of doing work here?" asked Hattie.

"Definitely not," said Damiel. "And if you need a break, just go through a door to your favorite spot and stay there for as long as you like. When you're ready, come back, and we pick up right where we left off."

"This two-dimensional time thing still goes over my head," said Hattie.

"I can understand it must be challenging," said Damiel. "You've lived your whole life in a projection of time into a single linear dimension. Once your training commences, you'll better understand the quantum mechanics of it and the other time dimensions. Those can get a bit trickier."

"More dimensions?" asked Hattie. "Two isn't enough?"

"Well, no," said Damiel.

Hattie wasn't ready for a science lesson at the moment.

"I'll stick with two for the time being," said Hattie. She turned to Adlai.

"Adlai, um, Commander, are you a Guardian too?" asked Hattie.

"Of sorts," said Adlai. "I do guard, but I am a guard of the Father's Heart."

He smiled with gentle eyes.

"I'm not sure what that means," said Hattie.

"I command the Justice of God," said Adlai, "but justice gains its strength from the opposition of truth, and that truth lives in the Father's Heart."

Hattie looked at Creator for further elaboration, which He eagerly accepted as an invitation.

"On Earth," said Creator, "you are used to the idea of good versus evil, right versus wrong, yes?"

"Of course," said Hattie.

"But sometimes evil looks like it wins. People are murdered, hurt, exploited, tricked, trafficked, and any other many evils. It might seem like evil wins in those situations, and those situations are devastating for those involved. But My Father is a Father of Justice. He does not let those wrongs go uncorrected. That's why He had Me create Adlai. Whether by the hands of humans or spirits, any violation of truth and love generates strength and focus within Adlai for correction. Some wrongs are corrected immediately. Others are elaborately orchestrated plans over generations, but justice is always released. Adlai is the Archangel that overseas My Father's Justice."

"Archangels like Gabriel and Michael?" asked Hattie.

"Among others," said Adlai.

"Together," said Creator, "they orchestrate, lead, and drive My will."

"You must be very busy," said Hattie. "The anger and rage on Earth is reaching almost unbearable levels."

"The Fallen are doing everything they can to distract humanity from the move that is coming," said Adlai.

"They already know what Your plan is?" she asked.

"And there's nothing they can do to stop it," said Adlai. "They even know that they have already lost, but they are set on attempting to ruin what they can on the way down. But that's where I come in."

"There's a reason why Adlai is the most powerful Archangel," said Creator. "The atrocities committed against My Father generate an imbalance, which gives Adlai his strength. As long as there is injustice in the world, Adlai has a mission."

"Once the world is perfect, does that mean you disappear or something?" asked Hattie.

"I will cross that bridge when we get there," said Adlai. "Justice isn't just about right and wrong. Father sits on a throne of justice. Justice is merely the support. When the Age we are in ends, the justice that is laid will merely be a foundation for what comes next."

"What does that mean, 'the Age?'" she asked.

"You needn't worry about the Ages for now, Hattie," said Damiel. "You will learn about them in time. But for now, we are in an Age that needs justice. It needs Adlai. It needs us to work alongside to accomplish what the Father has outlined. Our focus now is reconciling as many of the Heirs back to the Father as possible."

As usual, Hattie found herself fumbling over more questions with each answer she received, but she felt peace about it. For the first time since her arrival, she knew that she could simply rest in the moment.

Creator carved the dishes as the attendants passed out plates mounded with food. She could taste the food even before her lips touched a dish.

As the guests tore through the feast that lay before them, Hattie couldn't help but pause to savor the moment. She could hear the wind passing through the meadow of grasses and flowers as if an orchestra of violins played in harmony all around them. The breeze was warm on her skin, but comfortable.

She looked about the table, filled with joy and laughter, each adding to the complex composition of the ambient tones. Here, she sat with her deceased husband, the Creator of the universe, and some angels.

Hattie smiled to herself, knowing how many people on Earth probably thought she was sitting on a cloud in a white toga next to a chubby white baby angel. If they only knew what awaited, their perception of life would be so different. She sat here feeling almost too unreal for belief.

Her life was not boring on Earth, but she felt as though she lived in a fog, walking through the thick mud of life that never seemed to relent. How would she have lived differently had she known what was to come? What would others do if they could see what she sees now? The world would be changed.

She thought back to her favorite mystery novels. This is where the big twist happens, right? Just when everyone feels comfortable, the real twist happens. But no twist came. Just bliss. She ate the nameless food with pure delight. She chatted with Creator, broke bread with the angels, and laughed with George like she had never laughed before. It was perfection.

I must be out of my mind, but if this is a dream, I don't ever want to wake up, she thought to herself.

"It's not a dream," said Creator. "You died. Now you get to live. So keep eating."

38

He watched as the inferior presence approached.

"Your Royal Highness," said the chamber guard.

"What is it?"

"Baal Hadad requests your presence, Your Royal Highness," said the guard.

"Tell him I am preoccupied."

"There's a change in the plan, Helel," said Hadad, his footsteps echoing across the chamber as he stepped into view, approaching the throne, his illustrious garments flowing behind him.

"A change according to who?" asked Helel.

"A boy. I saw him today," said Hadad.

"There are no new boys."

"Not a human," said Hadad. "A Host. He's a new Archangel."

Helel paused to consider the statement.

"And what did you see in this new boy Archangel?" he asked.

"He called himself 'Adlai.' His markings were...unlike anything I have seen before. They were a peculiar mixture. The boy was traveling with a group of Heilen."

"They came to see you?"

"Yes, in my chambers to deliver the usual orders," said Hadad.

Helel huffed.

"Even in the face of defeat, He is fixated on His rules," said Helel tossing his hand with dismissal. "The boy can't be a Heilen. Raphael already holds that position."

"Some of his symbols were in fact Heilen, but I could see signature

Traces from at least 7 different Tribes and even more Orders. But what concerned me was this."

Hadad held out his hand as a singular ruby red floating symbol levitated in the air.

"This is when I knew I needed to come speak to you," said Hadad. He paused. "Do you think He is mounting an attack?"

Helel's eyes narrowed as he examined the symbols.

"No," said Helel. "He will not attack. He is still convinced the humans can be trained to be His actual Heirs. Imagine that. Those pitiful creatures."

"What should I tell the armies if they see the boy?" asked Hadad.

Helel leaned to the side, resting his chin on his hand, tapping his lip for a moment.

"Tell them the Creator and I have been in discussion, and He is fed up with the behavior of the humans. That they fall short of His expectations. This new Archangel will be his weapon against the humans as they continue to disappoint over and over. Tell them this is a good sign. Tell them all of our efforts are making a difference, and unity will be regained once again."

"Does this change our plan with the humans?" asked Hadad.

"Not in the least. Cain and his family will be our anointed. They will act as a beacon for us, to draw in the other humans."

"I already feel our strength increasing," said Hadad, flexing his broad shoulders.

"It will come quickly. He made them strong, but unaware of the strength. Their physical frailty will not be difficult to exploit in order to redirect them. We will use His persistent slowness against them. They will become upset very quickly knowing their prayers are not answered by Him. But us? We will be there. We will have what they need. We can show them things beyond their imagination. These generations will quickly become ours."

"Shall I call for a meeting with Cain?" asked Hadad.

"Yes. His most recent reports showed that he is distraught over the banishment. We will need to offer him something to ease the struggle. I will leave it to you to decide what that is. Once his needs are met, I will begin my training with him. He will be my primary focus."

"Shall I alert Molak?"

"Yes, call a meeting. Do not inform the others at this time until we have further information. For now, we need to focus on intercepting the work of the Heilen. I am not surprised that He assigned them here, but the damage to the relationships with the humans has already been done. It is only ours to lose. The tribe of Cain is our key."

Helel's grip tightened on the arm of his throne.

"Oh the plans I have for them," he said. "I will sit on His throne."

"As you wish, Superior."